THE HOUSE
ON THE RIVER

BY
DUNCAN R. SMITH

Printed in the United States of America

Nickel City Books

First printing, 2020

ISBN: 978-1-7351779-1-5

Interior Design by booknook.biz

DEDICATION

*To our daughters, Megan and Lizzie, and
to all they have taught us and
continue to bring.*

CONTENTS

1

APRIL, 2004

I t wasn't the first time a body had washed up in the tangle of mooring lines off the village of Youngstown. The Niagara River swept wide here, carving a broad arc in its eastern bank, before curling back and spilling into Lake Ontario. Bodies of people who plunged over Niagara Falls or drowned in the lower rapids were occasionally recovered, six miles after the river had calmed down, in the lee of a yacht basin set deep in the elbow of the river's last bend.

The diver, thirty feet down to reset a mooring, first thought the shadow was cast by a block of ice on the surface, although he hadn't seen ice on the river in a week or more, and the shape didn't drift with the current. A foot appeared to be hooked in a rusted cable, a head settled well below the foot, as if the head held extra weight. Puzzled, since it was too early in the spring for a boating mishap, the diver swam for a closer look.

The corpse was fully dressed, a denim jacket buttoned to the neck, a bit of crease still evident in the press of khaki slacks. Only the head looked misshapen, with tiny ears hung low on a huge head, and tufts of hair that were matted by a tar-like substance. Blood? The diver used his boat's radio to call the sheriff's department and was asked to stay with the body until the department's Underwater Recovery Team could get there.

The death might have escaped Linnie Carson's notice, had Main Street not swarmed with deputy sheriffs' squad cars when she got to Youngstown. On the road since five a.m., she had made great time on the westbound Thruway and had decided, on pulling abreast of her aunt's driveway, that she couldn't show up without flowers, so she'd continued two more miles down the road to the village. A deputy sheriff at the makeshift roadblock told her the town didn't have a regular florist shop anymore, but bouquets were often available at the B-Kwick Market.

"What's the trouble?" Linnie nodded at the landing down below.

"Found a body in the river — could be a murder. Sad thing. I hear he may be an idiot. Retarded."

It took Linnie a long moment to reassure herself that she had called her aunt's house not much more than an hour earlier, and no one was missing.

"'Handicapped,' I guess you'd say," the deputy corrected himself. "No driver's license, just a photo ID."

Linnie bought a bunch of flowers at the market before circling back to River Road. With the trees on its banks beginning to bud and the brush sparse, the river sprawled out beyond the road in all its breadth and splendor, the water green and shiny as cheap glass, the current and the wind both running north and forming little ridges of water that didn't crest. The house had been built on a point of the river, about a hundred years earlier. The road, steering a straighter course, cut away from the water and by-passed the crook of land, thereby marooning the house at the end of a long, well-rutted gravel drive.

The driveway curled through a low swale, where the so-called "bunkhouse" sat. Built to house maids as well as a bunch of children and their cousins, never winterized, the bunkhouse was shuttered, even those rooms her aunt, Evelyn Phillips, liked to use as an office. The main house had been fully winterized and upgraded when her aunt decided to sell her large house in Buffalo and move with her children year-round to Lewiston. Linnie drove to the circle that fronted the main house, parked, and let herself in, relieved that the front door was, as usual, unlocked.

Ted Phillips squatted in a corner of the entry hall, trying to make a stack of magazines and catalogues that kept sliding sideways, and didn't seem to notice her arrival. He moaned when the stack toppled, then drummed the length of his forehead with his fingertips. Ted was fifty-two.

"Ted!" She waved the flowers to get his attention. "Honey, it's me, Linnie."

"Busy-busy," he grumbled, keeping his eyes fixed on the magazines. She turned at the sound of footsteps hurrying through the living room.

"Linnie?" Nick bellowed, moments before he turned into the hall.

In her rush to greet her cousin Linnie almost crushed the flowers between them. She knew Nick would fuss if their hug lasted too long, but she wanted the contact and clung to him until she felt a tickle at her neckline. She hadn't expected to cry, not yet.

"Linnie," Nick cooed, backing away awkwardly, while she brushed away tears. "Evelyn's okay. We got this therapy woman, and she makes Evelyn get out of bed. You know Evelyn never likes being told what to do, but she gets on her feet."

"She can stand? On her own?"

"I lift her," he admitted. "The therapy woman has one side, she doesn't hold up much, 'cause I have the other side and all the weight."

"Jesus, you have to come with me." She started for the stairs, but Nick stopped her.

"She's in the den."

Among the consequences of her aunt's stroke that hadn't yet occurred to Linnie was the fact that Evelyn would be deprived of her bedroom upstairs, of its river views and richly carved mantel and attached bathroom. The downstairs den didn't even have a door in place, if she remembered correctly.

Nick led and she followed, running a hand along the familiar worn brocade on a sofa that divided the living room. He talked over his shoulder as he cut across the hall. "The doctor can't say if her left eye sees."

The headboard of a hospital bed was backed against the east wall of the den, so the left side of the bed faced the doorway. Since it was

Evelyn's left side that had been mostly paralyzed by the stroke, Linnie circled to her aunt's right side, but the older woman didn't seem to notice anything. Linnie lowered a side rail, at which point Evelyn's pale blue eyes settled loosely on her. "Is this okay?" Linnie asked Nick. "Does it bother her? If I sit on the bed?"

"Sit. No problem."

She laid the flowers on a side table, boosted herself onto the edge of the mattress, then extended a hand and cupped her aunt's cheek, the skin dry as chalk. The left side of Evelyn's mouth slumped open, as if all her worries had hung themselves on that corner of her face; her wrinkles had deepened considerably in the last year and were crisscrossed by smaller fractures. "Evelyn, honey," Linnie murmured, "you've been forgetting your moisturizers."

When her aunt failed to respond, Linnie turned to Nick. "I tried to think up jokes on the drive today, and nothing would come. Do you think she hears me?"

He shrugged with uncertainty. "Sometimes, maybe." Evelyn blinked a few times and raised her right arm, her fingers crawling aimlessly into the air, but when Linnie reached for her hand, Evelyn beat her to it, taking hold of her niece's wrist. There was no strength to the grip, but she didn't let go.

Linnie sat still for a while, briefly locking eyes with Evelyn, then bent over and kissed her forehead. "Evelyn?" She kissed her again. "I know you hate it, stuck in bed. I'm gonna get you back on your feet." What she didn't say was that no other alternative was thinkable: Evelyn was the last pillar left standing in the family.

Nick repositioned a curtain that had slipped from its tie and peered out the window. Outside, shadows of small clouds swept the backyard and the river beyond.

Linnie tried to fight back the lump swelling in her throat and stared absently at the junction of the cornice molding. "I'll stay a while," she managed. "I promise."

"You'll stay," Nick said, binding her to her promise. "Oh! You got a message. By the phone."

A couple of hours later, Linnie drove three miles upriver to a waterfront restaurant in Lewiston, where Evelyn's lawyer, Brendan O'Connor, awaited her. In his early thirties, he seemed too young for the relic of a bow-tie that he often wore with well-tailored suits and handsome dress shirts. She wondered, given his boyish good looks, if the bow-tie might be an affectation of modesty, an out-of-date fashion tacked onto a lithe, athletic body. Or maybe there was no conceit to it: she'd always found Brendan easy-going and charming, and even more so after he'd divorced a woman she never much liked.

Brendan stood to greet her and seated her at his table on the porch, which was spitting distance from the river. Linnie left her parka on: a steady chill blew from the Canadian bluffs across the water.

"Any trouble finding it?" he asked, reclaiming his chair.

"It'd be hard to miss." She nodded at the river; tiny eddies were darkening in the failing light, trailing tendrils of ink. "You said it was on the water."

"So what'd you think? When you saw Evelyn?"

"I didn't know what to expect. Have you talked to the doctor this week?"

"He isn't much help. He speaks in broad generalities. Never commits to anything specific."

Brendan must have noticed Linnie's disappointment because he changed his tone. "Well, he thinks improvement's possible, she might walk again, and you know Evelyn, she won't want anyone else messing around in her garden this summer, dead-heading the wrong flowers."

"Your father was her lawyer too, right? I remember him so well."

"He called Evelyn his dearest friend and smartest client. I inherited her from him."

"And your bow-ties?"

"Them, too."

"I'm not making fun of them," Linnie added, although in truth she supposed she had been.

"You wouldn't be the first." Brendan shrugged. "Anyway, thanks for coming. Your aunt had been dealing with some things before the stroke. About eight weeks ago she was in my office, having me draw up a new will and trust. Obviously, no one expected the stroke, but she's always had one issue that dominates her planning. Who's going to look after the boys when she can't?" He flinched. "Do you mind if I refer to them like that? 'The boys?' I don't mean–"

"It's fine." For as long as Linnie could remember, everyone in and out of the family had referred to Evelyn's two sons as "the boys." Nick and Ted would have been the last to take offense at the term, which Evelyn herself used.

"The thing is," Brendan continued, "your aunt wants to make sure they're both looked after. She's committed most of her assets to a trust to provide for their expenses and asked that I be the trustee."

"That's great." Linnie didn't see how the issue involved her and felt relieved that it didn't.

"That's the easy half. Her biggest concern is that Ted and Nick get to keep living at the house."

"That's a no-brainer." She understood, from his look, that it wasn't. "You're kidding?"

"It's complicated. The court will eventually require that a guardian be appointed. Someone to look after Ted and maybe Nick."

"Wouldn't that be Margot?" Margot was the eldest of Evelyn's off-spring, a year older than her brother Ted and nine years senior to Nick.

"You're the one she designated. I asked if she wanted to discuss the idea with you first, but Evelyn said to go ahead and draft the new will."

"Why didn't she ask me?"

"I'm sure she planned to."

"Then why didn't you ask?"

"It's not my job. I'm certain Evelyn thought there'd be a lot more time before any of this would be dropped in your lap. And there's nothing binding in the nomination. It'd need your consent and the court's. The court has final say, and you could always decline."

"Wait." Linnie had turned twenty-nine a month earlier. Though she'd spent much of the last year actively imagining a new life — and good friends were urging her to join them in Seattle — nothing that she had envisioned included caring for a child almost twice her own age. Ted's moods were impenetrable and ill-tempered, and he was subject to occasional incontinence.

"You think I'd pack up and leave Upstate New York," she asked, "only to move to the other side of Upstate New York? Is this another Buffalo joke? 'What's a two-time loser?'"

"I'm not presuming anything. I don't know what you or your husband would want. How is he, by the way?"

Linnie felt exposed by the naked disarray of her own life. Her husband's betrayals, not being ones of the flesh, failed to give her automatic grounds for divorce, and her signature remained alongside his on the apartment lease, the car loan, the credit cards and their bundle of debt. The only thing she could depend upon was that James wouldn't acquiesce to any simple course of action. "It's a mess," she admitted.

Linnie glanced at the docks below, where a few police officers had congregated, then looked at Brendan. His wavy blond hair swept back past his ears. He had lively green eyes, a strong jaw and brow, and a ridge on his nose that suggested a sports injury. His lips were, to her mind, perfect.

Linnie wondered if Brendan found her as attractive as she found him. Her bulky parka hid her figure, and she hadn't washed her light brown hair that morning and hadn't been to a hairdresser for "highlights" in months.

"My marriage is pretty well shot," she continued, "and I sort of told Evelyn as much." A thought provoked her. "God. Was Evelyn talking about my marriage? She'd 'rescue' me with this guardian business?"

"Not at all." Brendan cleared his throat and spoke softly. "Evelyn's acting in her interest, not yours."

"I know it." Linnie was irritated at her aunt's willfulness: it would be just like Evelyn to make demands from the grave. "Look, I'm owed vacation, I'll take a leave of absence from my job if I have to, but it's not about the boys. The only reason I'm here is her."

"Me, too." Brendan's eyes found hers. "When my father first got ill, Evelyn took charge, lined up doctors, you name it."

"I can imagine."

"Anyway, at the moment everything's, well..." he fluttered a hand, "in limbo. God willing, Evelyn will recover and there'll be a long time to figure out what happens next."

"And if she doesn't?"

"Christ, it's a pickle. Your nomination as guardian wouldn't be considered valid by the court. Technically, we can't submit Evelyn's will to the court."

"Why not?"

"Because she's still alive."

He paused when a beacon of light shot along the porch's rail. Beneath them, a policeman swept his flashlight across the docks and along the river's edge.

Brendan nodded at the officer. "They're trying to figure out where the victim went in the river. The poor guy they found today. You hear about it?"

"Not much."

"I was going to have my boat put in the water, but Youngstown was shut down. They found a body by the yacht club. The victim's about Ted's age. Also significantly disabled. Pretty much a ward of O.M.R.D.D." He spelled it out when he saw she wasn't familiar with the acronym. "It's a state organization for MRs — mentally retarded — and DDs — developmentally disabled. I don't know if the victim did any of the programs Ted does."

"He drowned?" Linnie looked at the river doubtfully; no one willingly went in the water this time of year.

"It's not clear. Apparently, the coroner found a hole in his head. Chilling, isn't it? Somebody drilled a hole in the head of someone like Ted."

2

An aging Buick flew up the driveway scattering gravel, with Ted's bicycle loosely fastened to its roof. Linnie met the driver out front as the woman hauled down the bike, the front tire of which had separated from the rim.

"He was a-ways out Creek Road," she said, nodding at Ted, slumped in the backseat. "Dragging his bike like a sled. I'd guess the rim's bad, not just the tube."

"Thanks." Linnie took the bike and looked at Ted; she hadn't realized he'd been missing.

"Ted's generally got Nick with him if he's out. So Nick can look out for him." The woman studied her closely. "You're Mrs. Phillips' niece, right? She's got photos."

"Yeah."

"She any better?"

"Hard to say."

The woman wiped her hands clean on the thighs of her sweatsuit, then extended a hand. "I'm April Becker."

"Linnie Carson."

"I know. Mrs. G., the housekeeper, she keeps me caught up. I live close by."

"I appreciate your bringing him." Linnie opened the back door and beckoned him to step out of the car. "Ted, we've got an appointment to make. Maybe you want to say thank-you to—"

"'April,'" the neighbor volunteered. "The boys call me 'April.'"

Ted stuck a leg straight out of the car and followed it once his foot had made contact with the ground, the movement so slow and awkward, so *elderly*, that Linnie reached for his elbow. He pulled clear of her and reclaimed his bike with a worried frown, then wrestled it sideways till it toppled beside the front porch steps.

"I live three driveways up," April said. "Across the road, not on the river. Tell your aunt I'm planning to visit tomorrow evening, if it's convenient. Might come even if it isn't. I'm awful fond of her."

Nick fussed and asked questions all the way to town: who was the psychologist, why did they have to visit one, and what did they want to know? Linnie had to explain that if their mother remained ill, the state's Surrogate Court would appoint a referee whose job would be to help the court determine what was in his and Ted's best interest. The psychologist, Judy Urbanski, had experience with the judges in Niagara County's courthouse, which was why their mother's lawyer had hired her.

When they arrived at her Lewiston office ten minutes late, the psychologist was polite but cool. "Judy" suggested that everyone use first names, to keep things "informal," and began by asking Nick if he'd like to talk with her. Shortly, the psychologist invited Ted to join his brother, and they spent what seemed no time at all.

Once the brothers were seated in her tiny waiting room, Judy asked Linnie in for her own private conversation, but this time she kept the office door open and her eyes on the waiting room.

"They'll be okay," Linnie said. The psychologist had tilted her eyeglasses for a slightly magnified view of the other room, presumably in case one of the brothers did something objectionable.

"They'll be okay," she repeated, by way of persuading Judy to close the door. "Nick keeps an eye on his brother."

"Poor Ted. Does he talk at all?"

"Hardly. I don't think he knows ten words."

"You and I didn't have a chance to discuss this beforehand, but the point of these sessions will be to see if I can get Ted to open up a little, let me know how he's coping. In a situation where the primary caregiver becomes incapacitated, we try to make certain we look after people whose interests might be overlooked or unattended to."

"In the first place...," Linnie paused, trying not to take offense, "well, I don't think Ted's needed to 'cope' at all. The housekeeper's been working five days a week instead of three, friends and neighbors stop by daily, and even though Ted senses the disruption, he probably doesn't understand the gravity of his mother's stroke."

"I'm not attacking. I'm trying to get a quick read on the brothers, the range of disabilities. But I'm starting with nothing." She held up a thin file folder. "How is it their family doctor doesn't have comprehensive records of clinical diagnoses? For fifty-two and forty-four-year-old brothers? Didn't their mother–?"

"She consulted everybody, that's Evelyn's way, but don't let her hear you going on about Ted's retardation and percentiles and speech pathologies, because she'll have at you if you're not going anywhere with it. Ted's alive. That in itself is an accomplishment."

"What do you think his range is? His capabilities?"

"They're very limited, I don't know how else to put it. He's always been there, a fact of my life, because I spent a good deal of it with Evelyn. He was born with Fragile X Syndrome, they did figure that out. Really significant disabilities and Quasimodo's face. Those poor ears." Linnie noticed Judy starting to write on a legal pad. "Wait. Ted was my 'Quasimodo.' You're not writing *that* down, are you?"

"Relax. I wrote down 'Fragile X Syndrome,' not 'Quasimodo.' He's got macro-orchidism, the list of afflictions?"

"I guess." She let herself settle a little deeper into the worn, spongy cushions of the couch.

"What about the younger brother? What's your relationship with him?"

"Nick is my big brother. I love him as much as anyone."

"He was pretty tight-lipped."

"Nick will fool you, the way he holds back. What I understand is, if he were born today, they'd categorize him as having minor learning disabilities, not minor retardation. With a little Special-Ed, he'd have been mainstreamed. Not that the 'mainstream' doesn't have its challenges."

"Such as?"

"Why don't they create Special-Ed classes for the mean kids: '*Miss Manners' Greatest Challenge: Remedial Etiquette for the Socially Disabling*'?"

"Did you experience adolescent hazing?"

"Who didn't?"

"Did you?"

"By seventh grade I had been the 'new kid' in a number of schools. I developed a sharp enough tongue to defend myself." Linnie was annoyed to see Judy write a few words on her pad.

"And then?"

"Evelyn took over. A good school here, then she sent me to her boarding school, which was great."

"As for Nick, I'm told his reading and writing skills are passable. The lawyer said he used to keep some sort of diary."

"His mother started him on it. Years ago. She pushed him pretty hard."

"I'd like Nick to start keeping a journal again. We should see he keeps up with it. He might be more open – forthcoming. Also, there'll be a document we can send to court to describe what he thinks, and how well he thinks. He can use a computer, spell-check, any of that, but have him make his own entries."

Unsettled by the realization that a measure of the psychologist's scrutiny had been reserved for her, Linnie drove back to the house on the river, where a bunch of cars were parked out front. Mrs. Gonanz, long known to anyone familiar with the household as Mrs. G., stood in the front hall, blocking the way of a gentleman in a brown suit and a clerical collar.

"Hi," Nick said, on seeing the visitor.

"G'afternoon, Nick, Ted," the man responded, patting Nick on the arm, before turning to Linnie. "I'm Robert Strickley."

"Reverend," Nick added. "You know Linnie?"

"I do now," the reverend said, with a tip of an imaginary hat. "Nick and Ted sometimes come to Sunday services. For years I've been after Miss Evelyn to join them. The Niagara Bible Church. Big stone building on the river."

"I know it," Linnie said.

"We let the community use our rec rooms. The state puts on a special-ed-type program that Ted goes to a bunch. Right, Nick?"

"Yes, sir."

"You may want to bring Ted this upcoming Wednesday." The reverend looked at the housekeeper, then at Linnie. "A service for one of the fellas in Ted's program. James Jannevich. Called himself 'J.J.' He must've been wandering in the lower gorge or fooling on the shore. He's the one they fished out of the river. Did you know him, Nick?"

"Not much, no, sir. He didn't speak to me."

"No family, or none that'll claim him. The state'll pay to bury him, but I thought we'd try to gather the others from his program and have a service."

"Any idea what time?" Linnie tried to imagine Ted sitting through a memorial service and couldn't.

"I'll have the program director keep you posted." The reverend started for the door. "And, Nick? Be great to see you and Ted on Sunday. You know you're welcome."

"Yes, sir."

Mrs. G. watched the reverend leave and waited to speak till she'd seen him reach his car. "He come in here, askin' to pay respects to Miss Evelyn, and all I can figure is he's gonna march right in and pray over her, whether she wants it or don't. I tell you what, Miss Evelyn would slap the evangelicist that started layin' on hands and gettin' loud with his prayers."

Linnie laughed with surprise. "Mrs. G! And you a regular at mass."

"Prayers oughta be quiet, that's why they wrote 'em in Latin. Anyhow, Reverend Strickley's not the only one rushin' to our rescue. Nick, your sister dropped in."

"Margot?" Nick looked towards the stairs.

"She's off on errands." Mrs. G. looked apologetically at Linnie. "Said she wanted to stay in *her* room, so I said *'Which one is that?'* and she says it's the one you're in, Linnie, and 'Will I please move your things to the spare room and change the sheets while I'm at it?'"

The blue room, where Linnie had been staying, had a large bed, a river view, and a private bathroom. The so-called "spare room" was smaller and shared a bathroom with Ted's room.

"You're the one's there, Linnie," Mrs. G. said, with evident irritation. "I can tell you what Miss Evelyn would say. And long as I been here, which is good and long, you spent lots more time in the blue room than Margot."

"It's okay." Linnie knew that Margot and Mrs. G. butted heads frequently, and she wanted to stay clear of it. "The other room's fine."

"Margot's askin' all kinds of lawyer and doctor questions, she must'a been talkin' to Brendan O'Connor, 'cause she's askin' me what I can do, and who-all tells Ted to shower and drives him about. Like all these questions is brand, spankin' new and she's the first to think of 'em. My goodness!" Mrs. G. huffed. "So I say to her, make no bones about it, I say, 'Margot, it's so nice 'a you to take interest.'"

3

NICK'S JOURNAL

April 12

Evelyn has words for the waves. Today the waves are big as trawler wakes, the water gray as battleships. The river is falling all over itself. I was on the banks.

Everything there grows worse than weeds. I cut maple shoots and sumac for Evelyn to see the river. They keep her in the den, a window looks right at the water if limbs and baby trees don't get in the way. Her bed has wheels and I keep it looking at the river, but mostly she doesn't see much if I can tell.

Linnie got here. I'm so happy. Her visits make Evelyn happy too, except maybe last summer. Linnie was worried thin, that's what Evelyn said. Linnie is so pretty, but not as much when you can see her bones.

She brung Jordan then, she always loved being with him. He runs funny, Jordan, hard out of breath, his mouth open. I told him he'll catch bugs, running in twilight with his mouth open, and he did. Last summer he swallowed the no-see-ums and choked them up and wouldn't believe we called them no-see-ums, not till Evelyn said so. He's not here this time.

4

It never would have occurred to Linnie, as a girl of twelve new to the town's school, that a boy from her classroom might be looking through Evelyn's windows. The house stood far from the road and well above the river. It was dark outside, unusually cold for May, and the boy had accompanied his father to drop off a load of topsoil. Linnie was jumping around the living room and conducting a make-believe orchestra, much to the delight of Ted, who mimicked her and stomped his feet and shook his head in spastic bursts of glee.

Nick had selected Beethoven's Fifth Symphony from the boxes of recordings that Linnie's mother had stored at her sister's house. Linnie had the sense that she was also being stored at the house on the river, but she didn't resent the notion. Evelyn's household was calm and orderly. Meals appeared punctually on the table, and if you wrote something down on a grocery list, even things like makeup and candy, someone was sure to buy it within a day or two.

Linnie's mother had moved with her fiancé, an architect, to his hometown in Sweden, and planned to bring her daughter over once she'd found an English-language school for her. It hadn't dawned on her mother that there wouldn't be any such school nor a mid-year spot in anything suitable. Linnie didn't mind the whole mess of her seventh grade year, her leaving the country-day school downstate and finishing the year at a public school not far from Evelyn's house upstate. She only hated the whole arrangement when the story about her performance was repeated to her by a girl in her class.

"You have to be careful," her acquaintance had scolded. "People don't know you hardly, and there're those people you live with."

"What?"

"Howie Desmond was outside your house, the night you were leaping all over the place leading the band with those retard relatives of yours in it. Howie saw the whole freak show."

Linnie felt the heat flash across her forehead.

"His father was working there or something."

That night at dinner, Linnie asked Ted if it would be too much trouble for him to please keep his goddamn mouth shut while he was eating just once in his goddamn life, when she knew of course that it would be too difficult, and Evelyn said nothing. She didn't even interrupt when Linnie started goading Nick, asking him if he'd like to help with her homework.

It was later that night when Evelyn walked into the blue room and sat on the bed beside Linnie, who was busy staring hard at the ceiling. "Ted's a queer bird, isn't he?" Evelyn said.

"God, you think?"

"He's a queer thing, I know."

"No kidding." Linnie kept her eyes pasted to the ceiling.

"And you're wondering how you got appointed one of the zookeepers."

"I know how I got here."

"It seemed best—"

"I'm not mad at anyone."

"Not even your mother?"

"What do I care?"

"You want to call her?"

"No."

Evelyn's hand found its way to Linnie's shoulder and gripped it firmly; it was Evelyn's voice that broke. "I just wish..." she began.

"Don't wish anything."

"I wish I'd been more available. Your mother's so much younger. I was away at college before she was even three."

"She thinks you're the great one."

"I wish I had her courage, her curiosity."

"Why?" Linnie was surprised by Evelyn's admiration for her sister. "Where would you go?"

"I'd wander somewhere. I'd put a boat in the river and ride it, through the lake and out to sea."

"You couldn't go. What would you do with Ted?"

"I'd pack him up and take him along. I've never been up the Saint Lawrence – except the stretch of it we took when I sailed from Montreal to Europe. What I remember is how cold it was when we hit the Atlantic. I think the Gulf Stream must turn east before it reaches the mouth of the Saint Lawrence. Do you know? The Gulf Stream? When does it head to Europe? Do they still teach that in Geography?"

"Earth Science." Linnie was irked by the ease with which Evelyn could switch subjects. One moment they were crowning Ted the king of misfits, the next they were worrying about the Gulf of Mexico's meandering currents. "We learned about it in Earth Science."

The snore rose out of the farthest reaches of her lungs, a rupture cracking through layers of resistance. Evelyn slept on her back, stuck there by the left-side paralysis and a disinclination to use her right side to roll left, into numb and undefined space. Linnie adjusted the bedside lamp to shine on the books she'd taken from the cluster on the desk. Her aunt had always been an avid reader, with piles of books on every available surface and in otherwise vacant drawers. These particular books had been dog-eared and highlighted by Evelyn, who preferred to do her own research.

On thumbing through an old book titled *Parent and Child*, Linnie found a marked passage about a court's jurisdiction in guardianship matters. Evelyn had underlined the declaration that the state Supreme Court has "*jurisdiction to entertain, for the appointment of a committee for the person, or of the property, of idiots, lunatics, and other incompetent*

19

persons." Her hand-written notes in the margin asked, "What idiot wrote this?"

Likewise, a statement in a handbook on mental retardation had also attracted Evelyn's attention; she'd put large exclamation marks around it: "_For most children in the U.S., socioeconomic status and maternal education are the best predictors of developmental outcomes such as academic achievement and cognitive function._" This passage, Linnie thought, must have struck her aunt as the cruelest of ironies, Evelyn a graduate of Radcliffe and descendant of a long-prominent family, the lot of which had failed to bestow any advantages on her male offspring.

Evelyn had a significant collection of books on the subject of mental retardation, many of which documented the abuses and deprivations once forced upon the "feeble-minded," the sort of mistreatment, Linnie supposed, that Evelyn had been able to spare Ted. She wondered if anyone had been able to shelter James Jannevich, the man dredged from the river, for whom there had been a service the day before. With Ted acting up, she and Nick had left him at home and gone to the memorial service held by Reverend Strickley, which was attended by all of seven people, three of whom worked for the church. Either Jannevich had been remarkably unpleasant or his counselors and caretakers were remarkably callous, for none of them were there even though the county had sent a special-services van. Linnie was glad that her aunt had been spared the sight of the cavernous church, all but empty.

A spell of coughing, a series of shallow hacks, startled Evelyn awake. Her eyes opened and she used her right elbow to crawl a little closer to the nightstand, from which she took a plastic cup of water with a child's training lid on it. She managed a few sips before dropping the cup onto the bed. Linnie retrieved the cup and stuck it back in her aunt's right hand, but Evelyn angrily flung it to the floor.

The cup rolled under the potty-chair set in a corner. "Feel better now?"

Evelyn groaned and looked at her niece.

"It's me, darling. Linnie."

Evelyn mumbled, ground her teeth in frustration, and tried again. "Blah ... blah-blah." The right side of her mouth fashioned a half-smile with which to mock herself.

"That's so great. You can speak." She saw the denial in Evelyn's eyes and hugged her aunt. "Everybody says you can't. Or won't. You keep trying."

Evelyn forced out a wisp of a laugh, then clamped her mouth shut. Her right hand waved off further effort. She used the bedpan, with her niece's help, and took a few more sips of water when offered, but seemed disinclined to further conversation, and drifted off to the sounds of classical music on the radio. Linnie was straightening out her blankets when she heard an odd whine from the rear of the house.

When she got to the kitchen, the back door, which she'd locked earlier, was rattling from the force of someone shaking it, and this time the whine was louder, two descending notes strung out in a yowl of frustration. She peeked out a window before opening the door. Ted was standing on the stoop, his clothes caked with mud. The clumps on his knees were especially thick, and they trailed odors of the deeper earth into the house, of dirt made rich by decomposing roots and insect matter long gone to rot. He had a filthy work glove on one hand; his other hand was bare but equally filthy, with dirt jammed under his long fingernails. He tried to push past Linnie into the house, but she grabbed hold of his coat.

"Where were you?"

He muttered something incomprehensible.

"Ted? Where were you? Do you know what time it is?"

"No-no-no," he said, walking past her and refusing to look her way.

"Leave your jacket and your shoes in the laundry room," she ordered. "Your jeans, too. You wash up before you go to bed."

5

Nick's Journal

April 20

You want me to write about Ted. Lately he's more backwards than forwards, which is what his bad days are like. He won't do anything unless it's in his mind to do it, he will shy himself away. Evelyn says these are the days he gets full out of sorts, and there's no telling when these days come or why. They arrive and are plain disagreeable.

You can't be mad at Ted the same as you can't be mad at a battery toy that bumps into the wall, but I lose my temper with him inspite. He is stubborn. Evelyn thinks he can't account for being stubborn and doesn't know better, but he knows he's stubborn and hangs onto it. Evelyn never gets angry with him, at least until she fell sick. Now, she gets mad with him. She doesn't say anything but you can see it on her when Ted's pesting around. She's jumpy, even stuck in bed.

Evelyn got angry when she wasn't sick, but never with Ted. I've heard her angry about Linnie's husband, and you asked how I like him. His name is James and you call him that, not Jim or Jimmy. Mostly he's quiet as a secret. I know he watches me if he asks me to do a job or a favor. He pretends not to watch but it's bad pretending.

He comes when Linnie does, most times, or when Linnie and Jordan did. I wish Jordan would come again. He likes to swim like me, and Linnie lets me take him swimming or off around. She knows it was me who took her swimming a thousand times, which is a low number for all the summers she spent here.

The summer before last Linnie was dog tired, sleeping anywhere all over the house and anytime. She said she was too beat to slap mosquitoes, and she was. James had his head bald because of his sister, who was sick. It's his sister that's Jordan's mom. I haven't met her and won't now. I took Jordan out on bikes. We'd ride to the fort and turn away from the lake, into the farms and fields. There's orchards no one tends and fields still being worked and marshes bound up with ribbons of forest. It's what Evelyn likes to call trees that ring a field, a ribbon of forest.

Jordan also thinks of names for things. Last summer we were riding bikes on one of those wet days without rain, the clouds low, and no breeze to dry things out. A mist can rise off a field, thick as steam, especially if there's trees around and no breath of air to blow it away. There was a field Jordan saw, with a patch of fog too deep to see through, and he just stopped and asked if it was ghosts in the field.

Was it ghosts he wanted?

6

The second corpse was discovered by a neighborhood boy who'd gone to the graveyard on a dare only to find boots sticking out of a pile of mud and composting leaves. When he looked closely, he saw that the boots were anchored to a rotting skeleton. With the story out – a body found in the long forgotten burial plot of a nineteenth-century farming family – the resulting crush of the curious had trampled a four-foot-wide path all the way to the perimeter's stone walls, which the sheriff's department had staked off with yellow tape.

The question, how long the badly decomposed corpse had lain half-buried, took a while to answer, with the forensic team from the sheriff's department taking soil samples and bone and tissue fragments from the body. The tiny graveyard lay next to the riverbank and was overgrown with towering oak trees and tangles of ivy, some of it poison. Pines, mostly red, had erupted throughout the plot, shifting headstones and buckling stone walls when the trunks toppled.

Linnie made Ted walk with her up the road a quarter-mile before they followed a neighbor's driveway to a stand of trees fifty yards short of the river and the graveyard. The day before, investigators from the sheriff's department had visited all the houses in the neighborhood. Linnie answered the door when an investigator stopped by with a few questions for everyone. Nick told him he knew of the tiny cemetery, but hadn't been near it in years. Linnie didn't know anything specific and was curious to see the investigator, so youthful he looked like a high-school student, interrogate Ted, the gray-haired babbler. Earnest, painstakingly deliberate, the investigator slowly repeated each of his questions to Ted, on the chance that repetition might secure a toehold on comprehension, only to have all his questions refused by a jabber of "boo-boo-boo" and a flurry of paddling motions Ted made with his hands, as if batting away flies.

Before leaving, the investigator pulled Linnie aside and jabbed his thumb at Ted. "We think the guy found in the graveyard may be like him. He has a head kind of big for his body. Maybe retarded."

Two nights earlier, Linnie had laundered Ted's splattered clothes and cleaned off the mud caked on his shoes. Had he wandered over to the graveyard? She decided to accompany him on a walk, on the chance that he might actually lead her to the graveyard. If he were familiar with the route, it might establish that he had used it.

"C'mon, Ted." He was dawdling behind her, dragging his feet through a wheel rut beside the driveway and plowing up the wet earth. "You know where we're going?"

Ted's chin was slumped into his chest, and his eyes were fixed on Linnie's feet. It wasn't his nature to take the lead in much of anything: he could resist, forcefully, if someone tried to shift his attention, but he rarely directed anyone or anything. He probably wouldn't guide her to the graveyard, even if he knew the way.

Linnie paused by the edge of the woods. Nick had shown her the cemetery, at her insistence, almost twenty years earlier, and even then it was wildly overgrown. She had wondered about all the packs of cigarettes stashed in the hollows where stones had fallen from the walls. Nick had explained that teenage boys sometimes hung out there.

On that first visit she'd examined the names and dates engraved on the plot's central monument, as well as on the scattered headstones. Apparently, the last person to be buried there was Jane Margaret Clark, dead at age nine, in the year 1887, which was the year that the Clark family sold their farm to a wealthy family from Buffalo looking to create a summer retreat for themselves and their friends. It had bothered Linnie, nine years old herself, that a girl's coffin could be consigned to such a forsaken spot; Jane Margaret Clark's headstone had been lifted completely out of the ground by tree roots.

Linnie left Ted by the edge of the woods and made her way to the cemetery. Although the police tape kept her at a distance, she didn't see mud anywhere. The underbrush, fallen leaves, and thorny weeds had matted together, thatching the ground with a carpet of stringy mulch.

Linnie watched an older man in a tattered windbreaker working a careful circle around the cemetery. He carried an ancient 35-millimeter camera and wore a press badge on which she could make out the words *"Niagara Gazette,"* as he cut through the trees and approached her.

"Morning," he called.

"Hi."

"Never knew this was here." He flicked his head at the low stone walls. "You a neighbor?"

"My aunt is. I'm visiting."

"I don't know there's much of a story here. Finding a body in a graveyard. I figure it must've been buried a good while, or the crows would've picked it clean."

"I guess."

"I can't make things out," he continued. "Somebody no one knows, buried clumsy. You figure if somebody wanted to get rid of a body, they'd drag it over the riverbank. Down into the river in winter, before any ice comes through, and that'd be the end of it."

Linnie nodded. She tried not to visualize a corpse pinballing off tree trunks in a thirty-foot drop down the bank, hard into the pebbles that lined the shore.

"And then I wonder how you get a body in here, unless it walked itself in. Even a wheelbarrow would have trouble with the fallen trees."

"You're a reporter?"

"Half-retired," he answered, "like everything else around here. You know our paper, *The Gazette*?"

"Yeah."

"I did the first story on this." He pointed at the police tape behind him. "I figure maybe there's a story about the cemetery, too. It was a family plot."

"The Clarks'," Linnie said. "There're fifty or more of them buried here. The graves date from about 1810."

"They stayed most of that century," he interjected. "Then, before the end of that century there were summer estates hereabouts, hard to imagine now. Something out of the Gilded Age. You should see the pictures, the town library's got some."

Linnie had seen the photographs: the stables, the polo field, the gardens, the enormous summer home built by Evelyn's grandparents.

"One big mansion burned down long ago," the reporter said, "and another fell down, probably thirty years back. Hard to tell what we've got around here now. Half suburban, half abandoned. Hell, we got the new century but not the new economy."

He scratched his balding scalp and looked back towards the clearing by the end of the driveway. "He with you?"

Ted was rubbing his back against a tree and looked, at this distance, like a small, scruffy bear. For a moment Linnie toyed with the mischief of denying kinship, of leaving him unclaimed. She wondered if the reporter would play good Samaritan and reel the stray in, or if he'd steer a wide course around him.

"I better get him home," Linnie said.

Margot and Mrs. G. were face-to-face in the front hall, in a stand-off, when the screen door slammed behind Linnie. Ted ambled back towards the kitchen, while Mrs G. uncrossed and recrossed her arms.

"I was explaining to Mrs. Gonanz," Margot finally told her cousin, "there are certain goddamn rights of occupancy, even in my mother's house."

Linnie saw the flush spread on the older woman's face. No one ever called her anything but *Mrs. G.*, not even Evelyn in a rare fit of temper; it was Mrs. G.'s given name within the family: distinct, respectful, familial.

"I keep things where Miss Evelyn has put 'em," Mrs. G. replied, then held up the disputed item for Linnie to see, a faded daguerreotype of a scowling ancestor that Margot kept removing from its spot on a bureau and Mrs. G. kept replacing. "I caught her bringin' it downstairs."

"I kept hiding the vile thing in a drawer," Margot admitted, "and, dear Jesus, it kept reappearing. Bloody black magic."

Linnie tried to imagine — and couldn't — a way to interrupt the argument. The profanity had unsettled the devout Mrs. G., who was trembling, and given Margot a clear edge.

"We should put it outside by the front door. It's so incredibly *totemic.*" Margot paused to confirm that the word confounded Mrs. G., before she continued. "We'll hang it as a totem and let it scare away evil spirits."

"Oh?" Mrs. G. took a moment to regroup. "You're off to Toronto?"

Margot looked at Linnie, as if to pull her into the argument, but Linnie wanted none of it.

"I give up." Margot smiled at each of them in turn and started for the door. "It's between you two. I'll try to get back next week."

Mrs. G. waited until she was gone. "Rights of occupancy? I put your things back in the blue room, Linnie, and changed the sheets, and I don't want no argument. Meantime, until Miss Evelyn says different," she held up the daguerreotype, "Mr. Totem's goin' back on his dresser."

"Okay."

"*Okay?* It'll be the first thing your aunt asks when she's up and about, she'll see eight things out of place and want a whole history and explanation."

7

I t was hours later, the household fed and Mrs. G. long gone, when April Becker stopped by with a flowering plant for Evelyn. She produced a bottle of wine from a huge pocket in her sweatpants. "Sweatpants are greatly underappreciated," she told Linnie as she handed her the wine.

Together, they fetched an extra chair and a pair of wineglasses, which they carried to the den. As Linnie reached for the light switch, she saw him, hulking in the corner of the dim room. His eyes were fixed on Evelyn, rooted by her immobility, while he shifted back and forth in a boxer's monotonous bob-and-weave, seemingly ready to duck a punch, maybe to throw one.

"Ted?" Linnie raised her voice. "Ted!"

He muttered a few stray syllables without acknowledging her and bumped into her as he hurried out of the room.

"Ted? Honey, are you okay?" April called after him, then waited till she heard the sound of his footsteps moving up the stairs. "I guess it's hard on him. It's lucky you're here. How long can you stay?"

"The firm is letting me take a bunch of time, but not a bunch of paychecks. They stop this week."

"What's your husband say?"

"He keeps emptying our checking account." Linnie's ATM withdrawal, for a mere forty dollars, had been declined that morning.

"My ex-husband?" April said. "He'd write checks and never record them. *Shit*, he'd say, *the bank keeps track, I'd lose any argument, so why bother?*"

"It's different," Linnie said. "He'd pretend it was careless, he does most of his damage passively, but James knows this damn state won't let you get a divorce without first moving out -- which takes money."

"I've been through it. You need a checking account, solely in your name, with a new address. That'll get the clock ticking if you go for a divorce. Heck, I can float you some money to open an account." April shooed away any possible objections. "Your aunt co-signed a loan for me once, when I needed it. If you know how to use accounting software, you can consider it an advance. I need good bookkeeping desperately."

April encouraged her to stop by the office as she uncorked the wine, while Linnie moved the spare chair beside Evelyn, who was sleeping. They both took a glass of wine and a bedside seat, but the loud labor of Evelyn's breathing drove them across the room, to the open window and the low rustle of the breeze in the riverside trees.

"Is her breathing always this troubled?" April asked, once she was settled beside the window.

"When she sleeps. We get her sitting up during the day."

"What's the doctor say? Is she recovering?"

"Who knows? The doctor doesn't answer questions directly. He talks about things — *aphasia, agraphia*, God-knows-what-else — in percentages. Like a problem isn't *global*, it's *forty-percent*."

"Isn't there a period, a timetable in which most people who are going to recover, do?"

"Three months." Linnie frowned. "That's when most spontaneous recovery happens. So far I don't think there's much to get encouraged about. Although it wouldn't be like Evelyn to do anything on anyone else's schedule."

"Is it her name you got? 'Linnie' short for 'Evelyn'?"

"Yeah."

"What's the name of your boy? The one you bring in the summers."

Linnie looked at her wine glass, wondering if she should have started with a full glass. "Jordan."

He'd been impossibly small when he arrived, six years old and he looked four, and he didn't have enough flesh on him to wrinkle, unless you counted the folds of skin that drooped under his eyes. He came for a short visit, at least that's what James had worked out with his junkie of a sister, and he stayed for years.

It took months to put weight on him, coming as he did from a home where he'd subsisted on ketchup sandwiches that he made himself, and it took months more to house-train him, to get him to use silverware, glasses, a toothbrush, his own towel, or any closet whatsoever. Linnie supposed he'd been shut in a closet as an infant, out of the way while his mother tended to her fix.

That first year Linnie taught him letters and numbers, at least till he'd caught up with the kids in his class, and she taught him how to pee standing up. It might have been a lesson better suited for her husband to deliver, but James would've made a long-winded mess out it, lecturing the boy on the mechanics of raised seats, lowered zippers, of arc and aim. She simply took Jordan, who'd only ever sat on a toilet, into the backyard and had him drop his pants and pee on a bush. Take dead aim. Shake, don't drip. Simple stuff, really.

It'd been a lot harder to get Jordan to stop hoarding food in his room. He'd leave half a sandwich under his bed, undiscovered until Linnie smelled it, rancid by then. Crackers got stacked in bathroom cabinets, cookies got stuffed in drawers, and he'd hide his money so well that he frequently couldn't find it. She reassured him ceaselessly, made certain he understood that food would always be available, but any habit of his was hard to break. He was stubborn. An addict, like his mother.

*James was conflicted about Jordan's parents, half the time trying to erase what they'd done (or hadn't), half the time trying to sanctify his sister for her son's sake. What irritated James endlessly was his nephew's complete disregard for a host of social conventions. Jordan would greet a complete stranger with an enthusiastic bear-hug; he didn't know about a polite handshake. He might meet a family friend and climb him like a pole, or flop into the lap of a visiting aunt; it didn't matter whose aunt it was. Embarrassed, James tried to articulate for Jordan the realm of the appropriate, used words like **propriety** as if a six-year-old boy who had all* *but raised himself would comprehend them. "Christ Almighty, it would be one thing if he were one of your cousins," James had whined to Linnie. "If he was Ted. Clumsy and fucking clueless, and none of it counting against him because he's got this carte-blanche disability and Special Olympics snot all over his face. But Jordan's really smart, and people won't forgive his being weird."*

More charmed than worried by Jordan's undiscriminating relish for all that was new, Linnie could not persuade James to let the boy's development take its own course. Jordan's only incivility that bothered her was the way he chewed food with his mouth open. It was the anarchy of the enterprise — milk poured into a mouth still packed with unchewed meat, bread visible on teeth newly employed in a casual grinding of cheese — that she found excruciating.

During their first summer visit, Evelyn had been resolutely unsympathetic when Linnie complained about how Jordan ate. "Every child is a vessel," she'd scolded. "Jordan is just waiting to be filled up with everything you can pour into him."

"It isn't that simple."

"Yes, it is. You may never understand it unless you have a special child. Then you have to keep pouring and pouring merely to keep him half full, and you'll resent the hell out of it if you start worrying about whatever spills."

"It's different. I've taught Jordan to eat. He's being stubborn – a boy who wants to find out if he's in charge."

"That sort of contest can go on and on." Evelyn snorted dismissively. "You don't appreciate the blessing you've been given. He's this beautiful, extraordinary, curious boy with this huge heart that's just waiting for people to leap right in."

"Jordan knows I love him." Linnie was irritated. "C'mon, Evelyn, get off your high horse. Or put it in its barn, will you?"

"This is one thing I know." Evelyn was unapologetic. "I'm not religious. But I believe in blessings."

"How long was Jordan with you?" April nodded at the wine bottle in case Linnie wanted to refill her glass, which she'd emptied.

"Almost four years."

"Did you have to go to court?"

"No. The parents granted us custody. I'd thought I might get to adopt him at some point."

"His mother was sick?"

"She quit the needle when she found out she had cancer."

"Jordan's father just reappeared?" April snapped her fingers. "Comes back a hero? Like he's been at the Trojan War all those years?"

"No. He'd stayed in touch. In fairness to him, he couldn't be around Helen — Jordan's mother. My sister-in-law was this consummate user. She'd suck him right in." Linnie, aware of displaying the bitterness she still felt, took a deep breath and spoke softly. "He got himself together. Clean and sober. Got a degree and a teaching credential in Oregon. Remarried. This time to a Mormon."

"Hell's bells. There's the Good Housekeeping Seal of Approval."

"Long story short. Jordan's with them now."

"You're okay with that?"

Linnie shrugged. It was the only answer she felt capable of.

"I didn't mean anything by it," April said. "My crack about the Mormons. I'm dating a man who was raised one and left the church, so of course he's twisted like a pretzel by it. He's a deputy sheriff. The chief criminal investigator."

"For Niagara County?"

"Yeah. You know the body they found in the graveyard?"

"I walked over there. With Ted."

"Dan — my friend -- says the pathologist's going to release a report tomorrow, and he figures it'll splash all over the news. Apparently that person in the graveyard had a puncture in his skull, not unlike the body they pulled out of the river recently -- with a hole in his head."

"They're the same?"

"I don't think they know. One body was in the graveyard all winter. But Dan says there's never been a serial murder in this county, and he figures that's what the buzz will be. Right or wrong, people'll be locking windows just when the weather would let us open them."

8

Linnie woke to a long, low-pitched groan rumbling through the house like wind stirring a complaint from the rafters. She was slow to recognize the source: Ted's bedroom. Her nightgown was thin for the chilly morning, but she hopped out of bed and rushed down the hall.

Ted was writhing on his bed, using the back of his hands to rub the blisters that crowded his face and neck. Fat blisters bulged below his knuckles and spread his fingers apart, and those which he'd raked with a fingernail trickled fluid, but he hadn't touched the ones on his eyelids that prevented him from opening his eyes.

"Ted, what..?" Linnie sat on the bed beside him.

"Itzy," Ted pleaded. "Itz-itz-itz."

"Stop scratching, sweetie. I know it itches." Linnie grabbed at his hands and held them away from his face, then shouted at the door. "Nick! Nick, come help!"

"God Bless America!" Brendan, who'd stopped by the house after breakfast, whistled at the sight of the inflamed poison ivy blisters on Ted's face.

Linnie explained that a neighbor had hired the brothers, but then separated them. "He had Ted, all on his own, pulling up weeds. For a stinking dollar an hour."

"What a rat." Brendan looked at Ted, then at a bottle on a counter. "Did you put rubbing alcohol on Ted?"

"Yes."

"God, it must've stung like hell."

"He was scraping the blisters. I didn't want the infection to spread," Linnie explained. Her face was reddening, too.

"The only thing anybody's allergic to," Brendan said softly, "is the resin in the plants. Once blisters form, they can't spread the allergic reaction. The damn things *are* the allergic reaction."

"So where were you at six this morning?" She turned to Ted and tried to take his arm, but he squirmed away. "Honey, I'm sorry."

"It's true you don't want the blisters getting infected, but I don't know you want them crimson, either. At least not on a day with a court date." Brendan turned to Ted. "Can we put on a little more Calamine?"

Ted moaned and swatted away any approach Brendan or Linnie made with cotton swabs doused in Calamine lotion. Only Nick was allowed to pat the afflicted skin with the viscous stuff, and he kept at it, even after they had all piled into Brendan's car for the drive to Lockport.

Brendan followed Ridge Road out of town, through farmland that buckled and rolled the farther one got from the flat basin of the lakeshore. Linnie was surprised, and charmed, by the dips and inclines of the highway, by the unexpected crests of small hills that laid out five-mile-wide vistas, the fields still fallow, the silos all peeling, the swatches of forest splashed yellow by the budding maples, and still thick as jungle.

In Lockport, the seat of Niagara County, Linnie expected to find a *downtown*, a cluster of buildings and activity, but all she saw were rundown buildings near the old locks of the long-abandoned Erie Canal. "This is it?" Two feet of water, cloudy with flotsam, lay in a stone-lined lock, beyond which a creek trickled through a bed barely wide enough for canal barges.

"It's been a while since that lock turned," Brendan said. On the way there he'd given Linnie a brief history of the canal. Its demise was just another example of the region's lost prominence and wealth.

Linnie read the large signs posted in front of a small office building: Armed Forces Recruiting Center; Eastern Niagara Ob-Gyn Group; Eastern Niagara Victims Law Center; Hayley Job-Training Institute. Most commerce had found its way to the main highways leading out of town, south towards the Buffalo suburbs. Linnie wondered what Brendan made of the constant display of economic contraction. Maybe one got used to it.

The Hawley Street Courthouse fronted a small square. It had three stories of limestone blocks and was nicely capped with a mansard roof. But when they circled the building, Linnie noticed the hideous addition tacked onto its rear, a long rectangular box striped with turquoise panels and horizontal windows. "I'm hardly ever here. I'd forgotten how ugly it was," Brendan said as he parked the car. "God, the building looks like a bad accident, one thing rammed right into another."

He led Nick, Ted, and Linnie to the entrance, where a deputy sheriff sat beside a metal scanning portal. A placard on the table specified: NO MACE, PEPPER SPRAY OR CUTTERS.

They followed a hall past doors to county legislators' offices, before climbing a stairway to the second floor, where the corridor walls were dark brown and the tan indoor-outdoor carpeting was seamed with cordovan duct tape. Backless benches lined the wall; a long row of bare fluorescent lights flickered beneath the cottage-cheese ceiling. They looked like lane-dividers, Linnie thought: even if they were overhead, the lights were as worn and dim as highway paint after a long winter.

A handsome atrium in the center of the original courthouse relieved the sense of creeping squalor. It rose three stories from the stone floors to a round cupola and was ringed by a walkway that separated two courtrooms. While Nick took Ted to the restroom, Brendan briefly ducked into a clerk's office. Linnie read the handwritten sign posted on its door: *Please don't ask for legal advise, we're not alowwed to give it.* Her eyes scanned the corridor and landed on a holding room where people in manacles and prison-issue orange suits sat on metal chairs.

She was glad when Brendan reappeared. "I've never been in a courtroom," she said. "Ever."

"Relax. You're not on trial."

Linnie couldn't explain why she felt as if she were. "Tell me again. What am I supposed to do today?"

"Keep everything simple. Make the judge think it's going smoothly, so he doesn't have to step in and figure out what to do with Ted."

"It's not going to fall on me, right? I don't want anyone thinking I want to be responsible."

"The judge won't do anything quickly if things are under control."

"You should let him know Nick can look after Ted and be his guardian."

When the brothers rejoined them, Brendan ushered them all into Surrogate Court. Soon, they stood for the entrance of Judge Hood, whose bushy eyebrows sprouted more hair than his scalp. Soft-voiced, attentive, the judge made short work of a few informal bits of business: hearings were postponed, a simple petition entertained, a sale of a ward's house approved, all before he addressed the court's calendar.

No sooner had the first case been announced than the courtroom doors opened, and Margot made her way to a seat across the aisle from her siblings. A man in a gray suit accompanied her, but it wasn't her husband. Linnie leaned toward Brendan. "Who's that with Margot?"

Brendan cupped his mouth and whispered, "I know him from Buffalo. A lawyer. Mostly a litigator, I think."

"Why's Margot bringing a lawyer?"

"I guess we'll find out."

Twenty minutes later, the clerk announced the matter-at-hand: "Phillips, Evelyn. Petition for Temporary Guardianship: Phillips, Theodore: Adult; and Phillips, Nicholas: Adult."

Brendan approached the bench and provided a brief history of the brothers, their differing capabilities, and the stroke that had incapacitated their mother, then outlined the legal issues and the rationale for maintaining the status quo until such time as Evelyn Phillips recovered or her disability was deemed permanent. Judge Hood held his pen like a drumstick, briefly tapping a pad in front of him. Linnie wondered if he was put off by Brendan, in his impeccably tailored suit and well-polished loafers. When he'd stepped up to go behind the bench, the judge had displayed pale blue socks between his dark trousers and badly scuffed shoes.

"How many family members are here? Let's bring them forward, find out what we got." The judge leaned towards the court reporter. "This'll be off the record."

Margot conferred with the gentleman next to her, then strode towards the bench, as if to assume the role of family spokesperson. But when her brothers and cousin approached and she saw Ted's face splotched with pink lotion, she gasped, "My God, Ted, what happened to you?"

"Poison ivy," Nick explained. "He was working for a neighbor. Weeding."

"*Weeding?*" Margot's enunciation gave the word a scientific stature — *nuclear physics?, she might have puzzled* — that made Ted's tackling of the chore that much more improbable.

Linnie had rarely seen Margot so agitated; she too seemed to feel she was on trial. Certainly, she acted like a defendant: questioning others and peppering the judge with challenges to a host of small procedural issues. "Can my mother even submit a petition to the court," she asked at one point, "if she's not currently competent?"

"What concerns us," the judge said, glaring at Brendan, the petitioner's lawyer, "is the circumstances of the person who may need the court's protection. It doesn't matter who files, a family member, minister, state agency, neighbor." He looked over at the brothers, who had returned to their seats. "I could use a little history."

Brendan, noting the impatient shuffle of her feet, deferred. "Margot's the eldest."

"Eldest, yes," she began. "I was born a year before Ted, who was immediately spirited off to an institution. It was a different time, it's what one did if one had money and bore a so-called '*Mongoloid*' or likewise afflicted child. So that's where Ted spent the first eight years of his life. I didn't remember him or know of him, no one ever spoke of him, until I was ten and my younger brother had been born. That's when my mother decided to bring Ted home. One baby home from the hospital, another one home from the institution."

Linnie, who knew that Ted had been institutionalized, was startled to learn that his stay had been so long. Judge Hood glanced at Ted. "Which institution?"

"I don't know its name. Certainly, the family never went. Anyhow, it made for an interesting year, me in fourth grade and suddenly I have two baby brothers, only one of them's taller than me. That first year, my God, Evelyn insisted I take Ted everywhere, to the movies or my friends' houses. Never mind that Ted's behavior and hygiene were awful. The friends I lost..?"

"Excuse me," Judge Hood interrupted, taken aback by the heat pouring off Margot. "Your mother? Isn't she the woman who's so active on behalf of the developmentally disabled?"

"When it suits her."

Linnie thought the retort terribly unfair but understood her cousin's resentment. As a child she, too, had often been embarrassed by Ted. She also suspected that Evelyn must have discussed the matter of prospective guardianship with her daughter. Whether she was inclined or not to the job, Margot clearly was fighting for something.

"Here my mother's two sons are in court," Margot snapped, "and she never took the first step to prepare for this. My mother wanted control but didn't want to confront lots of possibilities."

"This court entertains – I can't think of a better term for it-" Judge Hood said, "lots of wishful thinking. Aging parents with an invalid and grown child, and their last wishes are for the healthy sibling, who long ago moved to the Sunbelt, to come back to the Snowbelt and look after the helpless sibling. When that's just not going to happen. That's why the court's perspective is ward-generated."

"Exactly." Margot nodded deferentially. "Because this is a question for the court. Is what's best for one brother best for the other? My mother wouldn't be the one to ask. I have no idea if Nick can look after himself. Ted obviously can't. But Nick? My mother's never given him a chance. He's been swept up in her mission. Not just cared for, but turned into a caretaker, as if what he wanted to do with his life was to be his brother's keeper. Does Nick like the choices my mother's made for him? Or is he hopelessly saddled with them, like I was in fourth grade?"

9

NICK'S JOURNAL

May 5

We went to court. Margot got so bossy, I wish Linnie would.

I'm supposed to write about two things. One thing, do I like the time I spend with Ted and his day programs? Do I like other people there? Do I like going with Ted? Does Ted embarrass me? What do I want to do?

Most of the people at the day programs are friendly as can be, they smile and they hug, maybe too much if they have a cold. But I do not like people if they are mean. Ted went to ARTISTS ALL. The first day I went they made me a Proctor. The clients made art paintings, and one of my jobs was to have the clients use more than one color. Many people will do only one color if you allow it. We did art first, and music and dance after lunch. Ted won't ever sing or dance.

One woman client was trouble, one day foxing up to one man, the next day teasing up another. She liked it if one man would punch another for her, and I had to stop it. It wasn't much, because one man was tiny and I could hold him back with one hand and the other man would cry if you looked at him cross.

Evelyn will say I have a heart big enough for a whole family or two. She says I like everyone. I don't. I didn't like the woman and I didn't like a man there who used to act up. Two times I had to get him out of the bathroom when he was making a mess, smearing his filth everywhere, even on me. It's awful to have someone throw filth from the toilet on you, you feel so dirty.

Another man there would hit you in the head with anything sharp. They made those men go to another program, it was for difficult people. They weren't right for the artists group. They could hurt somebody is what I think, except nobody says it.

I don't tell Evelyn these things because she'd worry on them. She calls me a great blessing for Ted, she says every horse is blessed to have the right wrangler, and I know for sure Ted gets on better if I'm with him. Otherwise he is hard to understand and you might find him trouble. What else would I do? Generally, if somebody asks me that, they don't wait long before they start telling me what else I'd do. I don't know. That's true.

The second thing you want me to write about is harder. What do I remember of my father? Am I sorry about the divorce? My father left the house before Margot went to college. What I remember is he'd brush his fingers through my hair. He didn't like Ted. Evelyn didn't say so, but there's no other way to say it.

Here's one day I remember with my father. I like to swim, I love the water, and anyone will tell you I've always been a swimmer. Evelyn says I was a swimmer before I was born, I swam through the cord in her umbilical parts, and it made for a struggle when I was born. Born swimming. I know I couldn't swim as a small little baby, but I have no memory of days I didn't know how. We have a pool at the house.

My father didn't like it because Ted wouldn't learn to swim. He didn't care that Ted wouldn't go near the pool, he said a pool was a danger. I think it was the summer I was six because I could swim more than a length underwater, a fish my father called me. He made Ted go in the pool to learn to swim, he had to pull Ted into the water. My father wanted Ted to float. His arms were under Ted like you do with a little child, and all Ted would do was leave his face in the water, hang it there, like he didn't need air, until my father pulled Ted's head up, sometimes by the hair, and finally my father started screaming.

I swam under the water, but I could see Ted lying on top, he was large and had hair under his arms and his mouth was open and he wouldn't move an inch, not even when my father hit him. I could hear the slaps, even underwater, the slaps make a big echo. Then I asked Ted. I told him please breathe, please swim, and he just lied there till my father dragged him out of the pool. A hose was by the pool, sometimes the pool leaks and you have to top off the water, and my father hit Ted with the hose. He whipped him with the hose, but it was my father who was crying. Ted won't do some things, even things he knows how to do. My father wouldn't agree to that.

10

I ts pitch rising, Evelyn's cry was loud enough for Linnie to hear in the kitchen, and certainly the loudest sound she had made in a long while. When Linnie reached the den, Ted was hovering over Evelyn's left side, while her right hand stretched across her body and tugged on his sleeve. Her nails scratched Linnie when she pulled her aunt's hand free of Ted, who responded by pushing Linnie.

"Ted?" Startled by his strength, she knew that a question, rather than a command, might slow him down. "Are you okay? Hungry? What?"

"No!" He held up a pudgy hand with a thin clump of Evelyn's hair in it. "Nana-nana."

"Wait a minute, hold on." But Ted was gone, lumbering away like a bear on its hind legs, shoulders swiveling forward in turn with the feet.

Evelyn's eyes flashed at her niece, then turned to the far wall. Linnie lowered the bed rail, leaned over her aunt's scalp, and examined a small bald spot two inches above her left ear. A trickle of blood wove into the hair below and clotted there.

Linnie blotted away the clump of dried blood with a warm washcloth and exposed the small quarter-moon on the scalp where the skin had torn. Evelyn paid no attention. Her lack of sensation disturbed Linnie, as did the question of what Ted had been doing when he "scalped" his mother. Had he encountered one of Evelyn's increasingly pronounced involuntary tics and tried to suppress it? Or had he simply tried to get her to look his way? Linnie instructed Mrs. G. and Nick not to leave Ted alone with his mother, and she bought a nursery's child monitor for the den and two receivers, one for the kitchen and one for her own bedroom.

Late that evening, as the last rays of light crowned the high clouds, Linnie locked up the house. Ted and Evelyn were in bed, and she had a lot of work to do. She'd already spent many hours straightening out the convoluted entries that one of the associates had made on the books of April's business, which sold cellular phone services subcontracted from a large supplier. April had offered her part-time work, with the guaranteed bonus of a free cellphone and service, and Linnie had opened a checking account in her own name.

She set April's laptop and a fat folder of invoices and receipts on the kitchen table. Linnie liked the work, the simple linearity of using numbers, the satisfaction of arriving at irrefutable answers. At night the overhead kitchen light refracted off the slope of the stainless-steel hood above the range and shimmered on window panes, a tease of motion and substance. A fresh cup of tea beside her, she was sorting paperwork when she heard a clink on the window directly across from her. She looked up and saw her own face in reflection, eyes in a tight squint and hair in need of a brush, the whole image hollowed by the darkness behind the glass. Another face appeared, peering through hers, the second face grizzled by dirt or hair or shadows. Linnie stood up. The face evaporated, but a hand remained on the window, its palm facing inward, before it too disappeared into darkness.

Linnie heard the faint crackle of brush underfoot, the squish of wet grass, something retreating. Unable to find the kitchen flashlight, she hurried to the front hall, where other flashlights were kept. She called Nick and didn't open the front door until he'd joined her and they both had flashlights. He tried to persuade her to stay behind, but she locked the door behind them. She panned the property with her flashlight, the driveway out to the bunkhouse, the lawn back down to the kitchen, as Nick led, his own beam edging the house on three sides until they came to the kitchen window. Nick swung his light towards the river, let it flit by the willows along the bank, then settled it back on a spindly boxwood beneath the kitchen window, where a stack of screen windows leaned against the wall along with a ladder that belonged to the handyman who installed the screens every spring in place of storm windows.

Nick ran his light over the mulch and debris beside the house. What impressions that resembled footprints, if any, could have been made by the screen-installer. "You think you saw what? A face?"

"Like someone looking in."

"A face?"

"I think. It was so quick."

"Linnie?" A broad smile lit up Nick's face. "You a city girl?"

"God, Nick. Not anymore."

"New York City."

"I'm seeing things?"

"No." Nick scratched the flashlight barrel across his stubbly cheek, then honestly wondered, "Was it a pretty face?"

"No." She was surprised by the one vivid detail that had lodged: sideburns. "Old maybe, or in need of a wash. If it was a face."

Nick pulled out his house keys. "You stay inside. I'll swing up to the road and pool. 'Case it's not a raccoon."

Linnie was too relieved by the offer to object. She went to check on Evelyn and Ted, both of them smacking gums as they slept, loudly *tsk-tsking* her anxiety. Nick was back shortly, with a shrug: nothing he could find to worry over. The house on the river had always been a sanctuary, one extra curve off the beaten path, and never broken into. For Linnie, of course, the house had been more than that, bedrock when her own footings shifted, her unflappable aunt the tireless sentry, her mother chasing happiness so recklessly she chased it off.

Linnie couldn't get to sleep. She kept trying to ascribe an identity to the phantom face in the window. It was James, watching and scheming. It was a burglar, discriminating, not interested. It was supernatural, a wild-eyed, kindred angel guarding Ted. It was Ted himself, somehow aware that Linnie had an urge to run away from all of it and checking to see if she had. It was Brendan, waiting for her to undress.

She decided not to share the last thought with Brendan, with whom she was meeting the following morning.

The reception area of Brendan O'Connor's law office overlooked a glass-walled conference room, which itself overlooked the relatively new sports arena, the old harbor, and Lake Erie beyond. With the day warm and clear, and the view thirty stories high, only a thin arc of phosphorescence separated water and sky on the western horizon.

While Linnie waited to meet with Brendan, a girl flung herself on the couch across from her, plopped her feet on the coffee table, and pulled a teen glamour magazine from a canvas bag with a crest on it from The Chapin School.

"Chapin?" Linnie asked. "Do you go to school there?"

The girl considered the question, then considered Linnie, who was wearing sneakers and a well-worn jacket. "It's in *New York City*."

"I know," Linnie said. "On East End Avenue, isn't it?"

"Yeah, I guess." The girl reevaluated Linnie. "You know New York?"

"I worked there for several years. Then I moved north, up the Hudson." Linnie had forgotten, not that Brendan had a child by an ex-wife, but that the child could possibly be this old. She looked to be about twelve. "You're Brendan's daughter?"

"God!" The girl checked out her own clothes. "Is it that obvious? I don't tie a bow in *anything*."

"His bow-ties aren't .. bad."

"Do NOT encourage him. He pretends he inherited them all, but I happen to know he buys new ones, it's like he inherited the vice."

They were interrupted by a woman, appearing at the entrance to a corridor. "Mrs. Carson?"

Linnie recognized the voice from their phone calls: Lydia Kurtz, Brendan's secretary. From the cut of her dress, which hung from the lowest of her chins to the middle of her calves, and from the color of her dyed hair, which had the distinct tint of barbecued chicken, it appeared that Brendan may also have inherited her from his father.

Mrs. Kurtz noticed the girl and frowned. "Kiley?"

The child's response was equally curt. "Mrs. Kurtz?"

"Your father wasn't expecting you for hours."

"Hey? Really?"

"Not till late this afternoon."

"I got an early plane 'cause I knew Dana could meet me anyways."

"Your school has more holidays than the Church of Rome."

Linnie stood up and extended a hand. "Mrs. Kurtz, I'm Linnie Carson. Nice to finally meet you."

"I'm afraid Mr. O'Connor was stuck in court. He's running late. I expect him in thirty minutes, no more."

"No less," Kiley whispered, catching Linnie's eye.

"You have something for me?" the older woman asked.

Linnie handed over a package filled with Evelyn's bills and other mail. "We'll get this sorted," Mrs. Kurtz said, as she turned back down the corridor. "And, Kiley, I hope you brought homework. Your father's got appointments after lunch..."

As Mrs. Kurtz disappeared, her voice trailed off with her. Kiley faced Linnie. "She does that. She talks while she's walking away."

Linnie enjoyed the girl's energy and could remember herself at twelve, boisterous one moment, eerily silent the next. She wanted to keep the girl talking. "What's she like? Mrs. Kurtz?"

"Jesus, she can't really type or proofread. My mother says if Mrs. Kurtz had some money — and she *doesn't* — and if she were a little *less* helpless — and she's hopeless – she'd be one of my dad's clients."

"Have you had lunch?" Linnie saw Kiley's hesitation. "It's an invitation. I'm starving. Do you know somewhere nearby to eat?"

His jacket and tie discarded, Brendan waited till his office door had closed behind Linnie before reaching for his wallet. "That was nice, taking Kiley to lunch. What do I owe?"

"Forget it. I had fun. You're daughter's a kick."

"She's cool, isn't she?"

"Yeah." She imagined how difficult it must be on him, with his daughter spending most of her time with her mother.

He showed her into a chair before taking his own seat. "You're okay for money?"

"I can afford lunch."

"Forget lunch. It's a question Evelyn would want me to ask. I'm running her checking account, and I don't know what your financial condition is."

"It sucks. And you probably know that because Evelyn would've told you."

"She said your husband spent a while without a job."

"I hope she phrased it more colorfully."

"She wasn't sarcastic. Don't underestimate her affection for you."

Linnie sighed. "James finally has a job, thank God. He's teaching, full-time, at a community college. It lets us pay off some debt."

"And you? You're the officer manager of a law firm, right? The judge may ask about your obligations when we go back to court this week. He may also ask about your husband."

"Why? My husband isn't the judge's business."

"If it affects what you'll do..?"

"What I'll do? I'll tell you what I told my boss. I can't see past a month, I'm not even looking."

"I'm pretty certain Margot's going to press things in court. Her lawyer called, to 'confirm' Friday's court appearance, which he could have done without talking to me. He was fishing for information: what provisions Evelyn might have made; whether we'd looked into 'homes' for Ted to live in."

"A 'home' for Ted? How dare he? Do you *have* to deal with him?"

"Margot's entitled to counsel. I'm not sure what she wants."

"She's pissed off about something."

"Does Margot get along with her mother? She doesn't visit much."

"They're both really strong, opinionated women. You know Evelyn, how she can climb up on a pulpit and toss off a few holier-than-thou lectures."

"I adore your aunt, but she can rankle."

"'*Rankle?*' God, would she hate that word. It's what she'd say about Margot." Linnie noticed that her comment surprised Brendan. "Ignore Evelyn for the moment. What do you think should happen?"

"Evelyn's more family than client—"

"Forget the party line," she said gently.

"I mean it. She was my father's best friend. We spent so many holidays together. So she—"

"You, Brendan. That's my question. What do you want?"

Brendan took a while, visibly ordering his thoughts. "It isn't because it would make our lives easier, though it would, and it isn't because of her unfinished business, though she'd dearly want to finish it herself. I'd like Evelyn to recover. Maybe it's too hopeful, but I miss her. I want to sit on her porch, watch the river go by, and listen to Evelyn make sense of it."

It was Linnie's turn to be startled, the press of tears swelling her eyelids. Not long after her father died, she had found herself sitting on a porch-swing with Evelyn, watching the run of the water. *The river runs north,* Evelyn had said, *so I figure that's where heaven must be. Due north.* NOT IN CANADA. *My goodness, the Canadians have enough complexes as it is. Still, heaven's north, some little eddy where all rivers wash out. They don't take a lot of musicians in heaven, God knows not at first, but they make exceptions if a man played first chair. Your father..? I wish we'd both known him a little better.*

11

The last one to arrive in his chambers, Judge Hood tossed his robe on a coat tree and greeted the family, then Brendan O'Connor and Margot's lawyer, a man whose last name, Bridgewater, the judge kept shortening by a syllable: *Bridgewart*. Linnie supposed the judge was hard of hearing and disinclined to acknowledge it.

"How's your brother?" the judge asked, turning his full attention on Nick. "Where's he today?"

"At a program. Is that okay?"

"Sounds good."

"What'll happen?" Nick was clearly worried. "To Ted?"

"That's what we want to decide," the judge said. "You know why we're meeting, Nick?"

"Is it about Evelyn?"

"It's more about you. One day you might be able to live by yourself. You ever thought of that?"

Nick went blank for a moment, then tilted his head. "What about Ted? And Evelyn?"

"We'll think on them, too." The judge picked up a fat pen, which he rolled over his knuckles. "Right now we're thinking of you."

Nick's eyes swept the floor of the room. "Why?"

"Nick!" Margot glared at him, then at her lawyer. "We're trying to figure out who'll look after Ted, if Mother can't. Or you? Can you even look after yourself?" She lowered her voice when she saw how stiffly the insult had registered. "I know all the good things you do. But you've never been on your own."

"I don't think anyone's proposed that," Brendan said.

"I have a question. For Nick, if I might." Bridgewater stood up and turned his chair backwards, then straddled the seat and folded his arms along the top. "See, you need all sorts of things, I guess, to look after yourself, let alone to look after someone like Ted." Bridgewater tipped the chair and leaned into his question. "Nick, you got a driver's license?"

Nick blushed.

"A driver's license?" Bridgewater asked. "Do you have one?"

"It got taken away."

"The Department of Motor Vehicles? They didn't like the way you were driving? You got too many tickets?"

"I didn't ever get a ticket."

"I don't understand."

"Evelyn took it."

"Your mother took it?"

"She said I drove too fast."

"Did you?"

"No. She spilled her purse, with me driving, and got all mad about it."

"So you can't drive?"

Nick squinted, as if he might see through to the question's trick. "I don't have my license..."

"And the point of this?" Brendan inquired. "Evelyn's gotten a bit short-tempered? Heck, we all know that."

"My point," Bridgewater rocked on the back legs of his chair, "is we're talking about guardianship in the event Mrs. Phillips doesn't recover. And we got an adult who's lost his driver's license to his mother's pique and doesn't understand the law any better than that."

"If Nick elects to make peace with his mother—"

"We're not talking about peace. We're talking about coping in this world. And guardianship. Temporary. Permanent. For Ted, maybe for Nick. Counselor, you're the one who came to court to establish what will and won't happen with my client's brothers. So we need to factor in all levels of competency."

Linnie was astounded by the depth of her revulsion for Bridgewater: his belittling Nick was as repulsive as it was unnecessary. She poked the toe of her shoe into Brendan's ankle, hoping to prod him into a sharp retort, but Bridgewater broke the silence his last remark had created. "I don't know what decisions, if any, we intend on reaching today."

"We'll get to that." The judge looked at Margot. "Did you talk to your mother about this business of the license?"

"I didn't want to. To me, it just points out the power my mother has over my brothers' lives. How arbitrarily she can use it. She's made herself the functional guardian, without getting the court's approval."

"Why would she want to go through that?" Brendan was incredulous. "Surely, you don't expect her to ask the court's permission to care for her own children?"

"There are lines she crosses," Margot replied. "Like taking away Nick's driver's license. Maybe she had her first stroke sooner than we know. Maybe, even if Evelyn recovers, we're going to need to consider some sort of court supervision."

"There's a process," the judge said, "but ultimately any timetable will be the court's. So, first off, if we haven't had significant improvement in Mrs. Phillips' health in a month, we'll look to appoint a temporary guardian or guardians for the brothers. To do that legally we'll need to evaluate their capacity." The judge pointed at Brendan. "If you'd get me medical documentation, relevant opinions, and so on."

"Your Honor," Bridgewater was still swaying on the chair's hind legs, "Would it behoove us to start investigating the options? Of picking a guardian? We have two possible candidates here today –— that is if the cousin's interested and available. I know Margot Phillips' finances and personal life are stable."

Brendan put his foot on top of Linnie's when he saw her about to speak. "There's any number of considerations," the judge said.

"It might help," Bridgewater replied, "if the court discussed any 'rules of thumb' it has."

"There's no foolproof formula." Judge Hood put his pen down irritably. "Naturally, we've evolved to the point where we're looking at capabilities, not limitations. We're anxious to keep people in the community."

"And guardians? What makes for a good guardian? I'm asking because it's my understanding Evelyn Phillips tied a significant amount of property and income to the job."

"What's your point?" Brendan asked.

"I think that Evelyn Carson — or Linnie, if I can call you that — already got some money from her aunt. I wonder what happened to it."

It was the day after her mother had died unexpectedly. Linnie, having no idea where to bury her peripatetic mother, had flown to Buffalo and driven up the river: she'd spent as much time with Evelyn in the former summer house as she had with her mother on all her desperate globe-trotting. Evelyn was handling everything, the delivery of her sister's body from overseas, the burial, and Linnie assumed that she wanted to talk about those arrangements when she asked her into the den.

"This is for you," Evelyn said, handing her a check, drawn on Evelyn's account, for fifty thousand dollars.

"What?"

"I don't think it's right." Evelyn was clearly upset. "I'll never speak ill of your mother, but I don't think it's right for a parent to die and not leave a child something."

"It doesn't matter."

"It matters to me. Maybe you're right, and it doesn't matter, though that whole idea has been something of a refrain for you growing up. But it matters to me, and I can afford to do something." She thrust the check at Linnie. "We'll credit this all to your mother. I would've given her this. It's from your mother; it's nothing we need speak of again."

Delighted, Linnie took the check. As much as she loved having Jordan live with James and her, their apartment was crowded, and she had long ago resolved to postpone having children of her own until she owned property, however modest. She wasn't going to raise kids out of suitcases, the way she'd been.

Even better, she and James had been discussing the idea of buying his mother's property, a large house and a cabin on five acres with a distant view of the Hudson, a hundred miles from New York City, and a reasonable commute to her new job. The house was too large for the mother alone, and the cabin, if renovated, would make perfect mother-in-law accommodations. More important, James's mother needed the money, and Linnie was thrilled by the prospect of finally having a home of her own, better yet one that had been in her husband's family for a while. James handled the paperwork and Linnie the money: together, they would pay down the mother's existing mortgage until there was enough equity to refinance the property and rebuild the cabin. Full ownership would transfer to Linnie and James.

What James never revealed is that the property was already encumbered by more than the first mortgage, which Linnie was paying, and that he never recorded their $50,000 lien. When the holder of a third mortgage successfully sued to foreclose upon his note, Linnie's position – $50,000 and almost two years of paying the mortgage and property taxes — was wiped out.

If Linnie had chosen to dwell on it, the loss would have been incalculable: her "inheritance" and hard-earned paychecks consumed by the incompetence and chicanery of her husband's family, whose name she had taken; her mother-in-law acting as if she'd been the one cheated; James proving himself fragile, foolish, and -- worst of all — disingenuous. If Jordan hadn't been living with her, she would have cut and run, but Jordan was scheduled to join his father and stepmother, permanently, before the end of the approaching summer. Desperate to hang onto the boy, she stifled her rage and kept all doors open, on the chance Jordan might somehow slip back to her through one of them.

"You lost the money?" Bridgewater ran a finger along the top of the chair. "I assume there's some remaining."

"The whole issue is no one's business." Brendan slapped a folder across his thigh.

"It's the court's business," Bridgewater argued. "If Linnie Carson might be considered as a guardian, is she financially responsible? Should she post a bond? *Can* she post a bond?"

"Your Honor, no guardian will need a bond, since the guardian won't have a conservator's fiduciary duties." Brendan faced Bridgewater. "Most of Evelyn Phillips' assets will remain in a trust, which I'll administer, and my firm is bonded. And, not to mention, Margot, your mother bailed you out, did she not, when you and your *second* husband bought a condo in Toronto without understanding the staggering roof-replacement assessment that was imminent? She paid it. You didn't."

"Counselors," the judge admonished, "this session is amicable, or I won't waste time with it."

"Your Honor, we do want to keep it friendly." Bridgewater's smile bared a row of bleached teeth. "I must say, Mrs. Carson's husband, I think his name is James, he's been helpful and forthright in his conversations with my client."

Linnie looked at Margot. "James called you?"

Curious, the judge surveyed the cousins.

"He called," Margot said, "to catch up, and ask my view of Evelyn's health. He said he hadn't been able to reach you at Evelyn's house. Anyway, he sent his best to all and said he hoped you'd bring the car back soon. I guess you drove his car out here?"

"I would've driven my own car," Linnie replied, ignoring Brendan's squeeze on her arm, "because the car in my name was a lot newer, which was why we had to sell it to pay off the debts we got when he wasn't working."

Margot laughed. "Oh, heavens, I don't know anything about it. I'm sure James misses you, is all."

When they left the courthouse, Linnie was still seething. Nick laughed at the sight of her in the car: arms folded, legs crossed, mouth pinched, back pressed hard up against the passenger door, with the seatbelt looped around her sideways.

"What's so funny?"

"You're steaming hot mad."

"It's not funny."

"Okay." Nick, waiting for his smile to dissolve, tried to hurry the process along by frowning.

"Relax," Brendan advised Linnie. "You said it yourself. Margot wants control, so her lawyer's going to figure out who flinches and why."

"I don't need to be a goddamn guardian, and I didn't come here to be his target. I'd leave, except I'd have to drive home and James might get to use the car. You believe he said that to Margot?"

"Maybe he was fishing," Brendan suggested, "for news of you."

"Maybe he can keep walking to work. I wish to hell it were winter. Nick, where's your damn driver's license?"

"I don't know. I' been driving without it. Evelyn would've gave it back."

"Let's find it," Brendan said. "Or renew it if it expired."

Back at the house, Linnie made a point of looking for the license. Besides the den, which had been emptied of many documents when it had been turned into a sickroom, Evelyn kept an office in the ground floor of the bunkhouse. Linnie never spent much time in the "office," the ground floor a suite of three maid's bedrooms long overrun by Evelyn's collection of books and photos and grotesqueries, all of them detailing the horrors visited upon the retarded over the ages: an iron vise for the head, a sketch of an idiot's public flogging, old medical manuals describing the brutal cures inflicted by asylums on countless patients, photos of naked institutionalized children lying four to a bed and caked with each other's excrement. Evelyn had made herself an expert, armed with boxes of slides to take on any public speaking opportunity that presented itself, and in the process she had turned her bunkhouse office into a compact museum of horrors.

Linnie found the bunkhouse's office door unlatched, the mortise plate torn from the jamb by a forced entry. Unable to comprehend why anyone would break in, she pushed the door open with her foot. Stacks of books reached from floor to ceiling. The rooms weren't heated; shelter would be minimal. Nonetheless, a corner of a rug had been folded over upon itself. A seat cushion had been moved from a wicker chair and lay inside the fold of the rug. Someone had spent time there.

12

T his handle's only got a latch," Dan Pataki said to Linnie. "Used to be you didn't need a deadbolt, but you ought to think about adding one." April had told her boyfriend, the county's chief criminal investigator, about the suspected break-in and brought him over to the bunkhouse.

"How'd somebody do that?" April pointed at the dislodged mortise plate.

"I think someone leaned hard on the door, and it popped open because the screws had already worked loose. The wood's not rotted. It's fine, of a quality you can't find anymore. Whoever did this isn't sophisticated. No one used a tool or tried a window."

"Should I file a police report?" Linnie asked.

"Anything missing?" Pataki took off his pale green sheriff's parka as they stepped inside. "You need a report if you put in for insurance."

"I doubt much is gone. Only Evelyn would know."

"What do you think?" April swept an arm around the front room's dusty stacks of books. "Why'd somebody do this?"

Pataki looked through a window at the driveway. "You can see this place from the road, unlike the main house. All closed-up, no risk to breaking and entering. Out in Wilson we got kids, they look for anything closed for the season. They're after booze left in a boathouse, a place to party. Or electronics to pinch."

"We're a long-ways from Wilson." April turned to Linnie. "It's a good ten, fifteen miles out the lakeshore."

"There's troubled kids here, too. Though I don't know what they'd want in here," Pataki admitted, peering into a closet stuffed with frayed books and tarnished curios. "Linnie, you got those cousins."

"And?"

"I don't know." He picked through a shelf in the closet and found a box of slides, a few of which he held up to the light. "Dear Lord, here's a sore sight. Some boy in a harness and choke-chain collar."

"Families used them to keep a retarded child from wandering," Linnie explained. "Evelyn collected photos. Some more than a hundred years old."

"Grim stuff."

"Evelyn figured history needed a witness." Linnie looked at April, knowing she would understand.

"Grim stuff," Pataki repeated. "Your cousins ever come in here?"

"Not the ground floor."

"Ted? He's the older one? Word is, he's pretty hard challenged."

"I suppose."

"You think maybe he'd bust in here?"

"Why?"

"Curiosity. Anger. His mother spent time in here. Or maybe he wonders about the building. It's within his mental reach, right? Any child wonders."

Linnie felt her muscles contract, a tightening from the top of her chest to the wall of her stomach. The county's chief investigator, here as a favor to his girlfriend, was treating her cousin like a suspect. "I doubt Ted would come to these rooms," she managed. "Sometimes in the summer, if the house gets full of guests, Ted and Nick will sleep upstairs, in the boys' bunkroom."

"So maybe it gets to shelter. Someone breaks in, sleeps inside."

"I thought I saw somebody outside, one night a few weeks ago," Linnie said, "but we couldn't find anything."

"If anyone was here, he can't have stayed long." April pointed towards the bathroom. "No real heat, and the plumbing shut off in winter."

"You got a path down the riverbank?" Pataki asked.

"It's steep," Linnie said. "You can get to the bottom, but it's a climb either way."

"You see the border patrol cars all over the place now. The officers swear immigrants sneak across this stretch of the river. Mostly Asians, who get into Canada easy and come over."

"A bunch of horsecrap," April hooted derisively. "Nobody's as much as seen one."

"Got to be honest. We don't get calls on it either."

"My God!" April exclaimed. "Given all the lazy-asses around here, a group of twelve Chinamen set foot on River Road and they'd be hired faster than you can chop suey."

"I still think it's shelter," Pataki said, replacing the seat cushion on its chair. "Somebody spent a little time here." He picked up a periodical that lay on the floor, open to a diagram of a multi-chambered brain, each chamber a holding pen for a personified and caricatured emotion: *Anger* raged in a forechamber drawn to resemble a cellar. Printed on well-yellowed paper, the journal was titled *Behavioral Science for Subnormal Intellect*. "Here's some light reading," he remarked, tossing the journal on top of a pile of similar curiosities. "Your aunt actually read all these things?"

"Probably, to see if they were worth keeping. For her collection."

"Which is?"

"Things that didn't get it right. History's miscalculations."

"That could make an awful big library," Pataki mused. "Of course, the person I'd really like to talk to is your aunt. Jannevitch, the first victim we pulled out of the river, we know he spent time in local institutions, and everyone hereabouts says Mrs. Phillips is the expert on that kind of thing."

"She is," Linnie said. "She had Ted try all the day-programs."

"We can trace Jannevitch back twenty years, always living in a state-approved facility, but then his history dries up. Here he's your older cousin's age, and he didn't just materialize one day in some group home, yet we can't trace him too far back. If he's local, which I'm assuming, he must've had a family at some point, who stuck him somewhere."

"The state must have records," April said.

"The state's the problem," he replied. "All these laws, protecting privacy, especially for the disadvantaged. You run into firewalls when you try to go back into these lives."

"Why go back?" Linnie nodded at the shelves housing Evelyn's collection of lurid history.

"To find a family, for starters. With Jannevich we couldn't find a soul to notify. I don't know how or when he got committed to the state, but it's likely someone signed off on it, only those records are sealed. Or lost."

"What about the other guy? In the graveyard?" April nodded upriver, in its direction. "The newspaper said he was probably homeless."

"Looks like dental records gave us a match, which was hard because a lot of the guy's teeth had fallen out. A resident in the Pine Street facility in Niagara Falls wandered off a couple of years back, been missing since, and it looks like this guy's got his teeth, or what's left of them. How is it, with the retarded, you'd think they never saw a dentist? I was at the Pine Street home last week, and I don't think two teeth pointed in the same direction."

"How did the poor guy stay lost?"

"I don't know," Pataki said. "Maybe somebody put him up. We have so many retarded adults. I checked with the state, and the numbers in this county are disproportionately high."

"Do you think it's environmental?" April asked.

"I don't buy that. Most of the local MRs were born years before the first house was built on Love Canal. I think the problem here is economic. A couple of generations of brain-drain. The ones with college degrees leave. The ones who can't leave, stay."

"Well, I'm staying." April grinned. "What does that say about me?"

Pataki helped Linnie lock up the bunkhouse office. She hadn't found Nick's driving license in Evelyn's office there, but she'd come across a short stack of well-preserved leather-bound books: the collected poems of Yeats, an early edition of Joyce's *Ulysses*, a compact and complete

George Bernard Shaw. *An Anthology of Irish Theatre* was inscribed on the title page, as were the other books, in someone's handwriting:

> *Ev,*
>
> *I should have the pluck (foolhardiness?) of an Irish protago-*
> *nist or, failing that, an American-sized fortune and a yacht*
> *with the tonnage of a battleship and sufficient ordnance to*
> *still wagging tongues. Better yet, a brave new world and the*
> *courage to risk passage.*
>
> *What little I have I do treasure.*
>
> *Bless you,*
>
> *P-*

Linnie was intrigued by the note's intimacy but didn't get a chance to ask about it for a week.

13

The evening breeze chased away any bugs that had survived the extended dry spell. With the peonies swollen by long days and toppling under their own weight, Linnie and Nick wheeled Evelyn's hospital bed onto the huge side porch, that she might enjoy her garden. Evelyn's face brightened in the fresh air, and her eyes found whoever was speaking. She didn't attempt to talk, but she held her niece's hand tightly and squeezed it if she needed anything.

Brendan found them there, as she and Nick were trying to move the bed back inside. Linnie kept a troublesome screen door open and let the other two lift the bed over the threshold, then sent Nick off to check on his brother.

Reaching the den, Brendan dragged the bed in a sideways loop such that the headboard fit into its place against a wall. Linnie helped swivel the bed, then put a hand on the thin rise that Evelyn's leg made in the covers. "She was so happy to be by her garden."

"Yeah?" He looked at Evelyn, who was nodding off. "She's probably wondering why no one staked her peonies."

"You're hired."

He laughed. "You couldn't pay me enough, to risk screwing up her garden. I'd never hear the end of it."

"It's strange." Linnie swept aside the hair that had fallen across Evelyn's forehead. "Sometimes she wonders who's with her. Even me. Her eyes glaze over."

"Hell, I keep expecting her to shake free of it, suddenly sit up straight and tell us what's what." He took hold of Evelyn's arm, which was slipping off the bed, and carefully put it under the covers.

Brendan looked relieved when he and Linnie retreated to a couch in the living room. "It's difficult seeing her like this," he said. "She's always been the quickest study. She'd grasp an issue before you'd finish presenting it."

"Do you know anyone who called her 'Ev?' She has this little collection of books." She gave him the anthology of Irish plays. "Look in the front. Is this from your father?"

He opened the binding, read the inscription, and blushed. "It's my father's handwriting."

"I wondered. His name was 'Paddy,' right?"

"Yeah." Brendan flipped through the other books and browsed through the endearments in the inscriptions.

"So the two of them were more than friends?" Linnie smiled. "You know Evelyn, always so circumspect."

"They were great friends, best friends, I don't know why they didn't act on it."

"You think?" She picked up the volume of Yeats poetry and read: "'*Dearest Ev; I'm looking for the Irish in me, the fierce and the rash, me wee poor Irish left in the County or scrubbed clean by generations of your Episcopal cousins. With love to green, P.*'" Linnie raised an eyebrow. "You're telling me this — whatever it was, this 'love to green' – was unrequited?"

Brendan faltered. "Well, the timing was for shit. My mother died when I was in high school, and Evelyn had moved from Buffalo to live year-round here at her summer house. Her divorce had to have been bitter."

"Bitter? I think she made her break and moved on."

"Divorce isn't that easy."

"I take it yours wasn't?"

"You met my ex-wife. What do you think?"

Linnie had no intention of telling him. She'd met the woman several times at gatherings on the river, and she shared her aunt's opinion.

"She's Manhattan born and bred, and no doubt misses it," Evelyn had said. "Unfortunately, she's begun to feel the compunction to condescend to those of us who aren't inclined or able to live there."

"What happened?" Linnie asked.

"My father's health was failing, and the firm I was with in New York broke up. My wife agreed to try Buffalo. Three years was three too many. Jesus, she tortured everything. I thought I'd have time to sort it out, on my terms. Then one day my wife announces she's moving to New York and taking a graduate course in Art."

Linnie thought of Jordan, recently carted off to his rehabbed father's new home; Jordan would have taken Linnie to Portland with him if he could, and she might have gone. "You could've gone with them," she told Brendan.

"Kiley stayed with me."

"I'm sorry. I didn't—"

"To finish the school year. She was happy with me. I thought I'd get the lion's share of custody. I didn't figure on an old asshole of a judge declaring a pre-adolescent girl mostly belonged with her mother."

Linnie put a hand on his arm. "I'm sorry."

"I was so goddamn relieved when my wife left."

"I'm not buying it. Not with Kiley."

"That part hurts."

Linnie, who'd never thought Brendan's marriage a success, wondered about Evelyn's and how it had failed. Had there been gradual erosion, till there was nothing to stand on or for? Or were the shifts tectonic, violent and unavoidable ruptures? Linnie wasn't sure how to categorize her own marriage's collapse, except she knew there was a moment when she'd understood the finality of it.

When Linnie's job forced Jordan, James, and her to move north, to a town outside Albany, James had Helen shuttle up the Hudson as well, to move in with their mother. There, Helen's cancer stuttered, side-stepped vital organs, and entertained slight remissions.

It was Jordan's visits that unsettled his grandmother's household. Frightened by her appearance -- his mother was bruised, sallow, skeletal

— Jordan would cling to Linnie, so much so that James started to exclude her from the visits. But Helen retreated into herself when her son was around, and the grandmother's exuberance could be absolutely suffocating. "She won't ever leave me alone," was the way Jordan described his grandmother's attentions. "Even TV. Why can't I watch it by myself?"

"She's so happy to see you," James explained. "She looks forward to it all week."

"Why?" Jordan's question was sincere: not much happened on his Sunday visits, certainly nothing that generated his anticipation.

"It's blood," James had said, with a look at Linnie, who wasn't a blood relative and who somehow had no trouble bonding with Jordan. "You're part of her blood. She cherishes that."

"What?" Again, the child didn't get the logic.

"Just fly with it, okay? For now? Go with it."

"I'm flying with it," said Jordan, chicken-winging his way out of the room they were in. "Fly, fly, fly."

James waited till he was out of earshot before turning on Linnie. "You could help, you know."

And she did know, had always known, that she probably could help him in his effort to get close to his nephew, but James was stubborn, and his attempts were resolutely ham-handed.

"You could help," James repeated.

A week later James announced that Jordan's father, having gotten his teaching certifications in Oregon, would be visiting. Whose idea that visit was, Jordan's father's or his uncle's, was hard to determine. "Seems like it's about time," James had replied when Linnie wondered why a long absent father all of a sudden paid a visit. "Especially with Helen so much worse."

"Who's paying for the plane ticket?" Linnie regretted her question, flush as it was with resentment that she'd rather have kept private, the moment James let the question hang.

"God, Linnie." He whistled through his teeth. "It's not like you to be so small."

Inclined to dislike the father, and thereby to defend her own relationship with Jordan, Linnie discovered that Steve Wheelwright was not simply unobjectionable, but positively charming. He befriended Jordan

with an ease that made James's efforts look all the more clumsy and spent
vast amounts of time with his son. When the time came, it was James,
not Steve Wheelwright, who calmly delivered the gutshot to Linnie. "He
wants his son. I guess that's that."

Linnie wondered if Evelyn had experienced a similar moment, a
sickening recognition that her husband was no longer her ally. Evelyn
had never discussed her divorce or her husband with her niece, and
seemingly viewed the subjects with a detachment befitting ancient
history. However, Linnie felt much more in common with her aunt
than her mother, who'd been thrown from the back of a motorcycle
and killed at an age when -- well, neither Evelyn nor Linnie would
ever have been on one. Linnie wanted to know about Evelyn's marriage, especially on the chance it had been similar to her own, but she
didn't want to ask Margot, who'd have her own slant. She decided to
have Evelyn tell her all about it - as soon as she was speaking again.

Two days later, Linnie left a flash-drive full of corrected data at
April's office in Niagara Falls, then followed the river to Tonawanda,
where she'd dropped off Nick. She found him as she left him, his
shoulders planing across the surface of the pool on the surge of long
strokes, while his feet kicked up a slight chop. She'd brought him to
the YMCA, where he swam during the long months when Evelyn's
pool was closed. He looked odd, with the facility's mandatory bathing
cap pulled low on his forehead, but his pleasure forestalled any impa-
tience she might have felt with other errands to run. Nick could have
helped, since she'd taken him by the DMV office to replace his lost
license, but Evelyn's car was in the shop.

It was long after dinner - Mrs. G. gone for the night, Ted settled,
Evelyn's physical therapist ferried to the bus stop up on the Lewiston
Heights escarpment - before Linnie had a chance to spend time with
her aunt. She brought a book to read, but the lamp by the bed had
been knocked from its table. Evelyn's right leg, the mobile one, had
coiled the sheets around her calf, while her jaw twitched with audible
cracks; air bubbles formed in the milky fluid leaking from her mouth.

It took fifteen minutes for the paramedics to arrive, five minutes more than it did for April, who promised to spend the night. Nick would sleep with his door open, in case Ted stirred, and April would camp out in the blue room, its door also ajar.

Once the gurney was wheeled from the house and secure in the ambulance, the driver wouldn't allow Linnie to ride in the back of the truck with Evelyn and made her buckle up in the cab's passenger seat. She hoped that Ted had slept through it all, the ordeal oddly quiet thus far, no sirens, nothing except the ambulance strobe-lighting the house with crimson flashes, but in her last glance at the house she noticed that the window shade in his room was angled to the sweep of the ambulance's lights differently than the pulled shades in other windows. She wondered if Ted had drawn back the shade and was peering out. She couldn't see a face, but she could imagine his: eyes wide and gray, tongue clucking against a cheek, head swaying to the bob of nervous feet.

"She your mom?" the driver asked, as the ambulance sped back up the driveway.

Linnie was slow to respond. "Manner of speaking."

"She's got an okay heart muscle, your mom, decent pressure and rhythm, so I'm guessing she'll rebound, and you'll talk."

"We'll talk," Linnie concurred, overwhelmed by the flood of questions she had for her aunt. She wondered about the endearments from Paddy O'Connor, who had never been identified as more than a friend, and about her divorce. And Linnie dearly wanted to know what had happened to goad Evelyn to retrieve the baby boy she'd sent to an institution. Was it an image that she didn't need to see to imagine: Ted's haunted face peering from a window? "You can be sure of that," Linnie told the driver. "We'll talk.

14

NICK'S JOURNAL

May 29

It was five days, and then Evelyn got home from the hospital. I drove up there Tuesday and Thursday when Mrs. G was here, and the doctor told Linnie it was probably a bunch of quick little strokes, not one big one. Which is a better thing. The doctor wants Evelyn to go to a therapy hospital, but she'd want to be home, and that's that. The bad thing is there's a bag on a hook, and her urine runs down to it. Before we lifted her on a pan or the potty chair.

The nurse told us we didn't have to empty the bag every other minute, but Linnie can't stop checking and throwing any little bit out. She says Evelyn wouldn't want us looking at a big bag of her pee.

You asked of Ted. He didn't like it with Evelyn away. He went around and around the house looking for her. Mrs. G said it was like when a mother cat has its kittens taken away, it'll go all over the place mewing for them, and it doesn't know they can't be found, so I told him Evelyn was at the doctor. Did he understand? I don't know.

We can't take Ted to a hospital, he won't want to visit. One time we went to see Margot in one, but Ted couldn't walk down the halls without moaning and sticking to me like we'd lose him. I think it's the smell of a hospital that gets him. He gets real crazy.

On Saturday James made a surprise visit. He took a bus from the airport to Niagara Falls and a taxi to Lewiston. He gave everybody a hug, even Ted, and said he wanted to see how Evelyn was. James fell asleep in the tv room and spent the night on the couch.

Linnie didn't seem happy about the surprise, and the next morning she was mad enough to break things. I was awake first and showed her the note. James wrote he needed the car for his turn. The note sounded fair and square, but Linnie didn't think so. She says he stole the keys from her purse and took the car like a thief. And she says, which I forgot, Evelyn's car is in the shop.

Brendan was sailing Sunday and stopped by. He's got another car, a Mustang his father had, and Brendan uses it in the summer when he can put the top down. He offered to lend it, but April's got an old Jeep, which is what Linnie borrowed. Brendan laughed when he saw the Jeep with the big rip in the top.

I started cleaning the pool, the cover is off and water running through the filter, and I put in the hose to top it up. It makes me happy, the pool open. Except Linnie stayed mad all day.

15

The Niagara Day Care Center was chaos at eight a.m.: the vans coming and going, and four personnel yet to show up for work. Linnie found herself policing the lobby of the county facility. One of the clients was strapped into a hockey helmet and a narrow wheelchair, her cerebral palsy lurching her so violently that Linnie, afraid the woman would tip over, wedged her wheelchair between two upholstered seats. Another client, his face clumped with tiny knots of beard that his razor kept missing, repeatedly extended his hand to her for a quick squeeze, after each of which he'd sniff his fingers to smell the floral lotion she had rubbed on that morning.

Ted sat peacefully in his chair, so slumped over he could have been shot. But the man stomping around next to him worried her. Well over six feet tall, with trunk-like arms swinging randomly from his broad chest, he muttered a barrage of *fuck-fuck-fuck-fuck*, the cadence varying without ever establishing a noticeable rhythm, the hostility radiating from him like a child's tantrum. He wanted someone caught by the slash of his arms; he wanted a knife; he wanted to cut.

Linnie chided herself: she was well versed in the lingo and literature of the developmentally disabled; she had absorbed, through the osmosis of family, much of the behavior-modification creed; she had a revered aunt who was a goddamn martyr to the cause. She should — by nature, by experience, by any principle that she could grab onto and hold dear — have defeated prejudice, and yet she disliked the bastard in front of her, swinging his arms like a monkey, looking for somebody else's breast to beat.

She felt relieved when the center's director, a sweetheart of a man three hundred pounds large, returned to the lobby, fresh from herding a group of aluminum-walker-wielding seniors onto their own bus, and immediately confronted the angry giant. "Joseph," he declared, "we're gonna have some fun today, you're gonna be out there today earning good money. Billy's a bit late, he's on his way, and I bet he's hoping you spend some of your darn money at McDonald's later. Okay? You want some French fries, right? Let's keep those arms down. Let's not touch anybody, we're not getting in their space, okay? We'll sit till Billy and the darn van get here."

The director bullied Joseph into a chair, much to the relief of Linnie, who could imagine Evelyn's disappointment with her niece's misgivings: her aunt would argue that a court's definition of crime, the notion that informed intent had to precede perpetration, supersedes any simple definition of evil, particularly a religious idea that primal wickedness is rampant in a fallen world.

Evelyn had had a profound impact on Linnie, who believed in a world with goodness in great supply; but she also knew that evil, an inexplicable urge to violence, came into play. In college she'd volunteered to staff a domestic abuse hotline; nothing had prepared her for the horrors she heard, firsthand, on the midnight shift. And what else but evil could explain Joseph? As soon as the director had stepped back a few feet, Joseph resumed his litany of *fuck*s and swung an arm. Though she kept trying not to, Linnie wondered how deep Joseph would have stuck a knife. If he had one.

She hoped the investigators had checked him out.

The next day, Brendan picked through the mail that Linnie brought, then flopped onto a couch across from her chair. "So I hear," he said, "you had a nice heart-to-heart with Judy Urbankski, M.F.T."

"You're the one who makes me go talk to her."

"Wrong. The court wants a therapist's opinion. Judy's will do. On Ted, Nick, even prospectively on you. You're filling a role, even if it's temporary."

"'Temporary.' I don't know why the court needs anything." The preceding Thursday, she'd taken Nick and Ted to their sessions with Judy Urbanski, then been invited to spend time in her office. "Judy was asking all these leading questions" Linnie began. "She knows I'm married, or not yet completely unmarried, and she asked me, point-blank, if I'm promiscuous."

"Okay. Clearly you like punchlines, and she gives you an opening."

"'Am I promiscuous?' I told her I was flattered by her interest, but thought therapists weren't supposed to date their patients."

"I'm guessing here," Brendan raised a finger, in mock contemplation. "Her laugh wasn't from the belly?"

"She didn't react. She did that therapist thing, ignore the remark, hang a little silence, and then ask if I was feeling hostile. Hostile? I was insulted."

"Christ, Linnie. The issues for you — by which I mean the court's concerns — aren't simple. At a point the judge is going to want to know that you're staying here because you want to be here."

"As compared to?"

"As compared to staying here because you're avoiding somewhere else. By which—"

"By which you mean James." She exhaled the breath she'd been holding. "He won't put up a fight, he'll duck it, so the burden and expense of a divorce will be mine."

"Is it money? Is that what you've been waiting on?"

"That's been the hold-up recently." Linnie picked at her fingernails. "For a while it was Jordan. If it didn't work out with him and his father. James is Jordan's relative. I would've needed that. And a marriage in order to keep custody of Jordan. At least at the start."

"Jesus, Linnie. You think a court doesn't keep reviewing the custody..?" Brendan broke off when he saw how crestfallen she was. "It's working out? For Jordan? With his father and stepmother?"

"Yeah. Maybe it's like Kiley. We're supposed to be happy they don't need us to rescue them." She ran her hands through her hair in an unsuccessful effort to keep her voice from breaking. "It's all stupid..."

He waited for her to look up. "So now what?"

She rummaged through her purse and pulled out a used scratch-to-win lottery ticket. "I buy these," she admitted, flipping her worthless ticket towards a trash can. "I don't have to win big. A small jackpot would be fine. I could pay movers and afford a lawyer to handle the divorce."

"Where would you go?"

"Maybe Seattle. My two best friends from college moved there. But right now there's only Evelyn. It's not Ted or Nick or James or the damn judge in Lockport, or Seattle, it's Evelyn."

She'd almost always known that, when and if the need arose, she had her aunt to rescue her. Evelyn had paid for sending her niece to her own alma mater, a boarding school in Connecticut where Linnie also thrived. Two different times Evelyn, declaring that Manhattan would be more festive for the school holiday, flew with Nick and Ted to New York for the long Thanksgiving weekend, in order that Linnie could join them in a hotel there. Ted made a daily ruckus on those trips, but every afternoon Evelyn would organize a "girls' outing" to take Linnie on, shopping at Bergdorf's, high tea at The Plaza, a matinee off-Broadway. Every night Evelyn gave thanks that Linnie had been able to share her suite.

Evelyn window-dressed all of it beautifully, a holiday storefront on Fifth Avenue, and Linnie pretended not to mind that her mother couldn't share those holidays. By Sunday she'd get on a train for the ride back to school and entrance her friends aboard with stories with which to hold court: her severely retarded cousin screaming like a banshee on a subway platform and wetting himself, her aunt mad with Nick and her for trying to get Ted onto a train. Stories were currency at boarding school, and other kids' holiday anecdotes were yams and marshmallows compared to Linnie's adventures with her cousin Quasimodo, her faithful servant Nick, and her formidable aunt. The stories held at bay, however briefly, the crush of loneliness.

"My life is on hold," she tried to explain. "Evelyn needs to rally."

Brendan stood at the sight of her tears and searched his office. "Do not get me Kleenex," Linnie said, wiping away tears. "You're not my therapist."

Brendan circled to her chair and sat on its arm. Tentative at first, his hand sought and found hers, enveloping it in both of his. With no advice to give, and none wanted, he let the heat of her hand radiate in the press of his. Overcome, Linnie folded her head across his arms and sobbed in his lap.

16

On the road back from Buffalo, Linnie followed the interstate up-river and past the reservoir that separated the river gorge and a power plant from the Tuscarora Nation's reservation, where she and April had scheduled a meeting with April's star saleswoman, Edie Paterson, and her friend Ruth Cornplanter. A mile onto the reservation Linnie spotted April's Buick, with Mount Hope Cellular placards on its doors, parked beside a pair of rusted-out Camaros from the Sixties that would need a crane to move them.

The cellular phone business was particularly good here, largely because of a long-simmering dispute between the Council of Chiefs and the phone company that provided residential service. The Council insisted upon sovereignty over construction of and access to anything on the nation's land: phone company repairmen had been detained by reservation police for trespassing and, more than once, shot at. Thus, phone lines didn't often get repaired and new lines didn't get installed.

Ruth Cornplanter was on Edie Patterson's front porch, working her cigarette breathtakingly close to her fingers, when she saw the Jeep. She motioned for Linnie to pull onto the front lawn and park beside the Buick.

"You can park on your front lawn here," Ruth said, flicking away her butt as she moved to greet her. "We don't got curbs and no red paint to put on 'em."

Linnie grabbed a box of files and brochures from the backseat. Mount Hope Cellular contracted with one main provider that had an ever-changing array of new plan details for the sales associates to keep straight.

April and Edie stepped off the front porch of Edie's cottage, which listed slightly. Thirty feet from it, a small trailer was set on blocks. A garden hose and extension cord ran from the cottage to the trailer's underbelly; a propane tank teetered beside it. Although she hadn't seen it yet, Linnie knew Edie had outfitted the trailer as a display and sales office, open on Wednesday afternoons and Saturday mornings.

As the four women converged on the door to the trailer, a Niagara County sheriff's squad car braked hard in the nearby intersection. The driver threw the car into reverse, braked again, and took a right on Walmore Road, accelerating as he passed Edie's property.

"Deputies can come onto Nation land," Ruth said, noticing Linnie's puzzlement. "Who else are you gonna put in harm's way when Johnny Deerfoot gets lit and prowls around with his eight-gauge?" She looked at the receding squad car. "'Course, that twit must've gone the wrong way. It's the Hammers' place he's looking for."

"Why?"

"You didn't hear?" Ruth shook her head. "They found poor Early. Dead, that's no surprise, except it was his skull, not just his liver, caved in."

"Poor thing." Edie ran her thumb and forefinger along the perfectly pressed crease of her blouse, then turned to April. "You know him? Lord have mercy. Made a career out of being the town fool."

"The alcoholic? Always outside the supermarket when the weather was right. What'd he call himself?"

"'Injun Joe.' Bad enough he hated his sorry self, but he had to drag us in. Poor half-wit never had a chance, his mother drunk every day she carried him."

Linnie thought she knew the man in question. Disheveled, webs of ruptured vessels capturing the little steel pupils in his eyes, the stink of vomit clinging to him, he occasionally took a statue's pose beside store entrances. "Cigar-store Injun," he'd mumble, extending his palm for a handout. "Injun Joe say, 'How.'"

"What happened?" Linnie asked.

"He's been gone a while from the shack his dad left, I hope they tear it down," Ruth started, "a hole of filth, and nobody knows how many weeks he's missing. He always said if he got deadly sick, he'd go 'native,' grab himself a gallon or two and go die in the woods. They found him this morning in a stand of trees on the banks of the escarpment, his body rotting, his liver no doubt a ruin, his head woodpeckered like a bird wanted to feed on his teeny-tiny brain."

Edie fingered the large gold cross on its chain, which perfectly centered her silk blouse and the well-tailored suit that made the three other women look as if they'd just left the gym. Linnie knew, by reputation, two things about Edie: she was an unstoppable force, charming, persistent, smart; she was also extremely devout.

"Is it connected?" Edie asked. "To the other episodes?"

"It's likely." Ruth coughed out a caution for her friend. "But, honey? Don't go pontificating on us. Early Hammer died with a hole in his thin head. It's the ways of man, not the Man above."

In Edie's moments of earnest consideration, Linnie saw why few could withstand her sales pitch: Edie's goodness radiated from her. "What I think," Edie said, "is the Lord has called some of the lost to Him."

"He could've got to it a little sooner," Ruth hissed. "These men-child are fifty and sixty and they're dying outdoors like road-kill. Hard to take comfort in that."

"The comfort is there for those who seek it," Edie insisted. "And these people – 'men-child' you called them – they're at peace. Scripture makes it plain. The meek will be made mighty. And I won't be afraid."

"Well, I'm afraid," Ruth admitted. "Something mean's on the loose, and I'm sleeping with Mr. Smith and Mr. Wesson on my pillow."

"Lord have mercy." Edie's eyes widened. "Are you talking about that little-bitty starter pistol your daddy bought at K-Mart?"

"I only keep three bullets in it." Ruth saw, from the others' quizzical looks, that her logic wasn't self-evident. "See, I'm guessing I wouldn't be the one holding the gun if it got to a fourth shot."

"You throw that away!" Edie shook her head fiercely. "This sorrow, it may be spreading, but whatever it is, even the TV news isn't making hay out of it. But you with a gun? *Now* I'm afraid."

17

I n a front-page article the next morning, *The Niagara Gazette* published a brief account of "Injun Joe's" death under the headline MISSING LOCAL MAN IS NEW VICTIM. *"The cause of death is still under investigation. Deputy Coroner Dr. Katherine Gambino cited toxic blood levels, consistent with a lethal dose of alcohol, as well as repeated trauma to the skull. The presence of bone fragments in mature scar tissue surrounding the small cavity bored into the skull suggests the injury may have been sustained over a period of time."* The article's final sentence, with its depiction of a hopelessly scattered family, struck Linnie as the cruelest of all: *"Early Hammer is believed to be survived by a nephew, George Flowers, with a last known address in Beaver Falls, Montana."*

Linnie had read the various newspaper accounts, slim as they were, by the time Margot stopped by the house, on route from Toronto to Lockport, to give Linnie a ride to their court appearance. "What we should do," Margot said, as she turned out of the driveway, "is put Evelyn's car in Nick's name. God knows, she's not going to drive it anymore."

"You don't think she might recover?"

"I think we should keep the car from her if she does recover. She lost consciousness several times. She may never be able to renew her license." Margot fetched a pair of sunglasses from the top of the visor. "Nick's okay? Driving Ted to his appointments?"

"He's fine. Is your lawyer meeting us at the courthouse?"

"I don't know there's much for him to do. Rick was busy anyhow, and it gets expensive having lawyers drive all over to listen to Judge Hood's homilies."

Brendan was late for the meeting in the judge's chambers, so Margot helped herself to the only seat available in the corridor while Linnie leaned against the wall. By the time Brendan did arrive, the judge had been summoned back to court.

"Whatever we hope to finally accomplish today," Margot told Brendan, in her most nearly forgiving tone, "let's keep it brief. I have to get back to Toronto this evening, and I'd like to have supper with Mother first."

"Judge Hood wants an update. I don't think he'll make any big decisions unless we hit the panic button."

"I didn't bring my panic button," she said, grinning, before lowering her voice to mimic the judge's congested nasal delivery. "Mr. *Bridgewart* is tending to more pressing business." Margot reverted to her regular voice. "And, no, he's not chasing ambulances, if that's what you're worrying about."

"Plane crashes are just so damn rare," Brendan sighed.

"Good Lord, he's with a big corporate client. I'm sure he doesn't know why this process of ours is so complicated. Linnie, you've been through it, haven't you? With your nephew?"

"It wasn't exactly..."

"You had custody, I thought."

"We had Jordan, his birth certificate. And a notarized authorization from his mother, which was what the school system required."

"The custody?"

"It wasn't set."

Margot looked puzzled. "I thought you went to court."

"Initially."

"I don't understand. Certainly, you could've won custody. A father who abandoned the household, a drug problem to boot, and you were raising the kid."

Linnie didn't know where to begin, or where to stop if she did begin. She'd consulted a lawyer about a custody battle, but the lawyer hadn't been optimistic about her chances. *First of all,* he'd cautioned, *the natural father never formally relinquished his status or rights, and he seems to want the boy, so you'd have to be able to show that you and your husband were capable of* — *and, uhh, interested in* – *providing a substantially better community for the child.* It was the word "community" that damned her chances. What community James and she shared, by the time they'd be petitioning the court, was solely embodied in Jordan, and she suspected James's lukewarm enthusiasm would sabotage her efforts.

"From what I saw," Margot said, oblivious of Linnie's discomfort, "you certainly loved that boy. Why would a court have a problem seeing that?"

"Every court case is different," Brendan said, aware that Linnie was fighting back tears. "The natural parent has rights that any court's reluctant to countermand."

"And my mother?" Margot wondered. "At what point do a child's rights supersede a parent's?"

"I know Evelyn overreaches–"

"I think Mother's done a lot of remarkable things, but Jesus, she's a woman who's lived her life in penance, and she made all of us don the sackcloth. It's not just Ted, or the way we've all been martyred on that crusade. Look at Evelyn's relationship with your father, Brendan. How ridiculous, and how sad, was that?" Margot checked Brendan, who was speechless. "Does Linnie know about it?"

Linnie thought of the book inscriptions and the history they hinted at.

"Do you mind if I tell her?" Margot asked.

"No." Brendan managed a smile. "Go ahead."

"I don't know how much time you spent with Paddy," Margot told Linnie. "Eveyln's great 'friend.' Of course, the two were absolutely made for each other, mad for each other, and everyone knew it. Paddy had married a younger woman who — it's no secret –- had a drinking problem, and nothing happened until after Evelyn's divorce. Which was when Paddy started spending a lot of time in Lewiston. It's the only time in my life I remember my mother being truly happy. Anyhow,

Brendan and his sister were off at boarding school. It was the maid who found Sally O'Connor at noon on a Saturday, passed out on her bed, drowned in her own vomit. Paddy was in Lewiston – in Evelyn's bed so the story goes – when his wife drowned in vomit in hers. The entire city of Buffalo knew it. No one was surprised or scandalized by the tragedy, except for Evelyn, who acted as if Sally's passing was some sort of judgment rather than a goddamn random, upper-class drunken accident. My God, Evelyn and Paddy belonged together, and I don't mean meeting for dinner one or two nights a week. I mean they should've spent the rest of their lives together. But why be happy when you could be penitent? Evelyn rolled the clock back, as if she and Paddy weren't in love. Evelyn and her goddamn need for penance."

Linnie noticed, before Margot, that the blood had drained out of Brendan's cheeks, as if there were more urgent places for it to pool. She wanted to gather Brendan to her, to roll back the clock, like Evelyn, and undo this last minute.

"Brendan?" Margot chided him. "Surely you knew? Tell me you knew."

"Yeah," he shrugged.

"Everyone knew. Your aunts, uncles, your mother's whole family. Even they understood. It was only Evelyn who needed to fix the blame and claim it."

"Right." Brendan was rigid, poker-faced. "Of course, my sister and I were told my mother had a heart attack, but who'd believe that? A forty-year-old woman?"

"Oh, God, Brendan." To her credit, Linnie thought, Margot appeared embarrassed by what she'd wrought. "I can't goddamn believe you didn't know all of it."

"I think," Brendan said, and then struggled for a thought, "I think ... it only matters for them. Paddy and Evelyn."

"I always thought the world of your father, Brendan. The loveliest man. I would've enjoyed more of him. So would Evelyn." Margot stood up and scanned the corridor. "Jesus, I need coffee. Either of you want any?"

"No." Linnie waited till Margot had walked off. "Are you okay?"

"Yeah."

"You sure?"

Brendan attempted a wry smile but couldn't pull it off. Linnie put a hand on his shoulder. "You want to talk about her? Your mother?"

"What would I say?"

"You tell me."

"She was affectionate. Careless. High energy at times — her best moments."

"Does your sister know? How she died?"

"No. Should I tell her? I think maybe not."

"Then don't."

"The bitch of it is," he conceded, "Margot's right."

"The bitch of it," Linnie corrected, "is Margot."

"My father, he did his mourning, real or whatever, but I don't know why he and Evelyn didn't wind up living together."

"Maybe he didn't want to uproot you, move to Lewiston."

"He was lonely. My sister and I would've done anything to accommodate him."

"It wasn't your decision. Or Margot's."

"Look." Brendan waved his hands, chasing it all off. "I'm okay with it."

"Well, I'm not." Linnie was furious with Margot, the bull in the pen, goring them both, opening her old wound and a new one for Brendan, and acting as if it were their fault for being in the pen with her.

By the time Judge Hood invited them into his chambers, she was ready for battle. The judge was outlining the judicial process of a custody hearing, when Linnie interrupted him.

"Your Honor," she said, "I'm sure we can all agree on something that will get us through the summer. I've decided, if it's okay, to stay at the house, at least through August, in order to look after Ted and Evelyn."

"What about your job?"

"Well, I won't get severance pay, but I really think the next month or two we should focus on Evelyn's health rather than court issues. She's got a couple of corners she needs to turn. And the summer's pretty easy, because Nick keeps Ted busy working with him at the neighbors."

Margot glanced at the judge, then Linnie. "James won't mind your absence?"

"Oh, Margot, I'm sure you'll let me know if he does. I probably feel a lot like you did, when you got your first divorce."

"Ladies?" Judge Hood combed a few strands of hair off his ear. "Does this, whatever it is, have anything to do with Ted or Evelyn Phillips? Because if it doesn't..?"

Linnie turned to the judge. "I can put together a temporary schedule for the court, for Ted and Evelyn, their medical attention and supervision, whatever you're comfortable with."

The judge shrugged. "I'm happy to extend all of this, on these terms, if everyone is—"

"Wait. How dumb of me," Linnie apologized to Margot. "Your lawyer couldn't be here today. He's busy with more important stuff."

"It's fine," Margot insisted. "I'm comfortable without him."

"He could've requested a postponement," the judge said sternly. "You want to consult him?"

"No." Margot stared at Linnie. "He'd worry about the same thing I do. It's a lot to be responsible for. Ted and Evelyn's care, and their disabilities don't overlap."

"Should we talk to the other brother?" Judge Hood checked a file for the name. "Nick?"

"I think he'd be alright with it," Margot said. "And I feel okay, if this is a temporary arrangement. And if it works."

"Okay, then," the judge began.

"With one condition," Margot added.

18

No one could object to Margot's provision, since the neurologist had already raised the point. Everyone agreed that, should the doctors and therapists strongly recommend it, Evelyn would be transferred to a convalescent hospital for a regime of physical and occupational therapy that could not be accomplished at home.

Linnie put Margot to work when they got back to the house. Together they bullied Evelyn's uncooperative limbs through a series of exercises. "My God," Margot exclaimed, once they began rotating Evelyn on the bed, "it's like she's a sausage in a pan, and we're determined to brown every inch of her. I can imagine how she hates being a patient.

"At least it isn't Ted we're struggling with. You're so young, and Mother elected to spare you what she never spared me, the sight of an aging woman wrestling with a grown man to wipe his ass. As if a parent's role was to be an orderly." Margot looked at Linnie. "I'm aware Mother would like you to succeed her as my brother's guardian, not me."

"It doesn't mean anything. Nothing's admissible yet and—"

"I won't do it on my mother's terms, and I can't. But the business of Ted will fall to me one day, whatever Brendan or Evelyn hopes, and I can't live here year-round. We'll find Ted a place where's he's well cared-for."

Linnie prayed that her aunt hadn't heard, or at least comprehended, the blunt statement. She dressed an ulcer on Evelyn's left heel, then massaged her entire back and legs with an oil that soaked into her parched skin, while Evelyn hummed with pleasure. She sent Nick to fetch groceries for dinner. Margot had left for Toronto by the time the plates were washed and next day's lunch packed for Ted.

By ten that night Linnie felt tired, but righteous. She had temporary control of the household and was happy about it. The backload of laundry had been washed, dried, and folded; she'd even tackled other chores that Mrs. G. was behind on. The only thing she couldn't handle was Ted, who needed to bathe and wouldn't. Nick pitched in and drew a bath, and tried to steer Ted to it, but he'd have none of it, making a boulder of himself on the bathroom floor.

"What Evelyn does," Nick explained, as he settled for forcing a washcloth over his brother's face, "is she won't hear 'no.' She goes deaf to the word, so Ted gives up saying it 'cause she won't hear it. It's her magic. She'd have him in the tub."

Once he'd been lifted to his feet, Ted would only agree to brush his teeth if he could do it over the tub with bathwater. Linnie figured that once he'd gone to bed, she'd grab his clothes, which had a sour odor to them – like long-standing urine in a parking garage - and at least get *them* clean. She watched a little television with Nick, in order to give Ted a chance to put on his pajamas and get settled, before she returned to collect his dirty clothes. Ted's door was open, his bedroom empty.

Afraid for Evelyn, Linnie flew down the stairs to the den, where her aunt was sleeping soundly. Nick circled through the house, from the four dusty rooms in the basement to the clutter of the house-wide attic, then checked the path down the riverbank, before meeting Linnie near the garden shed. "His bike's here." He pointed at it through the open door. "So he hasn't gone far."

Linnie asked Nick to accompany her to the bunkhouse, which they found undisturbed: a few stray shoots from a climbing rose crisscrossed windows laced with intact spiderwebs. She punched April's number on her cellphone but got another busy signal. "April's phone must be off the hook. I'll run over, see if she can watch Evelyn while we search. For now, Nick, you check the neighbors' property and keep an eye on the house."

The lights were on at April's house when Linnie pulled up the driveway. She hadn't noticed the unmarked cruiser there and was surprised when Dan Pataki opened the front door.

"Hey," he said, propping the screen door open. "C'mon in."

"I'm sorry." Linnie took a step backwards. "I didn't know April had company. Her phone must be off the hook."

"She's online; the cable's on the fritz."

"It's okay." Reluctant to discuss Ted's disappearance with a senior officer of the sheriff's department, Linnie turned to go. "Another time."

"Get on in here," Pataki teased. "She'll chew me out if I chase you off."

"What is it?" April hollered, stepping into her hallway. "Linnie?"

"I was going to ask a favor. But you got company."

"So?"

"Not much company," Pataki added. "She's been lost online a while, bargain-hunting."

"You're letting bugs in," April scolded, pointing at the wide-open screen door.

"Ted must've gone out on a walk," Linnie explained.

"Who's with Evelyn?"

"I was gonna ask if you—"

"Okay," April said, grabbing a jacket off a hook. "We'll bring a couple of cars, and one of us will sit with Evelyn."

Linnie hadn't reached Evelyn's house when her cellphone rang. "I'm glad you picked up," Margot said. "What's happened with Ted?"

Linnie had the sinking feeling, from the tone of her voice, that Margot had the answer to her own question. "What?"

"Bev Sanders, do you know her? Closer to my age than Evelyn's. She was driving down Pletcher Road and saw Ted, all by himself. At this hour! She's keeping an eye on him. She called the house, but no one answered, so she called Toronto information to get me."

"Where on Pletcher?"

"By the park entrance."

"I'll call when I've got him." Linnie hung up and did a u-turn in front of April's sedan, flagging for her to pull abreast. "He's on Pletcher," she told April. "You can go back home."

"You want me to follow you?"

"I'll call you on your cell when I've got him."

In less than a mile, Linnie found a big Oldsmobile parked along the right side of the road, with Bev Sanders at the wheel, her window cracked open and doors locked. Ted was sitting across the road, thirty feet down a back entrance into Joseph Davis State Park.

"I figured he shouldn't be out." Bev Sanders rolled her window down further. "I asked him. Tried talking to him. He took a seat over yonder and that was that. How's Evelyn?"

"Hard to say."

"This'd be rough on her, I guess. You're the niece?"

"Yeah. Thank you so much."

"Goodness, never mind. I'll be getting home, unless you want me a bit longer."

"I've got it. Thanks." As Bev Sanders sped away, Linnie wondered why she hadn't brought Ted into her car. Apparently, he knew her and might have accepted the offer, had she been comfortable enough to make it.

Ted was stabbing a wet patch of ground with a stick he'd found, splashing mud on his hands and trousers. He kept at it even as the stick splintered, while his eyes tracked Linnie as she crossed the street.

"Damnit, Ted," she muttered, folding her legs under her as she sat beside him. "I don't know what's going on, and I don't care. It scares me when I don't know where you are. You get that?"

Ted's eyes, cloudy at best, made Linnie think of coastal fog: unpredictable, impenetrable, but then she was blinded by the beam of a strong flashlight. She couldn't see who was holding it, but he was at least ninety feet away standing under a tree further down the back entrance into the state park. "Hello?"

"Are you okay?" the man asked.

"Yes."

"You're looking after him."

Linnie couldn't tell if the man was asking a question or making a statement. "Ted is my cousin."

"Who was the woman in the car?"

"I didn't know her, but she recognized Ted."

"When weather allowed, some people here used to walk at night. Like your cousin. Maybe it's an adventure or maybe it's companions they want. And maybe it's dangerous as they get older and frail and the confusion builds."

Linnie was surprised by how atonal, even flat, the man's speech was, but wanted to reply. "I don't like it. I try to keep him home."

"Yes." The man turned off his flashlight, spun on his heels, and walked further down the back entranced into the park.

Linnie got to her feet, took Ted by the hand, and got him up. "C'mon, honey. We better get home, or Margot's going to have both our hides."

THE HOUSE ON THE RIVER

19

I wondered what was the first thing my father did for Evelyn, as a lawyer." Brendan pulled a document out of a folder in his briefcase and slid it across the restaurant table towards Linnie. "Years ago," he explained, "my father had all the firm's records put on microfiche."

Linnie studied the blurred letterhead.

"It's a letter he wrote on Evelyn's behalf. It's the first thing I could find with her name on the file."

Goodyear, Decker, & O'Connor
Attorneys-at-law
1 Main St.
Buffalo, New York

June 12, 1961

Dr. George Froman
Executive Director
The Storey-Davis Institute
1150 N. Grant St.
Buffalo, New York

RE: The Science Club

Dear Dr. Froman,
This letter is to confirm our understanding, as agreed upon in our meeting yesterday, with respect to The Storey-Davis Institute and its patients. This office represents a patient's family, which is concerned about a report that the Fernald State School for the retarded in Boston has recruited some of its inmate children for a so-called "Science Club," the purpose of which is to trace oatmeal laced with low-grade radioactive material on its course through the digestive tract.

We consider the source of the report, now living in the Buffalo area, to be reputable. However, we cannot confirm the details of this experiment with the Fernald State School, the Common-wealth of Massachusetts, Quaker Oats Co., or the Massachusetts Institute of Technology, all of which decline comment through respective legal counsel.

Nonetheless, this office takes the position that no retarded person, and most especially a minor, has the legal capacity to authorize his own participation in any experiment. Consent must be rendered by a competent, court-authorized adult. This protection, which should be self-evident for those patients who have been placed in your care by parents or guardians exercising their competent discretion, should likewise be extended to any patients remitted to your care by the state.

Accordingly, whereas this letter is not intended to prevent the Institute and its doctors and staff from providing established and necessary medical care, you are hereby cautioned to refrain from using any minor in your charge for any experiment without the express written consent of the minor's parent or guardian.

Respectfully yours,

P. J. O'Connor, Esq.

ds/PJO

"My God!" Linnie pushed herself away from the table. "Tell me no one really did that. Fed radioactive oatmeal to children?"

"There was a lawsuit in Boston, maybe ten years ago, when all this information was made public."

"God! Evelyn must've gone batshit when she heard about it. Can you imagine?"

"What I love," Brendan said, "and I don't know who gets credit for it, Evelyn or Paddy, is that my father included the wards of the state under the umbrella of the letter. Most lawyers would write a letter saying '*if you violate my client, I'll have your ass in court.*' These two got together, apparently for the first time, and stood up for everyone warehoused at the institute."

Linnie looked at the date on the letter and did the math. "Ted was at that institute another year or two. But I can imagine how fired up Evelyn would've been."

"Me, too."

"Don't lose that." She pointed at the copy of the letter.

"I won't." Brendan returned the document to its folder. "Screw Margot and all of Evelyn's warts she'd have us look at. I'm proud of Paddy and Evelyn for this."

Ted had spent the afternoon at the recreational center in the basement of the Niagara Bible Church. With pick-up time at hand, the program directors were busy shuffling clients into waiting vans and cars. As Linnie parked, Reverend Strickley waved and made his way towards her. "Had some excitement today," he said. "A couple of investigators from the sheriff's office stopped in with old photos of the fella turned up in the graveyard."

"Did anyone know him?"

"Don't seem to. They're checking every file and record, whoever went to what, where they'd be, who all slipped through the cracks. And they interviewed me and the program workers – interrogated, I was - in case someone who knows them is responsible. Now there's a thought that pains."

"They talked to everyone? The clients, too?"

"They talked a bit with them. You can sense the investigators' frustration. Half the people they talk to can't put a sentence together. A strange business." The reverend patted her arm. "I haven't seen Nick in church on Sunday in a while. Got lots of parishioners who come right down River Road if he needs a ride."

"Thanks. I'll tell him."

"You do that." He excused himself with a smile.

Linnie noticed a man she knew and called him over. "Hey, Lenin."

The man, whose real name was Leonard, cut between cars and responded with his pet name for her. "Hey, Lenny!"

Except for the addition of ultra-thin wire-rim glasses, Leonard was a diminutive replica of Lenin. He had the same jutting chin and thin-slit eyes, the same balding pattern and hair color, the same drab clothes, and an identical goatee and mustache. Leonard, however, was only four-feet, six-inches tall in boots, and it was unlikely that he had any real grasp of the significance of the man interred at the Lenin Mausoleum.

"Work hard today," he said, after shaking her hand. "Whew-ee."

"You always work hard." Linnie knew him from another program, where he had previously spent his weekdays. He clearly loved two things: working at chores and being praised for it. "What'd you do?"

"Clean the whole room." Leonard wagged an index finger side-to-side. "No help."

"You did it all? You're such a good worker."

"Yes, sir. A real good worker."

"Wait." She feigned surprise. "Ted didn't help?"

"Heeeee!" Leonard brayed with delight at Linnie's joke. Everyone knew Ted wasn't a worker. "He's not help!"

"Thank heavens you are."

"Yup."

"I heard the police came today? Deputy investigators?" She wondered if the program clients had been unnerved by the development. "What was that like?"

"Dumb, dumb." He made a face as though he'd tasted something revoltingly sour, then repeated something he'd clearly heard once too often. "Don't go with strangers."

If she read his reaction correctly, he wasn't concerned about the bodies that had been discovered. Even for Leonard, disabled himself, the crimes were alien, as if the victims were gang members in a part of town one never visited. "Hey, Mr. Lenin," she asked, "you know where I might find Mr. Ted?"

"In his chair." He looked at steps that led down to the basement door to the church. "He grumpy today."

"Oh, great. I better not forget him, huh?"

"No, no." Leonard cackled, happy to have the last exchange. "Don't forget Mr. Ted."

Linnie turned to notice Ted starting up the basement steps with a young blond-haired woman behind him, sheep-dogging him hard on either heel, tight on whichever one steered him to the parking lot.

Mrs. G. was waiting for them when Linnie and Ted got home, and visibly exhausted. "Miss Evelyn got herself slanted on the bed, halfway to sideways," she groaned, "an' only me to wrestle her back to the middle. When Nick gets back, you might want him to pick up a roast chicken at the market. I didn't get to cook nothin'."

"Fine."

"And I'm gonna be late tomorrow. I have to take my brother to the dialysis center. Might stay a bit. At least the boredom won't kill him."

"How is he?"

"Thin and then some. He tries to eat, beef himself up, but he don't got appetite. He's on the list, but they won't do a transplant if you're weak-ish."

Linnie felt remiss. She'd known Mrs. G.'s brother was a diabetic with renal failure, but she'd been so wrapped up in Evelyn's problems that she hadn't bothered to ask about him. At least she remembered that his eyesight was also failing. "Does he like those recorded books? I'd love to send him something."

"That's so sweet. He likes stories with history in 'em, not the gush and gore."

"Great. I'll be right by a bookstore tomorrow."

"If it's no big bother..." Mrs. G. brightened. "You know, it's just what your aunt would do, if she was full throttle."

"Does he still have his peach trees?" Long ago, Mrs. G. had taken Linnie to pick baskets of peaches from a tiny orchard on her brother's property.

"Those trees haven't been pruned since gas was a dollar!" Mrs. G. laughed. "Even birds won't touch that squirrelly fruit."

"I'll take him peaches when the season gets here."

Mrs. G. put an arm around her and squeezed her, the hug so brittle it made Linnie wonder at Mrs. G.'s own health and age. The roots of her hair, more visible of late, were white, not auburn; age spots freckled her hands; and on the way to her car a hitch in her gait revealed a deteriorating hip. Linnie was troubled by all of it: she couldn't imagine the household without Evelyn or Mrs. G. in charge.

Linnie had Nick pick up some prepared food, and he shredded a slice of chicken and added it to warm mashed potatoes for his mother's dinner. Evelyn could only chew on one side of her mouth and swallowed erratically, so her eating had to be supervised. Linnie took the food in to her aunt, lowered the bed's side rail, and raised its head. Evelyn squirmed as she slipped down the mattress, then grimaced and struggled to turn away from her niece as a fecal odor seeped from the sheets.

Linnie lifted the bedclothes to confirm the problem: Evelyn had defecated in a pile beneath her and had slid into it when the head of the bed rose. Cleaning Evelyn meant lifting her dead weight: if a shoulder turned, a hip didn't follow. Gradually, Linnie pried her up, using pillows to prevent her from toppling either way.

What Linnie couldn't undo was her aunt's fierce embarrassment, all the more stubborn because it had no voice. Evelyn had been faring fairly well on a strict regimen, but she wasn't due to get bathed for another two days, when the nurse came to check her skin for ulcers. Showers, like medical appointments, had to be scheduled.

One of the therapists had recently asked if there had been episodes of incontinence. This was Evelyn's third such accident, and Linnie hadn't mentioned the other two. She decided not to mention this one. She didn't know what repercussions might ensue, but Margot made no secret of her belief that Ted belonged in a group home, a prospect that Evelyn's presence in the house forestalled.

20

Nick's Journal

June 11

A funny thing about Evelyn is she says she never gets angry. But she gets mad at a few things, like if someone is mean to Ted, and she still says she never gets mad, like it don't count if you got a reason.

Now she gets angry for no reason. Her face gets red and she throws things, and then her mood can go away, or run itself into tears, and I don't know if she knows why she gets sad either. Linnie says moods can swing this way or that, even when nothing's steering them.

I got out old photo albums and showed them to Evelyn. One of them has photos of the first house built on the river, a little up the river from here. Evelyn's great-grandfather built it. It was really big, and some of the pictures show the carriages in front. There are stables, gardens, a dock, and people in long dresses or straw hats, and Evelyn's always glad for the photos so we can look at things that are gone. The album has pictures of her grandfather's Buffalo house, which has its own ballroom.

She liked looking at the albums, if I can tell, and I showed her the one of our Buffalo house, except it's mostly pictures of Margot and Ted and me. You asked me what I remember about growing up in Buffalo before Evelyn moved year around to the river. I remember I liked sidewalks because I could walk all over, or to a store. I liked the traffic and all the lights in winter.

One thing that happened was a snowball fight. It was wet snow, which turns to ice when you pack it. Those snowballs hurt like crazy. I was walking with Ted, and three boys started hitting us with iceballs. My ear got cut, and the boys kept trying to hit Ted right between his legs because he didn't know how to protect there. The boys were ten years old, same as me. Ted runs funny, especially in winter boots, but I made him run. Snow was all over, and one of the boys got hit by a car when he jumped into the street to chase us. His leg broke, people said it was lucky that was all.

The police came to our house. The boys said we chased them into the street when it was them chasing us, but Ted couldn't say a thing, and no one believes me. A policeman said it was because I was a little idiot walking a big idiot. They took us to a police station, and all Evelyn could do was cry. Just cry.

We were sitting with some lady from the county when Uncle Paddy got there, and we could hear him screaming two doors away. Pretty soon the head of the station talked to us. He was nice and said to go home and they would tell us if we were in trouble. Uncle Paddy talked to the families of the three boys. I don't know what he did, but one of the boys told what was true, and then a second one did, and that was the end. What I remember most is Evelyn crying. It's not her nature to cry or let anyone see. Uncle Paddy had to help her out of the station.

21

I 've never been fingerprinted," Linnie said, while the deputy rolled one of her fingers across the ink pad and placed it on the card. Fingerprints were now required for anyone who worked or volunteered at local programs for the disabled. "Or is that what everyone says?"

"A precaution," the deputy acknowledged. "We need to know if anyone's working with the disadvantaged who shouldn't be."

"I suppose."

"Even Little League does it with their dads now. Fingerprints. Of course, you people in Lewiston are in the center of this craziness."

A frequent volunteer, Nick had gone to get fingerprinted, too, and he was anxious to get back home. He wanted to clean and vacuum the pool before the guests arrived.

Later, despite the balmy afternoon, only Nick would swim. The weather had been cool all week, the sunshine sporadic, and the water temperature was in the high-sixties. Sprawled on a chaise-longue near her, Linnie's best friend from college was napping. Business had taken Carol Doherty from Seattle, Washington, to Rochester, New York, from where she had driven over for the day.

Seated beside Brendan on the flagstone border, his daughter dangled her feet in the water while Nick swam past. "I can't believe he's swimming," Kiley said. "He must be a seal."

"It's not that bad." Linnie stood barefoot on the steps leading into the pool. "I would've gone in when I was your age."

"Yeah, right." Kiley kicked water into the air. "And I'll swim in it when I'm your age."

"What're you going to do this summer?" Linnie knew Kiley would spend most of July with Brendan. "Camp?"

"I hope not. I'm going to *chill*."

"We're checking a few day programs out," Brendan mentioned.

"Rejected, rejected, rejected," Kiley said. "I want to work for you. I'll be your secretary. Mrs. Kurtz can go to camp. Fat camp. Unless there's a special fat-bitch camp."

"Your language?" Brendan had a hard time looking disapproving.

"English." Kiley faced Linnie. "That's what I tell him when he says that like a question: *Language?* 'English.' And, Jesus, I'm probably as good a secretary as her. I can handle the clients, all the widows," Kiley choked up melodramatically, "and orphans."

"Honey, your mother's in New York. You can always leave the sneer with her."

"That's what Mom says about Dad's practice," Kiley told Linnie. "Widows and orphans. She says my grandfather and he have had some big clients, but they prefer," she coughed out a few mock sobs, "the widows ... and the orphans."

"I wonder if there's a drama camp," Brendan mused, "that's like a fat camp, where you send young drama queens to lose the drama."

"How old are you?" Joining the conversation, Carol Doherty opened her eyes and sat up.

"Twelve," Kiley answered.

"I grew up in the Bay Area," Carol continued, "and when I was your age, two of my girlfriends would go to the sleep-away Stanford golf camp for a few weeks."

"Golf?" Kiley gagged. "Gawd!"

"They didn't care a damn about golf, but they figured out all these cute boys went and *no* girls. They liked those odds, so they'd con their parents into sending them."

"Do they let you drive golf-carts?"

"They let you paddle canoes." Brendan turned to Linnie for help. "Any ideas?"

"There's a program at ArtPark. And the country club runs a tennis camp."

"Girlfriend?" Kiley glowered at her. "Whose side are you on?"

"My own." Linnie decided to drop the subject. In hopes that Jordan might be able to visit her, she'd researched a variety of short summer programs for kids. But a few days ago Jordan had e-mailed her:

Linnie,

I'm going to a skate-boarding camp that Dad found. Annie's close to having the baby. You could come before the baby and stay in his room. But the paint is new and stinks and there's no bed.

Say hi to Nick and Aunt Evlin and Teddy Bear.

Love you XOXO Jordan.

Linnie's disappointment had not been tempered by her recognition that her nephew was in good spirits, and she felt foolish for having gotten ahead of herself, planning all sorts of activities on the chance of a visit.

Later that afternoon, Linnie and Carol were sitting on the porch, watching Brendan hurl small, fallen branches over the bank into the thick vegetation there. Kiley stood near him and waited for the occasional fishermen to drift past close to shore, then hollered at each boat to find out what, if anything, had been caught, mostly for the pleasure of dismissing any fish they held up. "*That's it?*"

"She's a pistol," Carol remarked to Linnie. "Of course, it's tough to date a divorced man with a daughter."

"Aren't you getting ahead of yourself?"

"Read the fairy tales, Cinderella. Stepmothers rank lower than witches and dragons."

Linnie laughed. "You know the least of my worries? My next marriage. If there is one. Besides, think of Jordan. Or Kiley." She nodded at the girl. "I was an only child. I'd like a roomful of stepdaughters."

"You're asking for it." Carol looked at Brendan. "He's cute, I'll give you that."

"Yes. But he's Evelyn's lawyer."

"So? No one's ever defined incest that broadly. Lawyers would never allow it." Carol shook her head. "The problem is, if you get tangled up with him, it'll be harder to leave. The economy is a disaster here, and you could get stuck babysitting your cousins. I think you should come out to Seattle, leave all this behind."

"I'm thinking of it, believe me."

"Good. It's great you can help Evelyn, but the day's coming when you'll have to put yourself first. I was talking to one of her therapists."

"Which one?"

"Speech, I think. She said the doctor didn't think Evelyn was trying to speak again. She'd do better if she spent time at a rehabilitation center and got pushed."

"What did you think? When you saw her?"

"She recognized me. I saw it in her eyes. She knew me. I think she's embarrassed."

The prospect of Evelyn becoming a virtual ward of anyone, especially a team of unfamiliar therapists at a convalescent facility, terrified Linnie. "I have to talk to her."

She waited till late that evening, after Evelyn had been carted outside and fed dinner on the porch, where they hoped she'd enjoy the flowering wisteria tumbling off the trellis and the garden rising with foxglove and delphinium stalks. The sunset had stirred up a palette of crimson across the river, and lightning bugs, increasingly rare, glinted beneath the nearest pines when Linnie left the porch and found Evelyn still awake in the den.

Lately, she'd appeared in a number of Linnie's dreams, the kind that occurred on the trailing edge of sleep and left the dreamer, suddenly conscious that it was all a dream, disinclined to disturb it. In them, Evelyn seemed ten years younger and was pacing on the far side of a room that Linnie entered. She appeared to be on the verge of speaking to Linnie, who let the dream play out as long as possible, on the chance that Evelyn might say something.

Some subjects, certainly, would never be broached. Surely, Evelyn would be loathe to discuss her regret and guilt for committing her infant to an institution, nor would she ever criticize her sister, at least not in her niece's presence. Linnie's mother had squandered her inheritance on two separate purchases of houses in Europe, both times putting her successive husbands on the title since as a non-citizen she couldn't buy the beachfront properties. Not a penny had ever been repatriated to this side of the Atlantic by either husband, who so far as anyone knew still owned the houses.

Unaccustomed to expecting much from her mother, Linnie didn't mind what her mother had done with her money. But Evelyn had to have viewed the careless redistribution of family assets as an unforgivable betrayal of one's offspring. Her disapproval, root-deep, would remain unspoken. Instead, Evelyn might comment on their family itself and wonder how genetic predisposition, supposedly nature's blueprint for species preservation, had resulted in such disorder for the Phillips and Walker clans. Ted was only the latest of several family members cheated by chromosomes. What Evelyn might joke about was the wild divergence of the Walker sisters, the elder the bulkhead, steady into any breeze, the younger a torn sail, flapping every which way.

Linnie wondered if she and Evelyn would ever discuss what she had learned courtesy of her nephew Jordan, that it hurt desperately to have a child you loved in your house and then to lose that child to the whim of imperfect parents. Never once had Evelyn expressed regret when she had to pack Linnie up, sometimes after a year, and return her to the natural mother. Never once had Evelyn said anything more than a teary farewell. "Dearie, you know you're the brightest light in this old house, and you're always welcome."

Linnie's figure cast a faint shadow the length of the bedsheets. As Evelyn stirred, Linnie announced, "Me. Only me."

She waited until Evelyn's eyes settled on hers before continuing. "I've had a couple of glasses of wine, so I'm going to say what I'm going to say, and I think you hear it. Here it is: you're not trying hard enough." Linnie ignored her tears, which coursed along her nose. "I know you hate the way you sound when you try to speak. You sound like some poor, speechless retarded kid, and you must hate that worst of all because you've always been their voice. The thing is, the doctors figure you're not trying, and they're about to put you somewhere where they'll make you work at it. So, not tonight, because tonight I want you to sleep on it. But I want you to talk, and I don't care what it sounds like.

"And another thing?" Unsure of what had registered, Linnie thought of the one circumstance that was certain to press Evelyn to greater effort. "Ted is getting weirder. It's gotten strange enough around here. Surreal. Dead bodies turning up - of people like Ted. And Ted's floating way, way out there. So I want you to find your voice and let him hear it."

22

Margot's appearance in the entry hall didn't distract Ted from the curiosity of cause and effect, the way the twist and turn of the ballpoint pen he wielded with his right hand resulted in the slow tear of the flesh of his left palm.

"Ted?" Margot calmly extended a hand and waited for him to put the ballpoint pen in it, then led him by his wrist into the downstairs bathroom, where she disinfected and bandaged his small puncture wounds.

"What I wish," she said, telling Linnie about the incident afterwards, "is that they still made those antiseptics that sting. You're too young, but I remember they used to put a splash of iodine or something on a cut, and it stung like hell. Something like that might stick with Ted."

"I don't know what sticks," Linnie admitted.

"Whatever. Do you have a list for us today? Places to visit?"

The neurologist had suggested that the family examine a variety of prospective convalescent homes for Evelyn, and Margot and Linnie's internet searches had proved largely unhelpful. The one local rehabilitation center devoted solely to patients recovering from strokes had a long waiting list.

The first stop on the tour that Linnie had arranged was a place called Calgary Glenn Residential Manor. A bright blue bagpipe was painted on the sign for the single-story building, which was across the road from the giant discount mall that could be seen from the Interstate.

"Great!" Margot blurted out, as they pulled into the parking area. "My mother will be near the mall, where I bet they find the ones who wander off. God, what a horrid-looking place."

Inside, the reception area sprawled out into a common area for the patients, two televisions blaring across an assortment of orange naugahyde furniture. A nurse's aide paged the manager, who led them on a tour. The heavily trafficked central corridor was clogged with elders in pajamas and nightgowns, pushing walkers or dragging IV bags on rolling stands. "Do the residents ever put clothes on?" Margot asked, "or is it a constant pajama party?"

"Lots of our residents dress meticulously," the manager said, pleasantly foiling the attack. "But it's their choice."

The corridor circled through the facility, she explained, so that the residents would feel a dormitory-like congeniality. Linnie had important questions to ask – the availability of private rooms, the skill level of staff therapists — but Margot was so put off by the first bedrooms they passed, three roommates confined to hospital beds in a room barely big enough for two, that she needed an explanation.

"Three people in one room? Is this Medicaid at work?"

"It depends. Somewhat."

"I can't see my mother tolerating even one roommate, the TV always on something she doesn't want to watch."

"Private rooms do become available–"

"My mother," Margot interrupted, "would hate to see three people squeezed in a room, even though she can afford a private one. She'd go off on some bloody crusade, saving the elderly from roommates and their monstrous, chattering TVs."

The other Niagara Falls facilities further depressed Margot. "I can't see Evelyn accepting this institutional privation. She'll sink from the weight of it."

The last two places they visited were more attractive, but they were in or near Buffalo, a half-hour drive from the house downriver. Margot and Linnie concluded the tour in Brendan's office. "Okay, do we have a first choice?" he asked. "And a second and third? You may have to move Evelyn whether you want to or not."

Linnie described their first two choices, one of them connected to Buffalo General Hospital, one in an affluent suburb. "They're nice and have good therapists," she said.

"Someone's got to bully Mother into talking," Margot added. "But as for a third choice?" She allowed herself an exaggerated sigh. "Euthanasia. And you can put my old horse down with Evelyn's. I couldn't bear seeing her in most of these places. She'd hate it, she'd rather die."

Linnie was surprised, and touched, by her cousin's sudden rush of emotion. Margot fished through her purse for a handkerchief and dabbed at her eyes, while Linnie handed Brendan the application packets. "We'll have the neurologist fill in his part," he said, "and I'll have both of you sign consents before you go."

When Margot went to the restroom before the drive back to Lewiston, Brendan asked Linnie, "How was it today?"

"Strange. Margot was so *protective*. I think she wants to take care of Evelyn and make sure her mother recognizes it. Margot the caregiver."

"You two drive together?"

"From Lewistown. Her car's there."

"I was going to see if you could stick around for dinner."

"Evelyn's doctor is driving up to see her after work. I'm free later, if you feel like driving."

Despite her remove from the city, Evelyn had continued to use doctors there, either those who had long served her family or their successors. Brendan was at the house by the time Evelyn's internist was ready to share his evaluation of Evelyn. "I like the neurologist who's on board," he began. "What worries me is the weight she's losing."

The doctor checked Ted briefly, then accepted Linnie's offer of a glass of wine. "Whatever happened," he wondered, glass in hand, "with your aunt and her collection of esoterica? On the treatment of the retarded."

"She's got a lot of material," Linnie acknowledged. "I don't know if she ever decided what to do with it."

"*One Hundred Reasons*," the doctor said. "That was the last thing she told me. She'd use that title for a book and list a hundred of the most egregious ways the retarded were mistreated. Floggings, imprisonment, surgical experimentation. The Supreme Court wanted them sterilized.

"What I told her is, I thought things she's told me about her own family were absolutely as interesting, maybe more so. Certainly, it was odd she married a Phillips."

"Why?"

"The families didn't get along for some while. Do you know the story of the flying? I think a newspaper account termed it *'Any Idiot Can Fly.'*"

When neither Linnie nor Brendan responded, he continued. "It was the summer of 1921. Buffalo was still wealthy, the Roaring Twenties roaring. As I understand it, there were three Walker brothers; the middle one would become Evelyn's father. The oldest brother, Lawrence, never married – too much of a playboy. He was one of the best polo players in the country. Also, he was a fly-boy who'd gone off and joined the Lafayette Escadrille with the other rich American playboys and flown with the French Air Force years before America got into World War I. I gather that on his return he had any woman he wanted.

"One of the big Walker summer homes up here in Lewiston had its own polo field, and Lawrence made sure there was an airstrip as well because he liked to fly one of the Nieuport bi-planes he'd flown with the Lafayette Escadrille. Apparently, he'd re-engineered the cockpit so a woman could fit in it with him, and when he'd return hours late from a flight with some guy's wife, he'd tell the anxious husbands stories about needing to put down somewhere for repairs, when of course everybody knew these women had been rolled in more than just the bi-plane.

"Denton Phillips was one of these husbands, and jealous as hell of all the attention Lawrence got –– polo-star, pilot, playboy. Phillips was a fair polo player, not of Lawrence's caliber, and he'd learned to fly, too. Anyhow, that summer the Walkers planned a huge July Fourth event up here at their compound on the river, with a polo game in the morning.

"Now we get to the youngest Walker brother, Bronson. He was pretty much a dwarf, and feeble-minded as a cow. Nurses were assigned to him around the clock. What this Phillips character decided to do was to fly over the Walkers' July Fourth party, to buzz it a couple of times in Lawrence's Nieuport bi-plane, except instead of Lawrence, Bronson Walker would be in the cockpit.

"The idea was to make it seem like the idiot had no trouble flying the plane. Denton Phillips would stay down out of sight and work the controls, and when Lawrence's plane buzzed the party, Bronson the idiot would be waving and giggling. He'd be flying solo. You see? *Any idiot can fly.*

"To prepare, Phillips brought a mechanic and went flying a couple of times in the bi-plane. He took 'the idiot' with him to practice. The morning of the party, Phillips had his mechanic sneak to the airstrip. The mechanic is used to seeing poor little Bronson around the plane, even in it. What nobody imagined is that Bronson had been paying attention and figured out how to take off. All on his own, with the mechanic checking the engine, Bronson gets the plane not just going, but airborne. Suddenly, the 'idiot' is flying solo. It's not what Phillips intended, but the poor boy is up in the sky flying, God help us. As I said, and the newspaper accounts referred to the incident similarly, 'Any idiot can fly.'

"So Bronson Walker flies the plane straight across the river, up it a bit, right to the first Canadian power station south of Queenston. The poor boy crashes into transformers, and he's killed instantly. The thing is, the explosion knocks out power, even up in Toronto. A quarter million people are blacked out for at least a day. To calm all the authorities down, the Walkers made a nice contribution to a Canadian veterans' group, and of course they tore out Lawrence's airstrip."

"Denton *Phillips?*" Linnie wondered.

"He's the uncle, not the father, of Evelyn's husband," the doctor confirmed. "You see why the families weren't close. You'd think they'd have known better than to get tangled up in marriage."

"Apparently not," Linnie said. "Did Evelyn ever talk to you about the institution? The one she and her husband sent Ted to?"

"Briefly. I did ask her once. She just said it was terrible."

"What did she mean? What was terrible, the place or the fact she sent him?"

"I don't know."

23

A few days after Margot and Linnie's tour, Evelyn's neurologist had her conveyed by ambulance to the convalescent facility in Buffalo. Ted became frantic when his mother was loaded into the ambulance and tried to get on board with her, then chased the vehicle down the drive.

Late the next night, with the others asleep, Ted ambled off on his own, and Linnie didn't discover it until she was awakened by the noise of his returning sometime after three a.m. A neighbor's dog was barking ferociously and kept it up, long after she'd put Ted back in his bed.

Though she worried about them, Linnie supposed that Ted's unauthorized walks, which he clearly enjoyed, represented accomplishments for him. He could wander off and find his way back home, independently.

Besides, it was impossible to lock Ted in the house, since Evelyn had ensured that he wouldn't be trapped in the event of a fire. All the exterior doors had interior handles like the ones on the inside of bathroom doors: a push of a button locked them, and a twist of the handle unlocked them. Only on the outside was a key necessary.

And Ted wasn't the only one to slip out at night. Once the warm weather arrived and the temperature of the river rose above seventy degrees, Nick often climbed down the bank and swam near the shore, where a slight back eddy curled through the shallows. A hundred and fifty feet out, the current ran at four-miles-per-hour or more, a speed that no swimmer was going to match. Having joined Nick for a few midnight swims when she was young, Linnie didn't like the rough rocks of the riverbed underfoot or the way slimy river grasses along the shore dragged across her arms and legs.

She doubted that Margot knew about Nick's river adventures, though Margot's announcement that she would take a week's vacation at Evelyn's house would give her a firsthand view of her brothers' inclination to wander. Linnie was glad to transfer responsibility, however briefly, and hoped to use that week to make a long-postponed visit to her friends in Seattle. But no sooner had she found herself a reasonable airfare than Margot called and made clear that the point of her visit was not to spend time with her brothers. "I do so love the house. I'm bringing three other couples, so I figure Nick and Ted can stay in the bunkhouse. If you think it's prudent – safer for Ted – you may want to stay in the bunkhouse, too. But I do think you'll want to come to the dinner parties."

"What I want to do," Linnie complained to Brendan, "is dress Ted up all fancy, rent some tuxedo and you can do his bow-tie, and show up at her dinner parties with him, as if - *of course, darling* - we're all invited. Have Ted waltz in with a gift-box of fancy chocolates and a bottle of port."

Brendan laughed. "You're not obliged to accommodate her."

"What? I'm going to put her guests out in the bunkhouse?"

"Yeah."

"Right! She'd take it out on Mrs. G., who'd have her own stroke."

"It's still Evelyn's house."

"Yeah? If you're so brave –– being the lawyer and all — why don't you be the one to tell Margot to bring some tents for herself and her guests and to arrive in an RV if she's hoping to use a bathroom?"

Brendan laughed again. "As Evelyn's lawyer I feel the need to recuse myself."

"Coward."

A temporary move into the upstairs of the bunkhouse proved a surprisingly pleasant distraction for Ted, who helped Nick and Linnie clean their long-ignored accommodations. A central staircase rose to a large common room, where an antiquated television managed hazy reception of most Toronto and Buffalo stations. On either side of the common room was a bunkroom and bathroom, the boys' bunkroom a shade of hunter green, the girls' a pastel that had faded to gray. As occasionally happened when Linnie put Nick to work, he startled her by his broad acumen: he knew how and where to turn on the water, how to air the pipes, how to light the water heater's pilot; soon, even the downstairs bathrooms had working toilets and hot water.

Margot arrived with a car full of flowers, one arrangement of which was exiled to the bunkhouse. Fortunately, Ted clearly enjoyed the chance to sleep on a bunk bed, at least if Nick slept above him, and he didn't sneak out once the entire week.

The second day of her vacation, Margot took Linnie with her on a visit to the convalescent facility, where Evelyn was propped up in bed and clearly exhausted. A nurse's aide was sponging her face but stopped when the younger women arrived. "She was just with the speech therapist," the aide said.

"Great." Margot waved at her mother, then crossed to her bed. Linnie hovered in the doorway.

"Not quite talking up a storm," the aide said, "but working hard."

"I'm here." Margot spoke loudly enough so that Evelyn's eyes gravitated to her. "I'm here," she repeated.

Evelyn studied her a while and managed a lisp. "Thhee."

"You 'see?'" Margot was stunned. "You see me?"

Evelyn struggled for it. "Yeth."

"That's so good, I'm so proud of you." Margot kissed her mother's forehead, then turned to Linnie, beaming. "She's working so hard."

Evelyn's eyes never quit her daughter. Her entire jaw shifted in preparation, but she didn't speak until Margot was looking at her again. "Thhorry."

Margot leaned closer. Evelyn studied her a moment, then used her good hand to tap her chest. Her voice was weak. "Thhorry."

"Sorry?" Margot looked at Linnie, then at her mother. "You're sorry? There's time for that, it's no matter now." She fought back tears. "You're doing splendidly. I can't imagine how tough it is."

Evelyn coughed and pointed at a water glass, which Margot raised and held to her lips. Evelyn didn't try to talk again. Margot brought a box of tissues out of the bathroom and worked through a handful.

Back at the river, Linnie returned to the bunkhouse. She resented its shortcomings: the lack of a kitchen, the persistent mustiness, the thin walls that couldn't muffle the boys' snoring, the heat unrelieved by cross-ventilation. She slept fitfully and woke at the slightest sound, real or imagined. The third night, she heard a slight rattle, the sound of a door shifting in its frame, and called out for Nick to get upstairs to bed, only to remember that he'd returned an hour earlier. She hopped out of bed and confirmed that both brothers were asleep. Increasingly dim, the rattle was supplanted by a faint metallic clicking, as if a locked door-handle were being turned. She tiptoed to the top of the stairs. The world went silent when she called out a tentative *hello*.

She found a flashlight and made a racket going down the stairs. She banged on the door but didn't open it. The next morning, Linnie put light bulbs in two outdoor sockets on the first-floor perimeter, and a man at the hardware store helped her connect a strong battery to a motion-activated light, which she attached high on a front corner of the bunkhouse.

That night she tried to dismiss the scratching she heard as a squirrel on the roof, a raccoon in garbage, a neighbor's cat hunting prey. The outdoor lights were turned on. She considered circling downstairs to Evelyn's office to see if a rodent had gotten inside, but the rooms' collection of oddities — a straitjacket made with wooden slats to restrain shaking from palsy, a photo of a dwarf with a cleft palate who became a carnival attraction — unnerved her even in daylight. The contents were exactly the stuff of nightmares: illustrations of a drooling fool of a goat-boy or a monk holding a cross over an unfortunate's bloodied head.

Although Margot didn't sit down for one meal with her brothers, she went out of her way, the three times she hosted dinner parties, to invite Linnie, who found excuses the first two times and only agreed to attend the final dinner, on Margot's last day in the house, when she discovered that Brendan had also been corralled. He arrived early and joined Linnie in the kitchen, where the boys were having an early supper.

Come dinner, seated at the head of the table, Margot had Brendan sit on her right; Linnie was seated at the other end of the table beside Margot's husband of eight years. Linnie liked him, inspite of her efforts to hold a stable marriage with Margot against him. As the evening wore on, Linnie paid little attention to how often her wine glass kept getting refilled until she knocked it over, at which point she decided to get herself to the bunkhouse before she conferred upon Margot another anecdote which she might use to her advantage.

Brendan, who'd been drinking coffee for a while, offered to accompany her, and they said their thank-you's and started hiking up the driveway towards the bunkhouse, where Nick had forgotten to leave the outside lights on. The cloud cover and overhanging trees made the path so dark that Brendan fished out a flashlight on a key chain and flickered its dim beam from the dusty gravel of the drive to the full flush on Linnie's cheeks. "Quit," she said, retreating from the light. He still held one of her arms but returned the key chain to his pocket.

Their world gone dark again, Linnie leaned in, brought his face to hers, and kissed him. He tasted of coffee and the berries from dessert, and she loved it that he left his tongue out of the kiss, their lips gently touching, until she used her own tongue, let it dart into his mouth. He responded in kind, then cupped her ass with both his hands and brought her close, a leg of his tight between hers. She pressed into him and felt her heat, a damp rush, but finally pulled back as all the obstacles presented themselves. "Damn," she whispered, "I can't take you into the girls' bunkroom or my reputation will be ruined."

He paused, amused by a thought of his own. "I can only imagine Margot counting cars in the morning and finding mine."

"Wait." She remembered that his daughter was in the city. "Kiley?"

"I have to pick her up at eleven-thirty. Tonight."

Linnie hated that he had to leave but saw no alternative. "What did Margot say? When she was bending your ear at dinner?"

"A short treatise," he said. "On why she should be in control."

"Evelyn's doing a little better. Maybe it won't matter."

The prospect, exciting as it was, made Linnie consider what she'd do, and where she'd move, if Evelyn did recover. She felt adrift in a sea of possibilities. And there was Brendan, to whom she was attracted. She pulled away from him to swat a mosquito. Inspite of the starless sky and the pitch-black of the driveway, she could imagine his smile without quite seeing it, his mouth pried open at the corners, his eyes lit up with mischief. She stepped back into the embrace and kissed him passionately, pushing her hips hard into his: she wanted him to feel a frustration equal to her own.

24

Nick's Journal

July 14

The bunkhouse sits in a low spot about middle of the way from the road to the house. The breeze off the river always blows by the house, but trees block it from the bunkhouse. It's hard to sleep when you're sticking to the sheets.

One night it was so hot I went to swim in the river. I told Linnie so she watched Ted. I swum well down the river and put in at somebody's dock where they have wooden stairs all the way up the bank, and their house is on the other side of the road so you can't wake them up. I walked back the river road and went through the part of the park on the river. A man was sitting in the park, like he was waiting. He was under a fat bunch of trees, which is where mosquitoes are worse. He saw I was dripping wet, he asked if the river was warm, and I said it was and the current isn't much close to shore. He said what about a towel, could I leave one downriver so I could dry off, but it's too much a bother. He doesn't look straight at you when he speaks, and I think I remember him from years back, when he'd help a bit like me at day-programs. Kind of quiet, if I remember. Was his name Edward?

Margot is here, and what's that like, you want to know. It's okay. If I say something, she says it back to me. Wow, it's hot, I'll say. Is it too hot for you, she'll say. I tell her I don't like Randoph Collins, he's the one had Ted weeding poison ivy. Are you mad with Mr. Collins, she says, well I hear you, she says. I don't know what she thinks. Linnie will laugh or get mad, she tells you straight. Mr. Collins called to hire me and Ted again, and Linnie answered. She said it wasn't even half a wage minimum he pays. She said we wouldn't work for him and called him bad names on the phone.

25

Hundreds of T-shaped gravestones were laid out in neat rows, as if they'd been put up for veterans. The flimsy markers were engraved with nothing but a number.

"It's an odd way to mark a grave," Dan Pataki said. He'd phoned to see if he could look through Evelyn's collection of oddities in the bunkhouse. Although Linnie was staying again in the house, she'd met him with a key and let him into the ground floor. He'd spent a good while going through the well-preserved books and pamphlets, and now he was sorting through a portfolio of artifacts about a particular institution. The Letchworth Village for the Feeble-Minded and Epilectics had been founded in 1908 by a philanthropist and eventually run by the state until its closure in the 1970s. Stapled to a piece of lined paper, which listed everything in this particular collection, was an index card with Evelyn's handwritten reminder on it. *Bourke-White photos? – needed.* The famous photographer had shot photos of the institution, and Evelyn wanted one for the history she had compiled.

When possible, it was Evelyn's habit to group topic-related items in a portfolio like this. A poster from Letchworth, demonstrating a variety of nude "cretins," had been presented at the 1932 Eugenics in America Conference. Their medical records were filled with an astonishing number of measurements; the study was titled "Anthropometry of Mongoloids and Dwarfs."

Pataki turned his attention to Linnie. "We had a guy wind up at Memorial Hospital in Niagara Falls yesterday," he said. "His father took him, and I've no cause to doubt what his father says. It seems the guy did this to himself."

He fished a photo out of a jacket pocket. "Is your stomach on the strong side?"

"I guess."

He handed her a photo. "Taken on admission."

The picture showed the side and back of a head with a nail driven into the skull. "The father said he walked in on his forty-year-old son when he was doing it, trying to hammer a nail into his own head. A slight fracture of the skull. Thankfully, he didn't get through the bone."

"Why did he do it? What's the father say?"

"He doesn't know. His son's had migraines, but he's not verbal. The father thinks maybe he was attacking the source of his pain."

"What do the psychiatrists say?"

Pataki guffawed. "They don't know. They've got no fancy German word for it, and no known disorder, so they just spin theory."

"You think it's related? To the other cases?"

"With the others a hole was made in the skull. Two of them were precise, although not in the same place. The victims could've been unconscious or even dead when the skull was finally punctured. But yesterday's business isn't the same."

"Maybe it's one of those 'copycat' things."

"Lord, you're watching too much television. 'Copycat?' The poor guy has an IQ of fifty, it's not like he's sitting around reading the newspapers and thinking he'll give something vicious a similar whirl."

"Then what?"

"That's my question. That's why I wondered about what your aunt has here. If she had a book that described something like it? The deranged or disabled mutilating themselves or one another. See, my problem is, this is not a smart guy who put a nail in his head. So, is this an original thought of his? I mean, where does he get," he paused to emphasis the noun, "the *idea*?"

He shrugged, then glanced back at the portfolio with the photo of the graveyard at Letchworth Village. "Did you notice? They just had numbers on those graves."

"Evelyn told me about it. The institution didn't put their names on them because of their families. A person could spend his whole life at Letchworth, but the families didn't want a record of it, not even a headstone with a family name. Too embarrassing."

"The families?" Pataki winced. "See, that's what I mean, the *idea* of it. It's not the retarded that came up with that awful idea, bury your relatives without recognizing they were even here. You had to be normal to come up with an idea that ugly."

He looked around the office at the stacks and shelves full of grisly material. "I'm getting an appreciation for what your aunt was up to here."

"Good." Linnie pointed down the hall past the bathroom. "Although sometimes I think there was even more of this stuff."

"Where would it be?"

"I don't know."

26

NICK'S JOURNAL

July 16

Ted liked the bunkhouse and being there. I thought it would make him cranky. I tried to think why he has fun there, maybe it's because it's like we're on a trip. If he was in the house, and Evelyn's not there, that's what he'd think about. But since it wasn't the house, he didn't worry on Evelyn or where she was.

After our time in the bunkhouse he didn't go into the house easy and stayed away from the den. It was two days later Linnie came up to me. She was trying so hard not to cry you could see it in the way her arms were crossed and shaking. She folded up the moment she started talking, and then she was bawling.

27

The woman cast her eyes everywhere except through the coke-bottle lenses of her glasses. Her lips trembled, her fingers absently strummed folds of her skirt, and she inhaled little puffs of air. Like the man beside her, she had the unmistakable physical characteristics of Down Syndrome, and she had the usual symptoms of a person, of any age, struggling not to cry. Her feelings were hurt, Linnie supposed, most likely by the client seated next to her, a young man working on his own pose, talking unnecessarily loudly to the man beside him.

Linnie might have interceded, but Ted was rocking on his heels, his shoelaces straying in all directions, and her cellphone indicated a peculiarly large number of new messages. Once in the parking lot with Ted, she began retrieving her messages, but the first was from the director of Evelyn's convalescent home, the second from the neurologist. Worried, she waited until she'd driven home, and forwarded through her messages until she heard a voice she wanted to hear, but even Brendan sounded stricken. "Linnie? Call me on my cell, okay?"

"They've taken Evelyn to Buffalo General," he began, when she called. "She's in the ICU. There's been another stroke. Worse than the others."

"Is she doing okay? Come on, she was doing better."

"I – uhh, they – at the hospital..." Brendan coughed, and then his voice broke. "They intubated her."

"Should I come?"

"Not tonight. She's in a coma."

"But I could talk to her. Don't they do that? When someone's in a coma? You have people they know — familiar voices – talk to them."

"Not tonight. She's in a coma."

"You already said that."

"She's on a ventilator. She'd almost quit breathing. I'm so sorry. Linnie...?" He paused at length to find better words and failed. "It's bad."

She understood that by declaring it "bad," Brendan meant "it" was "final." "I'll come," she declared.

"In the morning."

Her courage tanking, a sinkhole collapsing under her feet, Linnie managed a hoarse whisper. "Will you be there?"

"Yes. If you want."

Off the phone, she struggled to compose herself, then found Nick in the kitchen. When he looked up from his magazine, the speech she had intended to make disintegrated, the words scattering before her tongue could find them. She burst into tears and found herself, after he rushed to her, sobbing against his chest. She'd imagined she was supposed to be the adult, yet Nick was in control and instantly grasped the situation. "Evelyn," he said, and wrapped his arms around her.

Linnie was grateful when April stopped by early the next morning and offered her a ride to the hospital. "Brendan called last night. I thought you'd have enough on your mind besides driving. Or I can sit here if you'd rather."

"God, April. What did I do to deserve you?"

"Don't be silly." April retied a drawstring on her sweatpants. "Your turn will come."

"Wait." Linnie looked at the pajama bottoms she was still wearing. "Let me put myself together."

The ride to the city was so quick that Linnie supposed she'd slept most of the way. Inside the hospital, an elderly volunteer directed them to the Intensive Care Unit for the neurology department. At the nurses' station there, a post-surgical patient was being conveyed on a gurney to a bed. A dark pink scar zippered together by fat staples wove a semi-circle around his freshly shaven skull; the plate of bone that had been removed for the operation tilted upwards along the fault-line of the surgeon's cut. The man's eyes flickered open and blinked at Linnie, who was sickened by the thought that Evelyn, too, might be rendered a post-op Frankenstein.

Linnie brought April with her to the ICU desk. "We're here to see Evelyn Phillips."

"You're family?" the nurse asked.

"Yes." Linnie took April by the arm; she wanted the company.

A second nurse led them into an ICU ward to the last of a row of six beds, each one walled-in by glass on both sides and surrounded by a battery of machines. Evelyn's frail body was attached to an assortment of wires and tubes, drips and monitors, which the second nurse checked.

The gentle rhythmic huff of the ventilator was magnified by the rise and fall of Evelyn's chest and by her wheezing, wet exhalations. Linnie didn't dare touch her aunt's face, anchored as it was by an oxygen mask and tubes, and sought a hand, but Evelyn's left hand, once the blanket was lifted, had an IV needle in the back of it, so Linnie circled the bed and took hold of the right hand.

Linnie couldn't speak and couldn't cry. She didn't know if Evelyn's hand trembled a moment in hers, or if the tremor were her own, but she wanted the contact, her aunt's hand in hers, and the visit stretched well past the five-minute limit posted. Finally, when an aide joined the nurse to help turn the patient onto her side, Linnie and April retreated to a waiting room.

April had left by the time Brendan arrived. "Margot will be here no later than noon," he said. "Dr. Sheinman — the neurologist — did rounds really early this morning. He's promised to meet us here at 12:30."

Linnie glanced at the waiting room's clock: it would be three hours till the doctor showed up. Brendan turned off the television and pointed at the couch. "Why don't you try to rest? You can't have slept much."

"It's okay."

"C'mon." He pointed at the couch again. "Lie down, stretch out. That's what people do here. The hospital may send you home for a shower if you're still here in a few days."

At his urging, she put her feet up, and the next thing she knew Margot had joined them in the waiting room and Brendan had coffee and a sweet roll waiting. Margot had brought numerous packs of Kleenex, which she'd delved into liberally since visiting her mother in the ICU. Linnie felt a bit revived by the nap, and the coffee helped, but she was entirely unready for a conference with a neurologist. She might as well have been summoned to a court where an unfavorable verdict, long determined, would finally be delivered.

Margot paced feverishly and didn't let up when Dr. Sheinman joined them. "Have you seen your mother?" he asked.

"Yes." Margot sounded reproachful. "But she was speaking the other day. Improving. I wonder what exactly happened."

"This time the hemorrhage was more severe, and there's significant injury to the basic elements of the brain function, especially respiratory."

"Damage? There's already been that, hasn't there?" Margot was pleading. "Is this any different?"

"I'm afraid it is. The ventilator's sustaining her."

"Is there a chance? Of recovery?"

"Nothing's impossible."

Margot turned to Brendan. "What do you think?"

"I can't tell you what to do. Your mother has a Living Will – a health care directive. She prepared for this. I can bring the documents this afternoon."

"I presume the first thing," Dr. Sheinman said, "is to see if we can determine what the patient would want. Then the second thing is to see if the family agrees."

"Agrees with whom? My mother?" Margot's eyes swept across the others in the room. "Evelyn will take the high road, even if it's fatal. She'll want her bones lying alongside those of the other martyrs. I'm not willing to throw the towel in, or pull any plug, unless everyone tells me she's already dead."

When he had discussed the range of possibilities weeks earlier, Brendan had told Linnie that if such a decision were ever needed, the doctors would insist on a family's full complicity before removing life support. It's often the unhappy family member, he'd explained, who has the hardest time letting go. Whatever Margot needed from her mother, Linnie thought, she didn't have it.

28

NICK'S JOURNAL

July 22

Evelyn is in the hospital. In Buffalo. Except she's not there, not any part of her I know. You asked if God would worry about her. Is she alive? Is she dead? Evelyn wouldn't want God, or anyone, worrying on her. She does her own worrying, that's exactly what she'd say, and she'd want the last word on anything.

Yes, I will miss Evelyn if she doesn't come home. I miss her too much already, I missed her since the first stroke. Of course I know what death is. I think everyone does.

Evelyn wondered about Ted, if he knew about death. She asked me once when we were driving. It was the second day the raccoon was lying beside the road. I told her Ted sees the dead animal by the road, and he knows it's not going anywhere, and he doesn't need to know more, that's what I think. What will Ted do without her? It's already in him, a hole I don't know how to fill.

You asked if I thought Evelyn's life had ended. All I know is something is gone from us.

29

Ted was asleep in the back of the squad car. Alerted, Linnie had gotten back to the house on the river in time to greet the deputy sheriff, who ambled around to the rear door that Ted was lying against and opened it gently. "A woman who lives in the outskirts of Youngstown saw him in her backyard," he explained. "She was a little panicky when she called. She calmed down a bit when I got there."

"He's supposed to be at a day program in Niagara Falls."

"The guy driving the van stopped for a Coke, used the bathroom. Your fella here walked off, and the driver didn't catch it." The deputy stepped back as Ted clumsily made his way out of the vehicle.

"Ted, go get a glass of milk, something to eat." Linnie pointed him toward the house, then faced the deputy. "Everything's okay? With this woman?"

"She's elderly and all stirred up, wants to know what the heck's wrong with our world, this lost boy loose in it."

"What was he doing?"

"Nothing much. She's got a shed with a window, which is what he stood looking through." The deputy fiddled with one end of his sparse mustache. "He was pretty stubborn, made a little fuss at first. But I knew what we had."

"Thanks."

"Is he your relative? He walks real floppy, like his joints are broke. Is he in pain?"

"Not that I know."

"The day-care group put in a call, once they knew he was missing. You might let them know he's okay." He looked at the house. "It's a danger for the retarded to be out alone."

"I know. Thanks. I really appreciate it."

"Not a problem." The deputy glanced at Ted, then at Linnie, as if to gauge her capacity to restrain him. Finally, he tipped his head in farewell. Only when his car was halfway up the drive, the crunch of tires on gravel fading, did she turn to the house.

Ted stood by the front door with his head cocked so far forward he couldn't see more than his feet. "Ted?" she called. "Sweetheart, you keep wandering off and we'll have to put one of those wildlife tags on you, a big homing device stapled to your ear like a price tag."

Once they were inside the front hall, she noticed Ted's gaze wander to the table where his mother's purse normally rested. "Let's get some food," Linnie said.

After lunch, Edie Patterson stopped by with a tin of freshly made cookies. She'd offered to look after Ted while the rest of the family drove into the city for a meeting.

While Ted wolfed down a few cookies, Edie told Linnie, "His mom helped us get books for the school library on the reservation. A whirl-wind, the way she worked her friends. She said they'd be no cast-offs or paperbacks. Almost a hundred boxes she got: textbooks, encyclopedias, tax and legal libraries, a set of Dickens in leather. She's something special, Mrs. Phillips. Had her boys help with the unloading."

"You think Ted remembers you?"

"Seems it. Keep your cell on. I'll call if he starts to worry overmuch."

Linnie and Nick drove to the hospital and paid a brief visit to the ICU ward. Evelyn was pale as rice paper. A pillow had been propped under her knees, a suggestion of comfort at odds with the rigidity of her arms.

On their way down the corridor to a conference room, Linnie noticed Margot exit the room and confer briefly with her lawyer. The sympathy she'd been feeling for her cousin dissipated on the spot. Moments later, Brendan stepped from the room and said something to Margot, then something else to Bridgewater. Linnie hoped it was terse. Whatever it was, Bridgewater nodded a farewell and strolled towards the bank of elevators.

Brendan waited for Linnie and Nick and escorted them into the conference room. He didn't distribute copies of Evelyn's Living Will and her Durable Power of Attorney until everyone was present: Margot, Nick, Linnie, Dr. Sheinman, Evelyn's cousin Trudy Huntington, and a member of the hospital's ethics committee.

The first document was Evelyn's Living Will, which began:

> *This country devotes a shameful amount of its medical resources to its elders, many of whose lives are no longer recognizably human, many of whom pilfer medical attention that rightly should be conferred upon the young or disadvantaged. If I should become, on a presumed permanent basis, incapable of ...*

Margot's chuckle dispelled much of the tension in the room. She waved the sheet she'd been reading. "It's a lecture. You have to love her for it. My mother's in the goddamn ICU, and she'll still tell us what to think."

Everyone there, except Linnie, felt obliged to talk. Brendan outlined the legal issues; the doctor on the ethics committee explained the hospital's concerns and procedural guidelines. The neurologist, hectored by Margot's insatiable appetite for details, reviewed all possible outcomes of removing Evelyn from the ventilator: respiratory or cardiac failure, recovery; the only certainty was the lack of one.

"But if we focus on the positive," Margot persisted, "what are the odds of recovery?"

"And by 'recovery' you mean..?"

"Being conscious, cognizant. Talking again."

"Chances are very slim, I think."

"We have to preserve those chances, don't we? I'm told -- I don't know if this is right--" Margot glanced at Brendan, "that even if she's got a 'Do Not Resuscitate' order on file, we can argue--"

"Argue what?" Dr. Sheinman was visibly confused. "To keep her on the ventilator?"

"If it improves her chances of regaining consciousness."

"It stabilizes and manages her breathing. If you care to extrapolate beyond that, you might consider other risks. Blood remains from the intracerebral hemorrhage. If necessary, surgery might relieve the pressure of hydrocephalus — the swelling – but surgery has its own dangers."

"She looks okay," Margot said. "Swelling?"

"Inside the skull. It can result in herniation."

"Like a hernia?" she sputtered. "You're kidding?"

"The swelling," Dr. Sheinman explained, "can squeeze the brain out through the hole at the base of the skull, the foramen magnum. Like toothpaste. If that happens, the brain crushes the brainstem. Death is minutes away."

Margot, determined to quantify each and every possibility, grew silent. Linnie wondered if the doctor's unsparing depiction had been intended to quiet her clamor for attention and control.

The one surprise was that Evelyn's Durable Power of Attorney nominee for health care was a cousin of hers, and not Margot, Nick, or Linnie, apparently all of whom she neither wanted to burden with a decision about withholding treatment nor completely trusted to make it. Trudy Huntington waited till things had settled before speaking.

"Evelyn and I talked about it - in case it got to this. You know she wouldn't want tubes, paralysis, dementia. For her it's always been a matter of Ted: can she look after him? Because if she can't, if she has to be a burden, she doesn't want that. She'd want everyone to agree, and she'd want things as uncomplicated as possible. She wouldn't want to be where she is right now."

When no one disagreed, Margot struggled to her feet; her voice had lost its timbre and pitch. "It's all too sudden. I'll go along with whatever you decide. Right now I want to go be with my mother."

Back at the house, Linnie made her way to the banks of the river. All along the water the day's sunlight was fractured by waves into parallel sheets: green with the mirror of trees on the far shore, gun-metal gray when a bank of passing clouds blotted out the sun. Majestic, unstoppable, the river for Linnie was forever entwined with Evelyn and her place on it.

On the occasion of Jordan's first visit to the house, Evelyn had asked to accompany Linnie and him to Niagara Falls for a ride on The Maid of the Mist. The boats had been steaming, from both sides of the river, into the heart of the Horseshoe Falls for well more than a century, yet she'd never been on one. Ted would never have tolerated the boat-ride.

Jordan was nervous with anticipation, then giddy with excitement, as the boat chugged off from the wharf, yet the day belonged to Evelyn, enrapt as Jordan bounced around the boat's upper deck, firing off the full load of his disposable camera's photos before the immense horseshoe of the Canadian Falls was close. As the boat plowed into the thickening mist, the spray heavy as steady rain, Evelyn forced her free plastic raincoat on Jordan, who'd refused the hand-out and was cold in his t-shirt. She turned her umbrella into the mist and the breeze driving it, but couldn't keep the umbrella steady in the whip of the wind. Her squint kept water out of her eyes, but exaggerated the creases lining her cheeks. Her aunt, and it had mostly escaped Linnie's attention, was growing old.

The second thing that was clear was that Evelyn was having the time of her life. She laughed at the slapstick with her umbrella, and watched Jordan assiduously, lest she miss one detail of the child's elation. Rarely had Linnie seen Evelyn, so often restrained by a caregiver's role, abandon herself thoroughly to a moment's simple pleasures. She wished she had a snapshot of the day: no one could be erased from it.

At the house the cicadas in the riverfront trees were drumming up a racket. When had they migrated here and taken over the noisemaking from the ground-dwelling crickets? Evelyn could have explained it to her.

A kitchen door swung open, and Edie Patterson stepped outside and started across the lawn. Ted followed, but at a distance.

"You okay?" Edie asked, on reaching her.

"Pretty much."

"A hard business, deciding what to do."

"Ever been through it?"

"My father. Cancer got most of him. The most terrible pain. He'd beg my husband to bring the shotgun." She noticed that Linnie was crying. "I'm sorry. Here I'm hashing out old business. What're they fixing to do?"

"They're going to take her off the ventilator."

"I didn't know her well, your aunt. I imagine it's possible, what with her child, she's not looking for the Lord. But I know Mrs. Phillips is a keen woman, and the Lord will find her and keep her to Him. You remember that."

"I will."

She squeezed her arm. "I'll be off, if you're okay."

"Yes."

As Edie retreated towards the driveway, Linnie spotted Ted, dizzying himself, walking in a collapsing circle by the house. She tried to imagine what to do about him, and the notion that struck her was one she'd had before. It was a child's impulse, with equal parts of dread and resentment. Flight. She should flee.

30

NICK'S JOURNAL

July 29

The hospital moved Evelyn to a regular room. I think she might get drops of water if you put the straw in her mouth, but I don't know. Margot would live at the hospital if she could. She says she wants to stay, and then nothing much happens and she hurries back to Toronto for a day or two.

Ted knows things are strange. Mornings he wants to walk out by the road. Maybe he's hoping to get somewhere, or hide, or run off. We took him to the hospital. Evelyn was a statue, her breathing is whispers, and he didn't go near her. He looked her way once in awhile, but she's so thin and her face is gray, and it'd be hard to say he knew her. The room was so quiet Linnie turned on the TV for the noise.

Ted started walking back and forth until the room wasn't big enough for him. We gave Evelyn hugs goodbye in case Ted might do the same, but what he wanted was to go.

On her visits Linnie brings little jars of wax and chapsticks to rub on Evelyn's lips, which are so dry the skin flakes off. The lips have cracks that open wide and bleed. This makes Linnie cry, but she doesn't stop, and brings more lipsticks because they keep disappearing.

Margot says she wants to be there when things change, whatever it is, better or worse. What will it be if Evelyn wakes up? Will she say she's hungry?

And if it's bad, do I want to be there at the end? How do we know the end? Is the doctor right there won't be pain? I worry about pain because who could tell us what hurts other than Evelyn.

You asked if I pray. I dream. At first I thought it must be Evelyn's dream, only it was me on my bed waking up and thinking I saw a glass of water so full it kept spilling over. All these days, and Evelyn only drinks what leaks from the straw, and I don't know how that can't be bad.

31

W hat do you remember about your father?"
Linnie was thrown by the question from Judy Urbanski
and stuttered through a brief, evasive reply. Her father was
in his mid-fifties when she'd been born, and he'd always seemed a bit
frightened by the prospect of handling a young girl, as if his daughter
were a rare and unfamiliar instrument that he didn't dare play too
boldly. Linnie remembered being near him, within his reach if not his
lap, his gaze captive, his touch tentative.

She was eight when he was struck by a blood disease, and her
mother and father were separated. Although her mother expressed grief,
she didn't display much and was already involved with the Swedish
architect. Linnie remembered how mad she was with her father, so
much older than every other kid's father, and then dead. To this day
she disliked men who, at an advanced age, fathered children they'd
barely live to rear. Evelyn would have agreed with her.

Unable to avoid the subject of her father entirely, she mentioned
his career. "The Philharmonic played a short piece he'd written. Early
the next season. By way of honoring him. I think it's the only time
the piece was performed."

"You went?"

Linnie shrugged. The fact was, she'd felt ill and remained in the
hotel room rather than go to the concert hall; Evelyn had stayed with

her. The architect had accompanied her mother to the performance played in her father's honor.

Judy used a handkerchief to clean her eyeglasses, as if that might clarify Linnie's answer, then brushed wrinkles out of her slacks. "Back to the subject of Ted. I think he should see the body. If and when it's time. I recognize the possibility of a perverse — call it violent — reaction."

Linnie couldn't imagine taking Ted to see the body: on his last visit to the hospital he wouldn't glance at his mother; what would he make of a corpse? Besides, Evelyn had specifically requested a quick cremation.

On the ride back to the house it was the weather that turned violent. It had been humid for days, the haze settling and thickening, a dark mass of air now gathering across the river on the Canadian shore, turning the afternoon into twilight. The wind kicked up, raked through the trees, and sent pine buds flying, then calmed momentarily before the sky was splintered by dual prongs of lightning over the water.

The storm was close and closing, fat pellets of rain smacking the windshield, summer lightning crisscrossing the southern horizon, a bolt striking ground not far to the north. Linnie drove hard, gripped by the thought that Ted might have wandered outside, that he'd make a perfect target for lightning. The downpour arrived when she did, a sheet of water chasing her into the house.

Ted was in the front hall. He used the flashlight Mrs. G. had given him, in case power got knocked out, to try to trap its beam in a corner of the ceiling, and he squealed with delight when Linnie, aware of his game, made the beam that much brighter by flipping off the room lights.

When the phone rang, Linnie answered it fearfully, but Jordan was on the line. "It's me," he said. "I'm on Dad's cell. I almost broke my wrist." He paused a moment, lest she underestimate the gravity of the accident. "I had a *x-ray*!"

"What happened!?"

"It wasn't my fault." He proceeded, at length, to describe the skateboarding trick he had attempted and the wrist-guards he hadn't worn. "I have to wear wrist-guards now."

"Good. No more x-rays, okay?"

"How's Aunt Evelyn?" In the background his father could be heard advising him about what to say and how to say it, but Jordan plowed ahead on his own: "Is she dying?"

"Yes." Linnie could hear his father do more coaching.

"Dad says to tell you she must be an amazing lady and to let him know, if anything happens."

"I will."

"Linnie..?"

"Yeah?" She could hear the fear in the ten-year-old's voice and didn't know how to dispel it.

"What about you?"

"Honey, I'm not sick. It's only Evelyn." She imagined this was what he wanted to hear. "It's her age."

"But if you get sick..?"

"I won't get sick."

He took a few moments to mull it over, then changed course, describing his half-brother who'd been born two weeks ago. "He looks right at me, I know he does."

"That's so exciting." Genuinely happy for Jordan, who'd long been overjoyed by the prospect of a brother, she wished she were excited by the child's birth, but all she felt was that the timing was poor, the irony cheap, the circle-of-life metaphor impossibly sophomoric. A crater was opening in her life.

"Will you visit?" he said.

"Yeah. Of course."

"Will you?" He sounded doubtful.

"I promise."

Outside, the storm raged another few hours and had passed through before bedtime. Linnie took the brightest flashlight and walked the property. She wanted to make sure no limb was hanging on a power line, no tree split by lightning, no hazard undiscovered. She imagined the guard would change soon enough, but at the moment she was still captain of it.

Two nights later, Linnie kept nodding off in the chair in Evelyn's hospital room and waking, her back increasingly sore, in the middle of what seemed to be the same dream. It made no sense: a large tree out by the road, its top long ago shorn-off, needed to be cut down, but the trunk kept swelling or suddenly sprouting massive new branches.

Bored by the dream, and by repeatedly slipping back into it, she checked on her aunt before heading back to Lewiston. Evelyn was still, her mouth cracked open, breath trickling in and out, her heart racing frantically beneath the fragile wall of her chest — like a swimmer trapped under the surface by a thin sheet of ice.

Linnie was halfway to the house when her cellphone rang. Shaking, she answered it by saying "Wait," and pulled the car over to the shoulder before she could find the nerve to talk again. "Yes?"

The nurse explained that it had happened not long after Linnie had left the room. "I was with her. Her heart had been revving like a race engine, and then she just let go. It was easy on her, very quiet."

Linnie didn't know how long she spent on the shoulder of the road, her weeping interrupted by hiccups she also couldn't control. Eventually, she composed herself enough to pull back into the northbound lanes and drive home, where Nick was waiting. He ushered her into the house and kissed her forehead.

Ted was seated at the top of the stairs. His pajamas were inside-out, and he didn't say anything until she ruffled the top of his hair as she stepped past him. "Linn-whee," he mumbled, leaving her to wonder if he'd ever spoken her name before.

32

NICK'S JOURNAL

Aug. 18

The chapel is the small church at Trinity, not as big as the main one. The church is in downtown Buffalo if you don't know it. First we went to the graveyard Forest Lawn.

It's like a park with statues and trees. Evelyn didn't care about it, where she was buried, she said so, but as Margot says you can't put her out with the recycling, so she went to a family plot.

It was only ashes in the box we buried. Margot, Linnie, Cousin Trudy, Brendan, Mrs. G., me and the minister were at the grave. Ted stayed in the limousine. Two other people in black suits were there to help, and then afterwards was the service.

The church is where Evelyn went when she was young. Cousin Trudy arranged it and got the chapel, which was about full, I never saw half the people who were there, they were from Buffalo.

Margot's lawyer was there, talking to her before it started, and he was going to sit in the pew behind us but Linnie told him the seats were for family, but of course Mrs. G and Brendan were with us. The lawyer went to another seat.

I saw Reverend Strickley there, and he said hello. The church minister at Trinity didn't know Evelyn and started by saying how he wished he had known her, and others spoke, but Ted started banging his head on the back of the pew in front of him, not so as he might bleed, but hard, and he kept at it, so Mrs. G took him outside.

Brendan got up, because everyone was stuck watching Ted leave, and he talked about courage and love and generosity. I remember his dad and Evelyn together, him always being real nice, and Brendan said it was hard to lose someone who was a big part of his world and his father's. Evelyn reminded him of his father, very smart, very kind. Giants in a world gone small, he said, and I saw women start with the Kleenex.

Margot said something funny a doctor once wrote about a mother and a daughter, and did a reading from the Bible, she spoke so smoothly you could hardly see the shaking in her hands. Linnie had her turn and said Evelyn was the light at the end of all her tunnels, it's exactly what she said, and her crying got me started. I don't remember the last time I was crying, except I was little.

The chapel has stone floors and dark wood and windows that are cut like they're full of jewels. I never saw stained glass that beautiful, even Evelyn would admit they're really pretty. I started thinking if I looked at all the windows in the church I'd find Evelyn's face in one of them, even just for a moment, her eyes would be looking in and looking out, the way they do in stained glass.

33

"Ted's missing."

The program director was on the phone. The group from the church basement had gathered with clients from similar programs at Artpark, where they painted banners to hang by the outdoor stage, then set off on walks into the river gorge. "Another guy's missing, too," the director said. "Barney Lewis. He's a teeny little thing, a stick figure with cartoon eyes."

Linnie thought she remembered him from another such outing. Barney Lewis was bug-eyed, and one of his eyes turned out. Slight as he was, his arms were disproportionately short, and his hands tinier still; his elfin fingers dangled by his belt. His gait listed to starboard, the side of the walleye, and his pace was glacial, as if each step were a one-of-a-kind undertaking, like rock-climbing.

Linnie was mad with Ted for making a nuisance of himself and furious with the program directors. What were they thinking, sending clients on walks into the steep gorge?

She drove to Lewiston, followed a road through the center's parking lot, and left her car near Artpark's performance hall, which had been built right beside the gorge on the site of the old suspension bridge. She walked by a group of tents, where children were busy with their own activities, and past the outdoor stage. A row of metal-working sheds, shuttered at the moment, and a quarter-mile more of sidewalk separated her from the trailhead, where she met Ted's program director.

"Okay," he said to her, after conferring with an employee, "the big guy and the little guy are still missing."

"What happened?"

"Dave was in charge of Ted and John Hickley, who had an accident, so Dave took him back to a restroom and handed Ted off to Julie's group. And then, twenty minutes later, he wasn't following Julie anymore, and she couldn't do anything until she'd brought her crew back."

"Who's out looking?"

"Right now only Dave. We'll be able to spare other staff as soon as everyone else is put on their vans."

"Are they together? Ted and the other one missing?"

"I don't know." The program director grimaced. "I kinda hope not. That fella Barney, I don't know if you've seen him, but he's awful frail. You could break a bone just by hugging him."

"What trail was Julie on?"

"The lower one, but after the fork it splits and loops around." He nodded upriver.

Linnie started down the path. Once she passed the fork, the lower trail descended into the gorge gradually, curling through thick vegetation. A spell of dry weather precluded the chance of mud, but the path was narrow in spots where the shoulder had slid away. Down below the river glittered: luminescent and green, with circles etched by whirlpools so round they might have been drawn by a compass.

Scrub pines and tangles of oak vine might arrest the fall of anyone who slipped off the trail, except in spots where steep switchbacks or walls of outcrop created sheer drops. Ted should be able to handle the terrain and, if he were paying attention, would keep to the uphill side of the path. Linnie understood that what Barney would do, or how fragile he'd prove in the event of a fall, was more of a concern, especially if he and Ted were together and anxious enough to compete for a safe perch. Ted wouldn't want anyone crowding him.

A quarter of a mile along the trail Linnie felt as if she'd trekked into a wilderness. Overhead, a red hawk floated on an updraft, and the only sounds were the caws of gulls and the coursing of water along the rocks at the base of the canyon. Soon the trail split again above a wooden staircase, with opposed flights of stairs that helped manage a particularly steep section of the lower route.

Uncertain what Ted would make of this crossroads, Linnie paused and, feeling the undeniable tug of the water, descended the stairs. The trail doubled back past a sturdy black-walnut tree, downhill and downriver. She got glimpses of the clearing, a recess in the walls of the riverbank with a flat shoreline, and then lost sight of it. The path twisted around a thick wall of brush until the shoreline was visible again and she saw a fishing pole whipping back and forth.

The afternoon sun flashed off a rusty tackle box abandoned in a patch of brambles. Linnie climbed down a series of rocks that zigzagged along a steep chute, then followed the path around a final bend. She was certain that none of the program personnel would have allowed their charges to risk this route, ending as it did at a narrow patch of shoreline. Downstream, the gorge's walls were nearly vertical; the river was a torrent, roiling in the water-boils.

Linnie stopped thirty yards short of the gravel patch where the fisherman stood. Even at this distance, the stains on his clothes were visible, and his pole clearly wasn't equipped with either line or lure. The river was furiously loud, the upper Great Lakes emptying themselves through canyon walls not four hundred yards apart. She didn't know if he'd hear, but she called out anyway. "Seen anyone?"

The fisherman regarded her curiously and shook his head. Had he heard? His grin, expanding, revealed half a set of upper teeth; what remained were dark and jagged. His bottom lip bowed in. He raised his fishing pole straight up, then brought it down hard and struck the water. He whipped the water a few more times, then looked at her.

Linnie reversed course and hurried back up the canyon. By the time she got to the trailhead, Ted was standing with his program director, who explained that Ted had been discovered inside the performance hall, where stagehands were preparing for one of the last shows of the season.

"There's somebody else," Linnie told the director.

"We found him." He explained that Barney Lewis had toppled twenty feet down an embankment off the upper trail, hard into a web of exposed tree roots that had kept him from falling further. He'd sustained a broken wrist. An ambulance was on the way.

"Not him," Linnie said. "Someone's down by the river. Pretending to fish. He's weird, disturbed."

"No one's missing, not from our groups."

"Someone should check out who he is, what he's doing."

The director looked at Linnie as if she were a client and slow to understand. "He's not one of ours. If he knows his way down there, he knows his way back up."

Frustrated, Linnie was reminded of what Judy Urbankski had told her: parents rarely reported problems with personnel, most of whom worked for close to minimum wage, or with a program, for fear it might be shut down. The shortage, and it was dire, was of resources, not patients.

Back at the house, she turned on cartoons for Ted, then met Brendan at the front door. Ever since the night of Margot's dinner party, she'd felt awkward in his company and blamed him, perhaps unfairly, for her discomfort. She wanted someone else to help her sort through her confusion: where would she move, whom would she date? Brendan, who no doubt sensed her confusion, also reflected it.

"Maybe this will be good news," he began, after greeting her with a hug. "Although I don't know what you were expecting. From Evelyn."

"She wants me to look after Ted." The prospect, after the day's events, seemed increasingly daunting.

"She left you a sum of money."

"To look after him?"

"No. It's a simple bequest. I'd told her if she wanted you to be the guardian, she should make the bequest contingent upon your doing so, but she wouldn't hear of it. She left you a hundred grand outright. She knew it might run counter to her hopes of your looking after her boys."

"Jesus." Linnie started to do the math: she could buy a car, pay for a divorce, get out of debt, move anywhere. "When do I get it?"

"Anytime. I just have to cut a check."

"Do I have to share it with James?"

"Absolutely not. It's inheritance. But you don't want to screw up and put it in a joint account."

"What about Margot? Can she object?"

"Margot got substantially more, but that may not appease her. Whatever her objections are - and they're probably festering - they won't provide a legal challenge, at least not for your money."

"For what, then?"

"The rest of it. That money's in trust for the brothers, to pay for the house and other expenses. The guardian, when there is one, controls the house. And Ted. Margot will put Ted in a home."

"Can't the court stop that?"

"The court picks the guardian. The guardian figures out the rest."

"Christ." Her aunt had come, one last time, to her rescue, and Linnie was overcome by it. "I need a lawyer, somebody good at pushing a divorce through. And I need an advance. Enough for a trip to Seattle." She could see his dismay at the prospect but didn't know how to address it. "And Portland, to see Jordan."

Mrs. G. had taken a week off, and the house looked it. The no-see-ums, flocking towards the bright lights of the kitchen, had flown through the screens and died by the hundreds along the windowsills. No one had raised a sash and vacuumed up the bugs in a month or more.

"You have a nice break?" Linnie asked, when she found her cleaning the kitchen floor.

"Break?" she chuckled. "No such thing. I was lookin' after my brother. His wife can't no more. She's got the Allheimer curse, and her head's gone soft as a two-minute egg."

"I didn't know."

"Greg tries to watch her, but he don't got energy for himself. Estelle belongs in a home, except Greg's not keen on the idea. And she's stubborn and don't know she's a danger."

"I'm sorry."

"It's coming to that with Ted. There was always Miss Evelyn and me and Nick to tag-team 'im. Darned if I know what'll work now."

"With Nick and you—"

"No." Mrs. G. blinked away the tears forming. "See, I gotta go, too. Stayed longer than I would've, 'cause I wouldn't leave Miss Evelyn like that. But it's long past time for me to quit."

"You can't."

"Honey, you know how old I am. Greg won't live a year without a transplant, and the operation's likely to kill 'im."

"But...?"

"Estelle can't boil a pot of water safe. You're my other family. I'll hang on a bit, or till we know what's what, an' then I'll visit when I can."

34

L innie saw him as she crossed the supermarket parking lot. The deranged fisherman from the gorge wore the same soiled red sweatshirt he had on days earlier, and his sneakers were untied. His gray hair was cut into a platform of bristles.

He was quarreling with the younger man beside him, who finally grabbed his arm and tried to drag him towards a nearby pickup. The fisherman pulled free and stalked off, but stopped when he saw Linnie and stared at her. His eyes were rheumy, his mouth twisted into a fish-lipped pout.

"Will you get in the damn car?" the younger man said, catching up and snapping him backwards with a tug on his sweatshirt.

The fisherman muttered bitterly as he was spun around and marched towards the battered pickup, then shoved up and into the passenger seat. The younger man slammed the door shut and circled to the driver's side, while the fisherman slapped the dashboard with his hands.

Linnie started for her car, parked a hundred feet away. She wanted to follow the pickup, or get its license number, but the pickup backed out of its space and squealed off.

Linnie used her cellphone to call the sheriff's department. After Dan Pataki heard her description of the "fisherman" and his odd behavior, he asked, "Would you recognize him from photos?"

"I think so."

"We've got some individual and a lot of group shots. We've also got the names of anyone in a program. It's the ones we don't know about that we can't investigate." He sensed, from the delay, Linnie's perplexity. "Look at your cousin. He spent most of his life looked after by his mother. If she hadn't enrolled him in a program with state funding, we wouldn't know about him. We'd like names and photos of anyone known to a program; the regional office of OMRDD has a list of facilities. But..?"

"But?"

"A couple of residential facilities haven't been forthcoming when a deputy stopped by."

"Why?"

"They'll argue, 'Privacy.' But my guess? Their records, and maybe accounting, are a bit shoddy. If you had a little time, maybe you could stop by, chat them up: you're a close relative of a prospective DD client of theirs, you wonder who's there, would you put your relative there?, get names and photos, whatever."

The prospect intrigued Linnie: she was curious about the facilities and the people who ran them; also, she might learn something that argued against putting Ted in such a place. She made appointments late in the day at both homes, when the residents would all be there, in case photos were needed, and mid-day with the managers at their offices. Dan Pataki had been right. The record-keeping was poor: files overflowed with inconsequential, often handwritten notes; photos of residents, if there were them, could be twenty years old. Lists of residents who attended day programs, for whom bills would need to be sent to a variety of government agencies and foundations, were scrawled on a sheet of paper with absentees later scratched out and some clients were identified only by first names. The offices' accounting lacked the clarity that good software – and good input – provided, and a lot of the records would be easier to maintain digitally. Hearing this, one of the managers was happy to suggest that Linnie help. Linnie dropped off a list of client names and photos at April's house for Dan Pataki, as well as a note describing the residents as mostly calm and orderly.

Linnie returned to the house on the river to discover Margot there with a van to cart all of Evelyn's clothes off to the Salvation Army. "It's so important to do this," she said, as she stripped Evelyn's room of Evelyn. "Clean things out. Instant therapy. I know it's good for Ted. And I don't want to share the house with the ghost of her clothes. Anyway, if I get the bedroom cleaned out, I'm hoping you'll tackle her office."

"What do I do with her ... things?" Linnie imagined driving around with a truck full of her aunt's collection of curiosities and finding herself unable to unload them.

"Someone else must collect them."

"You know of anyone?"

"A medical school might have a library. I don't know. It's gruesome stuff. At a point I'd throw it out."

The second load Margot put in the van was full of things she was taking back to Toronto: all of her mother's good jewelry, two sets of antique silverware, the four most valuable paintings, and a Sheraton couch and table and Chippendale desk, all of which were museum quality.

Brendan was furious to discover that four of the items Margot took had not been bequeathed to her; technically, they belonged to the trust and were, in principle, the brothers' property. In fact, they likely would one day have belonged to Linnie, as a designated remainderman of the trust, but she was unable to summon much outrage. She was leaving early the next morning for her own unannounced raid on the apartment she had shared with James. She wanted to retrieve her things before divorce proceedings commenced, and she'd rented a large SUV and recruited April.

At three a.m. the following morning, April arrived at the house toting a thermos of coffee. "Might as well let me drive the first shift," she said. "I'll get past Syracuse if my bladder holds out and the coffee holds up."

Three hundred miles later, with each of them having caught a couple of hours sleep, they circled north of Albany to Glenville. James was scheduled to teach at the community college from 11:00 a.m. to 1:00 p.m. Although they were in the apartment shortly after eleven,

Linnie hadn't counted upon the disarray. If she'd wanted anything from the kitchen, she'd have had to clean it before packing. Stacked several feet high, dishes were lightly rinsed, pots soaking, everything started, nothing finished.

She'd brought garment bags for whatever was on hangers, garbage bags for the rest, yet clothes in the closets had slid off hangers and were clustered in piles on the floor or hung four-deep on hooks. James's clean clothes had been dumped wherever there was room: his underwear and shirts were piled with hers.

April circled through the apartment, doing her own reconnaissance. "Four of the pots are Calphalon," she reported, "which is worth something. The TV, if it was a flatscreen, I'd haul it outside myself, but it's even older than the computer."

"Leave them."

"Possession truly is nine-tenths of the law, I've been through it."

Linnie steered April to a table by the front door that was piled high with unopened mail. "What I want is bank statements, bills with my name on them."

Linnie would take only what was unequivocally hers: keepsakes, family portraits, articles of clothing, three small bronzes that had been her mother's, a demi-ronde table with exquisite inlay and other long-ago gifts from Evelyn. All of it would fit twice over in the SUV, and yet she was slowed by the hunt for a few pieces of family silver.

The moment the SUV was loaded, Linnie climbed into the driver's seat and headed for the Thruway. A helicopter couldn't have sped her away fast enough.

April sorted through the eclectic batch of CDs she'd brought, but was interrupted by the ring of Linnie's cellphone, which she answered. She turned it over to Linnie after listening for a moment.

"Havin' a bad day here," Mrs. G. said, clearly upset. "Don't know when you're back."

"Not till after dark."

"Ted was carrying a plate and fell. Old china. Broke like glass. Cut his hand up, an' he'd hardly get in the car to run up to the hospital. He's home now."

"Nick?"

"Couldn't get hold'a him. Still can't."

"He's working, right? At the Majikowskis today? There can't be many in the phonebook."

"I can't spell that." She caught her breath audibly. "Had the doctor wrap up the hand, so Ted couldn't get at the stitches. Seven stitches, it was."

"Call Brendan. Evelyn has him on speed dial on the phone in the den."

Once they reached the Thruway, April held up the CD she'd selected. "This is called 'My Fatherland' or something like that."

"By Smetana?"

"Parts of it are kind of military, and parts too lovely for words. I should've played it this morning. You hear it driving over hills into a sunrise, and you'll swear Creation would've been a bigger hit with a soundtrack."

"Play it."

The first movement, as April had noted, had its martial passages, but the next section was ethereal, lyrical, majestic. "Die Moldau." If Linnie recalled correctly, the Moldau was a river that ran through Prague, and she was mesmerized by the composer's rendering of it: a swirl of quickening currents become a rogue waltz; the soft, glittering notes of first light on still water; the pulse of commerce, accord and discord; the rush of cataclysm, water over a dam, a flood spreading.

Linnie wanted to visit Prague, to see its river. She couldn't imagine a composer trying to capture the Niagara. Was any major river so short? Thirty miles long, eight of them impossibly violent; the upper river flat and scarred by industry, the lower river framed by gorge and steep banks, its water spectacularly green with the excess of oxygen churned into it by the Falls and rapids.

She wondered if a river flowed through Seattle. Headed there next week, on an open-ended visit, she knew about its beauty, its wealth. Islands, bays, mountains, and a robust economy of the sort that had quit Upstate New York long before she'd been born. Seattle didn't need a river and was probably so well-endowed it had several.

Although April had chided her for not taking enough from the apartment, Linnie was beginning to wonder if she'd taken too much. If necessary, she could store some items at Evelyn's house, but she liked the idea of being able to fit all her things, and herself, into a car. It offered what several of the beautiful passages of music seemed to — immersion, regeneration. Weightlessness.

35

NICK'S JOURNAL

Sept. 10

Sheriff Pataki is a friend of April's. He came by with about a hundred photos of people in programs like Ted's. You'd think I'd have seen most everybody, but I haven't. Linnie didn't see anyone who looked like the man she saw by Artpark. I said when the weather's right and I'm outside late, what do people think if they see me? Someone's been in the state park at night, I told him. But why is he out? I think it's the weather.

Your questions are about Ted. Is he angry? Is he hurting himself? Is he hurting someone else? Who's watching him all day long?

Ted says no a whole lot, even if there's nothing to say it about. Is that angry? It's like rain falling, only this time it keeps falling and falling, and if you can't do a thing about it, you don't have to stand out in it.

Would he be better in a home with people like him? Ted doesn't like people like him, he doesn't like people, except a few, so I can't see him happy because he's with others and somebody else plays with the TV remote.

You talked about order, things being clear for Ted, like a day could be the alphabet, ABC, but Ted's alphabet doesn't start with A, is the way I'd say it, and it doesn't go the same way two days in a row. He wants food or sleep or TV, and anything he wants he wants right now, it won't matter if he just had it.

Ted left the house last night. On the back door we put an alarm. You put it at the top of the door, and if you hold a button and go out, it won't make noise, but it's hard to hold the button right. Mrs. G couldn't reach it, she said the alarm made her deaf, worse than an airplane, so we took the battery out.

My bedroom door stays open and I hear Ted sleeping. But last night he made noise in the kitchen. I went out looking for him, in case it was a danger, but saw him by the road. Somebody else was way down the road by the park, walking the other way, and Ted was near the driveway, so I didn't let him see me. He went to the bunkhouse, like he forgot he wasn't staying there, and didn't get in, so he went back to the big house. I don't know where he'd go, except I don't think he'd tell me if he could. I think he knows people watch him, so maybe he wants a secret, something that's his.

Brendan came out two days in a row. He asks if I know what Linnie's going to do.

36

The clock's ticking," Judge Hood began, showing Brendan and Linnie documents on top of his desk.

Brendan looked at a front page, then told Linnie, "Margot filed a petition in Erie County. I found out yesterday. She's seeking guardianship, jurisdiction in its court."

"Sounds like an end-around double-reverse." Amused, the judge flapped one of the thick bird wings that his eyebrows had formed. "That'll teach us to dawdle. She may try to bounce the trustee – you, Mr. O'Connor - whilst she's at it."

"The brothers have lived in Niagara County for decades."

"I have no ego on this. If they're better served in Buffalo-"

"They're not," Brendan replied.

"Then we ought to start figuring the keener points here. What I've done, so it's on record, is to adjudicate the older brother incompetent." Judge Hood turned to Linnie. "That'll get things going, for whichever court. What I'm having trouble with, is I'm told he's having a rough go of things. An accident, cut up his hand?"

"He fell," Linnie said, trying not to sound defensive. "Something Ted was carrying broke."

"Reports state that he's hard to watch over, goes off everywhere."

"He likes to go out walking. I can't chain him up. If Margot gets control, she'll lock him away."

171

"If I go outside the family to find him a guardian, what d'you think they're gonna do? Give him their master suite? Ted would wind up in a group home quickly. It might be best for him. A lot of folks have great experiences at these homes."

"They're twenty when they go there. Young," Linnie said. "Ted's fifty-two."

"The only thing I can rule on is his welfare. And with his mother having passed, we need to look past temporary arrangements and gather within a month." He looked at Brendan. "Assuming we still have jurisdiction."

Brendan waited till they were in the parking lot to revisit a familiar subject. "Have I talked about your trip?"

"You hope the weather sucks." Linnie was leaving the following evening for a two-week trip to Seattle and Portland and had a plane ticket that would let her delay or suspend her return for a modest fee.

"Torrential rain all across the Pacific Northwest."

"Fog, gloom, see the sun so little I miss Buffalo."

"I'm looking ahead here, but global warming?" Brendan squinted with seer-like concentration. "The Great Lakes are the place to settle."

Linnie noted how he carefully avoided the possibility of a relationship with her: he was affectionate, attentive, and if he said something amusing, his eyes automatically gravitated to her to gauge her reaction. At times his interest was as transparent as a teenager's, but he didn't own up to it, as if Evelyn's death, by having made the demands on each of them permanent rather than temporary, had created an insurmountable barrier.

Another possibility was that he had no interest in a relationship that would become, were she to move, long-distance. Neither did she.

On the ride back to the river Brendan seemed oblivious to everything but the car radio, choked with endless chatter. Finally, he turned it off and pointed at a country café. "You have time for lunch?"

"Sure."

He pulled into a parking lot crowded with pickups and escorted her inside, where the smells from the bakery's take-out counter were overpowering: baked apple, hot yeasty bread, burnt caramel. Brendan bought a box of butter tarts, still warm, each one leaching its own grease spot through the cardboard bottom. "Nick likes these as much as I do," he said.

Once they'd been seated at a booth, Brendan slid the paper casing off two straws and held them like chopsticks, trying to lift a packet of sugar. "Your visit to see Jordan?" he asked. "Are you nervous?"

"Yes. Who knows what he'll think about my divorce?"

"He won't resent it. He's not living in your house, he won't punish you for leaving."

"Kiley?"

"Doesn't understand I can't pack up my life and move to New York. She'd have me do it, not because we'd spend more time together, but for her convenience." He dropped the sugar packet and slid the straws aside. "You can do anything you want."

"You can't?"

"Our joint custody specifies that each parent stay in the state. Kiley's mother would go back to court if I moved, just to screw me out of my share of custody."

"So you're trapped?"

"I don't know. The thing is, I don't feel it, not the way I would if I were in Manhattan."

Brendan was clearly anxious when they reached Evelyn's house. He hopped around like a parrot with clipped wings checking every perch in its cage. In the kitchen Mrs. G. confirmed and reconfirmed her promise to work two weeks' worth of weekdays while Linnie was gone. An agency would supply nurse's aides to help look after Ted – and, no, Mrs. G. didn't know much about the agency, except a niece of hers hired out with them. Nick was in the living room and carefully recited the schedule given him for the weeks ahead.

Next, Brendan found Linnie in the den. Resolved to find a home for Evelyn's collection, they'd sorted the items and files from the bunkhouse and den. Linnie pointed at a composition book on the desk, open to a page of neat notations. "Did you know Evelyn kept detailed catalogues of what she had? Every journal, manacle, picture. But sometimes she refers to things I can't find. Did she ever share her library?"

"No idea."

"There's stuff missing."

He shrugged. "If you could get me a list of what we have..? I'm talking to the historical society to see if they want the collection. As of last week, I'm a lifetime member of the Buffalo Historical Society. So are you."

"You're kidding?"

"Nope. I paid your first installment of dues."

Linnie laughed. "God, do I have to memorize a list of all the Italian and black mayors to get inducted?"

"First off, as members we can propose an exhibit about a prominent woman from Buffalo, mother of a severely disabled child, a reformer, champion of the dispossessed. Keeper of the grim history."

"It's brilliant."

"No. I suspect they're like a lot of small museums: no exhibit space, no storage, no money."

"But we're *members*."

The next day, Linnie turned on all the exterior lights at the house and bunkhouse. She told Nick to leave them on day and night and made him promise not to let Ted out of his sight while she was gone.

That evening, Linnie accepted a ride to the airport from Brendan, who had to pick up Kiley. Her plane arrived hours before Linnie's departed, so Brendan took them both out to dinner between flights.

Kiley wasted little time filtering through her father's restaurant suggestions. The Country Club of Buffalo was nearby: "Everybody who eats there has a walker. And the waitresses need them."

As ever, Linnie was charmed by the girl's energy, if hostage to it. Like Brendan. When they were seated in a restaurant, and he excused himself to find a restroom, Kiley leaned towards her. "I'm really sorry about your Aunt Evelyn."

"Thanks."

"She was so nice, and Dad says super frigging smart. Plus, she was so good to her son, the weird one. Do you ever wonder what she'd do, if she was your age?"

"She'd work, she'd probably wind up running a big company."

"No, I mean if she was pregnant and found out her kid would be really disabled - you know with the tests they have, what would she do? Would she get rid of the baby?"

"I don't know." She knew that, later in life, Evelyn would not have been offended by an abortion, per se, unless it was done in response to abnormality: she would tolerate the procedure for most purposes, but not eugenics.

"Would you?" Kiley wondered. "Get an abortion?"

"I think so, although I'm not sure."

"Why?"

"It's tough." Linnie didn't want to admit how much time she'd spent thinking about it. An only child, she wanted several children - with no Ted among them. However, closing in on thirty, she no longer knew what she'd do if she were four months' pregnant and faced with the choice. "What would you want your mother to do, if she had that choice?"

"She wouldn't keep the baby, no way. I don't think my dad would, but I don't know. He is absolutely the nicest person I know. Period. All my friends love him!" She looked off in the direction her father had gone. "He's so nervous. He's trying to be so cheerful. I think he doesn't want you to leave."

37

NICK'S JOURNAL

Sept. 22

The house is too quiet, nobody could be home except the TV. Mrs. G isn't talking hardly at all. She's here a lot, but it's different. Was it Evelyn kept her talking all the time? And silence Evelyn would play away, two radios on, one in the living room, one in the kitchen.

April brought dinner last night, chicken with cheese and ham in it, and Ted had seconds. She made me promise not to let Ted go out or take him out at night, it's too weird now. She calls him "Teddy Bear" and me "Honey Babe" and makes me laugh, and now she sends the online jokes. Linnie wouldn't leave till I had my own screenname and would use it, so I do, I love the computer. We e-mailed her hello.

Yesterday I was walking Ted up the driveway, and he pulled me to the bunkhouse, he wanted to go in. I got the key and let him watch TV till it was dark, he would spend the night there if I was with him. There's no phone, and not enough heat for a cold night.

Margot came today. She asked me to do a test they use in Canada, she wants to see if it works. It was questions about news and money. She wasn't here long.

38

innie's spirits had lifted at take-off and stayed high throughout both flights. Carol Doherty met her at the Seattle-Tacoma Airport and took her to her one-bedroom loft with a view of Puget Sound.

The next morning, they met Beth and Rick Jauron for breakfast near the public market. Like Carol, Beth was Linnie's close friend from college, and she and her husband owned a construction firm that needed someone to handle the accounting and office management. "God, Linnie," Beth enthused, "if you're serious about moving here, you'd be great for the job."

Linnie suspected that Beth was pregnant. She'd always been thin as a model, but her hips and waist were expanding, her breasts swelling. Linnie asked Carol about it, when the two of them had set off on a tour of the city. "I don't know," Carol said. "I've wondered the same thing. Beth's been really hormonal lately."

Linnie envied the hormones. Nothing new had tugged at her emotions since Jordan had moved in with her and James. Maybe a new city, handsome as Seattle, would provide a rush.

The clouds were low, capping the mountains to the east and west of the city, and water was everywhere, Carol's car constantly crossing or skirting sounds, bays, lakes, inlets, marshes, ponds, canals, streams and river mouths; the terra firma seemed a patchwork of peninsulas and islands. Linnie imagined living on an island and commuting to the city by ferry. She'd learn to fish, or sail, and she'd buy rainslickers and boat-shoes and creams that would keep her hands and face from getting too weathered. She'd inhale ocean salts and forests' resins, and hike in the mountains when she needed thinner air.

Downtown Seattle had more new skyscrapers than all of upstate New York: Albany, Buffalo, and the three-hundred-miles of cities and towns between them. Carol circled through Bellevue, drove past universities, pointed out the billionaires' mansions. "Of course, it's Saturday," she said. "So you won't see the traffic, which is absolutely horrendous."

That evening, Carol took Linnie to a restaurant where other friends were gathering. Linnie quickly understood that one of the men had been brought there on her behalf. He had rugged good looks, and his name was Ken. Carol huddled with him and Linnie at the bar, then seated them beside one another when their table was ready.

Ken had an affinity for regional wines, several bottles of which he ordered for all to try, and he clearly liked telling stories, which were laced with self-deprecating asides. Linnie didn't mind when later, with the bill settled, his hand wound up on her leg.

"I'll give you a call," he said.

The prospect pleased her, a couple of days in a striking new city, and someone interested in her.

Back at Carol's, she checked her e-mails and opened Brendan's, with the subject line of "*News*," reluctantly.

Linnie,

I hate to bug you, but you'd asked about Nick and whether or not the court might consider him, possibly as a guardian, or a co-guardian who could be the one to live with Ted. Margot plowed through town, unannounced, and gave Nick a test to complete. A bunch of the questions are apparently about banking and bill-paying, since the test is used by some jurisdictions in Canada to determine competency of elders and whether or not old coots soiling their trousers need a conservator. Nick's never had to know much about money and bills (which the trust handles anyway). Margot sent me a copy of the test results, which also went to the court and to Judy Urbanksi, who should have been the one to administer any test.

Nick's score wasn't good, and I know you're thinking you could prepare him for such a test, and you absolutely could have, but now there's this fucking test score in the court records that probably kills any chance of appointing Nick to any partial role in the whole business. Worse, it highlights his "need" for stewardship, whereas I think he'd be okay in the summer house by himself. Lonely, yeah, but he wouldn't set the house on fire. And now, who knows? Judy Urbanski is useless. She doesn't want to do any testing that might dispute Margot's, especially as it might "make Nick feel belittled," which is exactly what he's been.

I went to court in Buffalo yesterday to argue that Niagara County's court was the proper venue, and got Margot's petition dismissed, and then this afternoon I get hit by her latest blitz. I won't press the issue of Nick in a guardian or co-guardian's role unless you want me to; that ship has probably sailed. But I don't know if we can keep Ted in the house without someone there the court trusts. Please advise w/ your thoughts.

I bet you're glad you're at a remove from all this, and I know Jordan will be thrilled to see you.

Peace (Bridge),

Brendan

Linnie didn't know how to reply or if she needed to, but the Peace Bridge connected Buffalo to Canada. She wrote back:

Peace, Brendan.

Keep pressing for Nick; he'd be okay for guardian. And if that doesn't fly, someone else could do it with him around, or I could

*do it long-distance. Tell the court I'll stick around a while longer,
if that helps.*
  The Whittler Narrows Causeway,
  L.

Two days later, Ken invited Linnie to dinner.

"This is fast," Carol remarked. "I was here months before I had a real date. Unless you count a vibrator."

Ken took Linnie to a wine bar, then to a restaurant that specialized in fish. They didn't finish dinner till midnight, at which point he briefly tried to steer things to his apartment, but Linnie was nervous about the next day's trip to see Jordan and exhausted.

Ken dropped her off outside Carol's apartment and handed her a business card. "It's got everything on it," he said. "Cellphone, e-mail. I really want to hear from you if you move here."

Linnie was pleased that the evening had gone so well. Ken wasn't as good-looking or funny as Brendan, but his clear interest relieved a little of the anxiety she felt about being newly single. Dating, something that had always been made awkward by the loneliness at the core of her, loomed.

Linnie rented a car the following morning. She'd wanted to do some exploring on the hundred-and-seventy mile drive to Portland, maybe swing out to the ocean or lunch at a vineyard in the Willamette Valley, but her anxiety got the better of her, and she found herself speeding straight down the Interstate. She arrived in Portland hours before Jordan's school was out or anyone expected her, so she checked into her motel early.

She had no trouble finding the Wheelwrights' modest house in the southeast quadrant and didn't venture from her car until she saw Jordan get off a school bus at the corner and hurry down the sidewalk. No sooner was she out of the car door than he raced to her and leapt into a hug that elevated him a foot off the ground.

When he finally let go, he grabbed her arm. "C'mon, c'mon, c'mon! You gotta see the baby, and Annie-Mom's waiting!"

The front door opened before they reached it. Jordan's stepmother, Annie Wheelwright, greeted them with a baby held to her shoulder.

Jordan slung his backpack to the floor and reached for the baby. "Let me show him, let me show him."

Annie made him sit down before she handed him the infant.

"This is my brother, Bradley," Jordan said, one hand perfectly supporting the baby's head as he tilted him towards the guest. "He only cries if he's real, real hungry. Right, Annie-Mom?"

"Must be," she said. "You pay him such good attention, you'd know." And to Linnie: "Jordan is an AMAZING big brother to poor little Bradley. Amazing! Every child in the world ought to have a brother like Jordan." And to Jordan: "Not that you're available for loan, Sweetie, you are way too important here."

Later, Linnie walked Jordan to a nearby park where there were paved hollows for skateboarding, and watched as he attempted, with increasing desperation, a variety of tricks. He managed a few twists and hops, but the board went flying anytime he tried anything complex, and each failure was tackled with the earnestness of an engineer whose rocket refused to launch. He spun a suspect wheel and mumbled, his heart so obviously on his sleeve that it tugged at hers, a boy chasing approval long ago won. He would've kept at it till after dark if she let him.

Back at the house, Steve Wheelwright had returned from his teaching job, and the women found themselves alone in the kitchen, prepping dinner. "Jordan's been so excited," Annie said, "to get you here. He's such a lovely boy. He does have – and I'm sure you know it – fear still in him."

"Yes."

"It makes Steve nervous, my saying that. He doesn't trust enough yet in his own strength to know the boy will find his. And Steve really doesn't have much use for his former in-laws. Even his brother-in-law."

"We're getting divorced."

"I heard. But I recognize you were family and then-something to Jordan. If Steve ever gets started, he'll thank you till you're sick of hearing it, you'll get Twelve long-winded Steps of gratitude."

"It's okay."

"You earned it."

"I don't want it." Linnie didn't hide her irritation. "It would make me feel like I was being dismissed: '*Thank you, that'll be all.*'"

"Well, then..." Annie studied her guest, and her inflection stiffened. "At least you can take comfort knowing Steve and I are devoted to raising him."

Whatever comfort there was in knowing that proved elusive, but she managed a concession. "Yeah."

"Look." A hand waved, as if to banish the mutual discomfort. "He loves you; that's a blessing in his life. So anytime you can visit, or we can arrange for him to visit you, it's all to the good. And it's a comfort to Jordan, knowing he has you. In the wings."

In the wings. The phrase slapped at her life, that of an understudy. A stand-in. That night, Linnie plotted out the rest of her visit with Jordan so that she'd be center stage with him: a horse-ride in the country, Western saddle, as requested; a movie; a trip to an electronics store, sky-not-quite-the-limit.

The weekend flew past, dawn to dusk activity; the ensuing weekdays dragged until school was out. Linnie found herself running out of time, the visit not so long that she could avoid its countdown, and not so short as to be effortless and easily repeatable.

The plan was for her to leave Portland Wednesday night, once Jordan was asleep, although he was crying before bedtime, begging her to stay just one more day and take him to school in the morning. Linnie understood the tears were the product of fatigue and promised to lie on his bed with him until he fell asleep. "Where will you be?" he asked, just when she thought he'd dozed off. "So I can visit."

"Home."

"Where? Auntie Evelyn's?"

"Maybe I'll just take you to Disneyland," she said, not sure herself where home was. "There's a plan."

"There's a plan," he concurred, his voice a faint echo.

Linnie hated the ride back to Seattle, shuttling between two elegant cities, neither of them home. Any fantasy that she'd entertained about Jordan needing her to rescue him had fizzled like stale soda.

The sky was dark, the black belly of storm clouds, and she couldn't see anything but the asphalt tunnel of the road and the cabs and backsides of countless tractor-trailers. She tried to imagine what she'd seen on the drive south — water and woods and mountains — but recalled instead a group she'd seen at the airport when she'd arrived in Seattle.

Five developmentally disabled adults were greeted at the baggage claim area by three people obviously responsible for them. Two men in the group were wheelchair-bound, one of them impossibly slight: discount-store sacks of rice were bigger than he was; toothless, his mouth contorted into off-center ellipses as he flopped with reckless delight at the hugs and greetings bestowed upon him. The other man in a wheelchair, high-functioning though still clearly afflicted with cerebral palsy, was high-fiving everyone and laughing, adept with all the patter: *How' you been?, What a deal, You're a sore sight.*

The handlers - and Linnie couldn't think of a better word for them - were younger than their charges, and they were gracious, loving, expansive. They touched those who'd be touched, and reassured the others, only one of whom was overwhelmed. Middle-aged, bovine, the woman would have backed inside a wall if only there were one behind her. Her panicked eyes were all but swallowed by the bags around them, each the size of a teabag. Aware of her struggle, one of the handlers began the gentlest of barrages: smiles, comments, questions, a brickworks of reassurance with which to bridge the torrent of fear.

Linnie couldn't help comparing these charges with Ted. The high-functioning guy with cerebral palsy would be a breeze to care for, and a pretty good companion. Even the malformed one, the poor rice-sack of flesh, might need to be lifted, dressed, and diapered, but his days were spent in a wheelchair that he couldn't move. He was hostage to his caretaker, not vice versa.

Linnie marveled at the way the handlers smoothed over the late-night airport madness, a crowd elbowing themselves to and from the baggage carousel. Was it that easy to dial up the love? These folks were family to their charges, nothing less. Family, Linnie reckoned, without any of the accompanying conflict, and theirs was an enviable eight-hour shift. She wondered how they'd compare to the people who'd worked in the institution where Ted had lived as an infant. Had those workers mustered the glib familiarity of family? Had Evelyn and Paddy O'Connor's letter badgered them into showering their charges with nothing but love? Or was it something else?

39

Nick's Journal

Sept. 29

Linnie is back, in her bag she brought a magazine of apartments to rent in Seattle. I don't ask her why. She didn't say anything except the judge here was jumpy to do something and we have to see him. He said the month's gone by, the summer is over.

You said he'll ask me, just like you, what would I do if Ted lived in a home? But whose home would it be? How many would be there? Is it a home with more than one van that has to come every day?

He won't want to move, he won't want a roommate, don't let him have a roommate. The only person he could share a room with is me. He will look hard on it if he has to move.

Would it be just me alone at Evelyn's house? You asked who would I want in my home? A woman, a partner, a wife, a friend. Do I know what sex is? Yes I know, but I don't think on it much. Who would I love, would they love me? What I don't want is trouble, what I don't want is wanting something I can't have, I know what that is. What I don't want is to be dumb in these things.

I like things I know, even if I don't want to do them. I have to help close the pool for the winter, and it's sad. The water is so beautiful with the sun on it, especially if you're in it. The light makes diamond webs that slide all over the bottom, but a cover goes over everything in winter, and it seems wrong, water without light. I always think will I be the one to open the pool next summer?

40

Linnie turned off River Road onto Pletcher, but the street was blocked by a garbage truck backing out of the Stella Niagara parking lot. She wouldn't have seen the disheveled fisherman if she hadn't been stuck. He slowly circled around a parked car, the windows of which were cracked open. The large dog left inside it must have started barking, because the startled fisherman stumbled backwards, stopped, and stuck his tongue out at the car window.

Linnie drove into the nearly empty lot and cut the engine. The fisherman flapped his arms at the dog, which hammered its paws against the car window so violently that Linnie worried the glass would break. She stepped out onto the pavement briskly, as if she had business of her own.

Across the parking lot a man yelled something and motioned for the fisherman to join him. He wore a knit cap pulled low on his forehead and ragged khaki pants too short for his lanky frame; he was taller than the person she'd seen with the fisherman by the supermarket, but he seemed calmer. As he approached the fisherman, he gestured for him to calm down.

The dog in the parked car snarled through the gap in the window. The fisherman swiveled and looked at Linnie, then started towards his companion, who also had turned his attention to her. Linnie stared back at the second man. She didn't want to retreat, but she didn't want to follow them if they headed into the woods. She hoped they'd enter one of Stella Niagara's buildings, which lined River Road.

The complex, which housed a convent and school, seemed far too large for its diminished mission. With no boarding students anymore and few nuns in residence, dormitory rooms were shuttered, fifth-story attics lurked, basements long ignored. Linnie thought the place would make a good B-movie set – one too many dark passages, one too many elderly nuns to watch over - with one possible exception. The neighborhood Quasimodos lived at home.

The two men cut across a narrow grass plot and continued east, into the woods at the back of the complex. The fisherman disappeared quickly behind head-high brush, but his companion paused and glanced back at the parking lot. At Linnie. She wondered if he meant to reassure her that things were okay. Then he wove into the woods.

Linnie didn't know where the woods ended, and doubted she'd seen anything worth reporting. Back in her car, she continued to the Robert Moses Parkway and up the escarpment, where she tried a shortcut, curling past Niagara University and cutting into Niagara Falls through the handsome Deveaux residential section. It was the adjacent business area that had been hollowed by a maelstrom so severe that it was impossible to imagine it as the work of economic mischief: block after block of shuttered buildings were standing but empty, as if some airborne catastrophe had chased off those who hadn't succumbed on the spot. Chernobyl. A fire would have been kinder, would have quickly razed what surely would all one day be razed, only at a pace so glacial and intermittent as to preclude any chance of regeneration. Linnie didn't understand how a small city could lose block after block after block. Did one ever get inured to the blight? And could she?

April had been lucky, opening her main store not far from the convention center that, now converted to a casino, was doing fabulous business. However, she was glum when Linnie joined her, and waved a letter from the phone company from which she subcontracted cellular service. "They want the whole goddamn enchilada," she said, echoing a complaint she'd been making recently. The company, one of the remaining giants, was keeping services from her customers and picking them off. "*V-cast, the web, Get-it-now.* They promise we'll have access to anything new, and we lost twenty customers last month who wanted things the phone company's not providing us."

"Anti-trust."

"Anti-human. Six months ago I would've said I can keep this business running, especially if I had someone like you full-time." She sighed. "But I recognize you have to figure out what's next for you."

"You have a Ouija board?"

"I got dice."

Upon her return from the Pacific Northwest, Linnie had told Brendan that she was resolutely irresolute. Her friends in Seattle were lobbying for her to move there; it didn't help that her local employment was part-time.

Several days later, Brendan stopped by to pick her and Nick up on the way to the Lockport courthouse, but Nick balked at going. "Will the lawyer be there?" he asked.

"Maybe," Brendan said. "But the judge wants to know what you think."

"He knows, I told him, I told Miss Urbanski. I wrote it." Nick crossed his arms. "I got work to do. The Majikowskis' leaves."

Brendan waited until he and Linnie were alone in the car. "What was that about?"

"Nick doesn't want to go. He knows he's getting steamrolled. And Ted'll get run over too, if the judge is leaning towards Margot's view of putting him away."

"I think he's leaning towards getting things settled."

"Why can't you hire a guardian? Someone who'd get to live in the house for free if he'd be guardian?"

"Christ, Linnie. The court's not going to go outside the family, not when a sister is seeking the role. She sent in her own petition."

It was the first day of October, and the trees were beginning to turn. Linden, ash, silver maple, locust, black walnut, beech, Norway maple, hickory, rogue cherry-trees grown forty feet high: every shade of green would soon be slivered with every shade of apricot and plum. Forests were taking back land farmers had once cut to their crops. Linnie settled back into her seat and wondered where she'd be once the season was over.

The winters on the Niagara Peninsula were more temperate than many imagined; it was their length that was intemperate. At the house on the river everything was brought closer once the foliage had fallen: the neighbors' houses became visible; across the river, with the dense greenery of the banks sheared, the road and its houses were revealed, and headlights streamed for miles, especially when new snow lay on the ground and the river was still as glass.

Brendan and Linnie found Margot and Bridgewater already inside Judge Hood's office. As the judge rose to greet them, Linnie noticed his pale green socks, exposed beneath wrinkled sharkskin pants. Though she was curious to know who on earth bought his clothes, she decided she liked Judge Hood for wearing them.

"Nice to see you," the judge said, waving at them to be seated before looking at Linnie. "You have a nice trip?"

"Thank you, I did." Linnie recognized that Margot must have mentioned her trip and decided to be anything but apologetic. "It was tremendous. Great fun! Old friends, and it's always so good to get away."

"Yup." The judge winked. "I go fishing. Way up in Canada."

"Where's Nick?" Margot looked to the door.

"He wasn't feeling great," Brendan said.

"He felt okay," Linnie corrected. "He didn't want to be here."

"You were supposed to bring him." Bridgewater turned his palms up. "We could've stopped by."

"Could you?" Linnie clasped her hands in mock excitement. "Maybe you could've brought more tests." She turned to Margot. "Are there any tests you want me to take today?"

"Pardon?"

"Maybe you'd like to surprise me with an aptitude test? See if I'm competent? Here's an idea." She nudged Bridgewater with an elbow. "Let's make it a contest. You and I will take aptitude tests, right this moment, and the loser has to strip and run naked around the court-house. See, the loser is revealed to be both dumb and offensive. You're a lawyer — do you think you could draft a binding contract?"

Judge Hood laughed. "Wait a second. You two?" His first and second fingers pointed at Linnie and Bridgewater. "You sure you're not related? Because I see a lot of brothers and sisters scrap like that."

"Do they give each other IQ tests?" Linnie asked.

"No relation, Your Honor." Bridgewater's smile was a testament to cosmetic dentistry.

"The brother Ted?" Judge Hood opened a folder and spread some papers. "Can we skip the fireworks and talk about him? Two of the day programs report declining standards of behavior, even before his mother passed."

"He's getting old," Brendan volunteered.

"So am I," the judge replied. "And the day may come when I need to be in a facility equipped to look after me."

"Anyone who hopes to keep Ted in a private home is ignoring his prognosis." Margot glanced at Brendan, then nodded at the stack of papers in the judge's folder. "Evelyn didn't tell you or me what she told his doctor. Ted's had several seizures in the last few years. Evelyn was fortunate: he was on his bed, or didn't fall far, and the seizures weren't violent."

"Evelyn, a woman nearly eighty years old, managed to deal with them," Brendan said.

"She was incredibly lucky." Margot rolled her eyes and let them settle on the judge. "You've got the literature. The frequency and severity of his seizures will increase. He'll need trained staff, long-term care."

"That's half the question," the judge said. "If he'll need a group home or institution one day, we have to take into account he won't be a good fit for some of what few we've got. And any place he'd fit might get a vacancy next week or not till three years out. We're critically short of spaces. If a vacancy occurs, it won't suit itself to our timing. Therefore, we ought to wait-list him anywhere he might fit, with a view towards trying it."

"This isn't what his mother wanted," Brendan said.

"I understand that." The judge fiddled with his pen. "Problem is, we're looking for some resolution within a month or two, and I don't know what options we'll have." He looked at Linnie. "You should have him visit a place or two, to familiarize him."

She didn't talk until she and Brendan were almost back to the river. "Teddy won't want to go to a strange place. I don't know what that first institution was like, but he won't want to go."

"I tried to find out about it," Brendan said. "The institution closed the same year Evelyn took Ted out. Some of the indigent patients might've wound up at the big state hospital, if their parents didn't claim them."

"You'd think they were lost suitcases."

"I can't find a trace of the place. But I found a local association for professionals in the field. With a website and online discussion board. I put in a few queries to see if anyone remembered it."

"It isn't right. To start and end your life in an institution. A crappy life with shit for bookends." She expected Brendan to say something, to induce a little guilt, but he refrained. And she thought of Ted that morning, so slow waddling from the riverbank to the house that she'd wanted to send a golf cart to fetch him. "Would you?" she asked.

"What?"

"Would you be a guardian?"

"I couldn't. The possible conflict with the trust–"

"If it were you, if it were your family?"

"I don't know. Maybe I would if I were married and my wife wanted to take it on."

"What kind of answer is that?"

"If I knew what it would do to my life."

"You can't know."

"If I could..."

"It could chase off a lover, scare your kids, make you the jailor and the jailed. You know what it would do." It pleased Linnie that she had painted Brendan, who seemed inclined to guide her into an identical corner, into one of his own. "You wouldn't do it."

41

The court recommended that Ted make a trial visit to a group home, Brendan's legal objections notwithstanding, after a vacancy suddenly developed. A man Ted's age had died at the LoveHope Home of a heart attack attributed to an arrythmia associated with his mitral valve prolapse. Ted also had the condition, but his had long ago been ruled mostly benign.

Linnie hadn't yet found the nerve to schedule the visit, nor to discuss it with Nick or Ted. She'd invited April and Dan Pataki over for dinner, and the evening was warm enough for them to sit on the porch and enjoy the view, while Nick fired up the grill.

To her surprise, Pataki knew of the opening at the home and had his investigators reviewing the death that created it. The coroner, though citing the heart attack as the cause of death, had noted two small cavities in the man's skull that had been "neatly chiseled or drilled." The injuries had been incurred well before the man's arrival at LoveHope.

"Who was the guy?"

"He was Ted's age. He lived with a woman who'd adopted him way back, till she got senile. When the county got wind of it, they put both of them in separate homes a year ago."

"Where'd the woman live?"

"Not far from here. Out off Swan Road."

"The wounds?" Linnie touched her own scalp. "Nobody noticed?"

"No. They never needed stitches. It wasn't a serious attack, whatever caused the holes, because if someone meant business, he'd crack a skull or splinter it."

"You think it's related to the other victims?"

"Must be." Pataki tapped the back of his skull. "Not a lot of nerve endings here. Still, it's odd it never got anyone's attention. It gets to my question: Would anyone sit still for such a thing? Would Ted?"

Linnie imagined what Nick would say. "He wouldn't sit still, unless somehow it was in his mind to do so."

"Maybe that'll spare him."

"Do the victims know the person responsible?"

"That's the question that stumps all of us," Pataki said. "We don't have incidents of abduction or evidence of outright attacks. The FBI sent its task force a while ago, and they can't find 'serial methodology,' the 'psychopathic footprint.' The injuries aren't identical or severe, and we can't get complete histories on some of the victims."

"Did you ever hear of the Storey-Davis Institute?" Linnie asked.

"No."

"Ted was kept there for the first eight years of his life."

Pataki took a sip of his wine and lowered his voice in confidence. "What's with the new place, and him trying it?"

"I've been hoping he could stay here. Maybe we could fix up the upstairs at the bunkhouse, bring in a few other clients, hire staff."

"No," April interrupted. "If you hire someone to be in charge of the disabled, one who isn't your relative, you'll be subject to state overview. Then it's certified staff on duty twenty-four-hours a day, and not only can't you afford it, but you're gonna paper your walls with regulations. You'll have your own halfway house."

"Christ." Linnie watched Nick scrape the grill that the flames now crested. He loved manning the barbecue, even in winter. Maybe she should pack him and his barbecue in her car and take him with her – wherever she ended up living; he'd be an unsalaried caretaker if Margot wound up with the house.

When Linnie brought Ted to the program in the church basement, Reverend Strickley asked how things were going and was surprised to hear Ted might be sent to a group home. "He ought to be in his own house, is how I see it."

"His sister and the court don't see it that way. I think Ted would be okay, if Nick was home with him."

"He would be. I see Nick with the clients, he's got the gift."

"You want to write a letter to the court saying as much? I'll get the address."

"Sure I'll do it." The reverend smiled. "I admired your aunt, though she chewed off my ear more than once."

Linnie laughed. "Evelyn?"

"If I ever drug up a phrase from the Bible or the like, I heard all about it, old Pope Leo Ten livening up a party by torturing mentally retarded, and if I tried to suggest it was *Cat'lick* mischief, I got another earful, Martin Luther wanting them all drowned. I admired Mrs. Phillips, a woman with a mind and God-given purpose."

"Thank you." She paused, trying to guess his age, and supposed he was five years Ted's senior. "Did you ever hear of the Storey-Davis Institute? In Buffalo?"

"Nope."

"It closed, more than forty years ago. Ted was there as a boy. I don't know what happened to the other resident kids."

"That's curious. Come, I'll show you." He continued, as he led her inside. "A farmer, ordained as well, had hundreds of acres of orchard, just in from the lakeshore, plus a big cold storage building, and he had this huge shed that once had sheltered seasonal fruit-pickers. Come W-W-Two, with so many soldiers stationed at Fort Niagara, the Army requisitioned the shed, plumbed it, heated it, and turned it into a barracks. It was empty after the war a good while."

As they entered the reverend's modest office, he pointed at a photo hung on a wall, in which a farmer stood in front of a peach tree with three hired hands, all fifteen to eighteen years old. Each boy was holding a tall, upright ladder on the ground in front of him and looking at the camera between rungs. A goofy smile lit up one boy's face. Another boy's gap-toothed mouth drooped wide open, and his eyes were vacant.

"In the late Fifties, with his 'barracks' empty and some kids aging out of facilities, the farmer took in twenty or so boys, a lot like Ted, but sharper, and he'd hire them out. Piece work so no one overpaid. He thought he'd give retarded kids old enough to work a God-loving home. My grandfather – him in the photo there – tried to crew some of 'em on his farm, but it didn't play. The workers meant well, but too much supervision was needed."

"When was this taken?"

"It was like forty years ago. Probably soon after that institute closed up."

"What happened to these kids?"

"The farmer couldn't make ends meet, twenty young men in make-shift quarters. I suppose neighbors complained, or *govermit*, and it all come to naught. I guess they scattered. Don't know, although probable we still got some of 'em hereabouts."

"I'd love it," Linnie said, "if you'd write that letter to the court."

"I'll do it. For Ted. And for your aunt."

Anxious to present the court with anything that argued against Ted's return to an institution, Brendan forwarded Linnie the e-mail he'd gotten in response to his query about the long-shuttered institute. A psychologist, newly retired from Buffalo's school system, had written:

> *I worked at Storey-Davis part-time when I was in grad school. I wasn't there when it closed, but I wasn't sorry it did, given the rumors. I always thought John Storey, who ran the place, pompous. Didactic, anxious to make a name for himself. I could show you where it was, if you're interested. I'm pretty sure one building is still standing.*

That evening, Linnie heard the front door shut and caught sight of Ted walking his bicycle up the driveway. She grabbed a large flashlight and hurried outside.

She followed Ted at a distance, curious to know where he'd go. Fortunately, he pedaled slowly, the pace never quicker than a brisk walk. He headed south and turned down Pletcher Road, away from the river and past Stella Niagara. An elderly nun was struggling to get out of her car in the parking lot and didn't make much of the lone figure riding clumsily into the night.

A few streetlights cast hazy cones of illumination along Pletcher Road until Ted crossed over the Robert Moses Parkway, at which point the woods and the darkness closed in. Linnie felt the chill when his pace slackened, and he dropped the bicycle on the road's shoulder. He walked further towards Creek Road before stopping under an oak that had carpeted the ground with leaves. Past him were a few driveways, macadam or gravel, which cut into farmland, some of it chopped into tiny suburban plots. Sheds, barns, stables, kilns: outbuildings were scattered, at least one per property.

Ted sat on the ground and waited, though for what would remain a mystery, because he got back on his feet after fifteen minutes and returned the way he had come. Hidden by a garage, Linnie waited until he had reclaimed his bike. He jumped, agitated by her sudden approach, but calmed when he recognized her, and let her walk the bike home.

At breakfast the next morning, she choked out the news about the court-ordered weekend at LoveHope and suggested the boys join her when she stopped by a bit later. Nick, instantly sullen, said that it would only make Ted more anxious to tour a strange facility and it would be best if he, and he alone, took Ted there on Friday.

The LoveHope Home was near the city limits of Niagara Falls. A small Quonset hut, painted with rainbow stripes, was connected by a covered walkway to a ranch house, one end of which had been extended by a prefab doublewide. Linnie found the Quonset hut's recreation center empty, but the daytime manager answered the front door of the house.

A quick tour ensued. The kitchen was clean, but the adjacent family room was carpeted, and it smelled as if no vacuum cleaner, in its many passes, had been powerful enough for all that had soiled there.

Linnie took out a store-bought peanut butter cookie she'd brought and tried to show the manager the trick that helped Ted take his morning medications. "Oh, gracious," the manager responded, "I got a dozen tricks of my own. Nobody gets by me."

"Ted gets so ... particular." Linnie smiled sweetly.

"There's a waiting list," the manager replied. "Your cousin could leapfrog it because he's old and his circumstances are unsettled. Lucky for him."

"What would the timetable be? If Ted were to move here?"

"It can take a month or two for the state to sign off. Plus, our central office is 'understaffed,' which is a nice way to put it. Accounting's about a month off current." She picked up the papers Linnie had brought. "'Phillips?' Is his mother the one with the property on the river?"

"Yes."

"Years back we had a fire. Everyone got out, but it took six months before the damage was fixed. Mrs. Phillips put up four or five clients in that other building."

"The bunkhouse?"

"She didn't charge a cent."

That evening, Nick wouldn't discuss the next day, when Ted was due at the home. By bedtime both of the brothers were missing, and Nick's cellphone was turned off. Linnie was looking for her car keys when she found his terse note: *In the bunk house*. He'd taken his brother and his packed bag up to the bunkhouse for the night, thereby leaving her at the main house, alone. She felt it.

42

Nick's Journal

Oct. 18

I tried to tell Ted about the home he had to go to. He was bothering, but about what I don't know. Some days he can't trouble to know what he knows. A horsefly can make him jumpy and he swats the air, or he can just watch it settle on his shoulder, like maybe this will be the time the horsefly don't bite, and then the bite surprises him. Doesn't he know he's going to get bit? I think mostly he knows, it's his memory that's slow.

It was afternoon, that's when I took him. Cars were in all the parking spaces, I was waiting for a space, when somebody said to pull off by the basketball hoop. A client was there with the ball. He dribbled like his hands were paddles, and he couldn't get it to the hoop. I bounced him the ball a few times until Ted would get out of the car.

I would have delivered him easier with a dolly, it's like I couldn't get him to pull his feet forward. Inside, he sat okay on a couch, except his eyes stayed with me. Janet cooked dinner, but Ted didn't eat what I didn't make him, and he wouldn't let anybody else say hi or any of that.

This is the room they gave him, it's a single, but not really. It's in the old part of the house, a door goes into the room, but there's a wall in the middle of the room which you walk around, and another tiny room is on the other side of the wall which a sneeze would blow down. I was there past bedtime, sitting on a chair, trying to talk Ted into sleeping. The man on the other side of the wall sings a tune all the time, no words to it. The man snores too, so you know he's asleep, but Ted was watching the wall, like the man might come as easy through it as around it. I couldn't make him still.

Janet, who was spending that night, come in and said to let Ted be a little, let him settle in, let him sleep. She told him we'd be right outside in the living room, but she went back to her room while I lay on the couch. This is the sound Ted made all night, woo-woo-woo, soft like a baby bird not yet with a squawk or its real voice.

43

S aturday morning, Brendan showed up early. He knew substantially more than Linnie did about cars and the range of mark-ups,
and they made quick work of her search for a new car. She spent
a little more than she'd hoped to, but on Monday she'd pick up a car,
registered in her name without a lien-holder or co-owner listed, and
it would take her anywhere she wanted to go, "Key West or Prudhoe
Bay or Go-Fucking-Figure," as she put it.

The car cost less than what the divorce lawyer had predicted would
be the legal costs of the divorce and settlement of the marital debt. A
little less than half of Evelyn's bequest would remain, a thought which
made her alternately giddy and terrified.

They got back to the house on the river the same time as Nick
did, who explained that the day manager had discouraged daytime
visitors, in hopes of allowing Ted the chance to adjust to the home. Her
afternoon now free, Linnie agreed to join Brendan for what might be
his last day of sailing that season. They parked opposite the small yacht
club in Youngstown, from where a tender ferried them to his 35-foot
yacht, which fading italic letters, in shamrock green, identified as "*Her
Royal McNavy.*" The J-Boat was sleek, with a low roofline for the cabin.

The wind was hard out of the west, and cold. Once free of the
mooring, Brendan had her steer into the chop rolling in from the lake,
while he unfurled the main sail and rigged a spinnaker. She'd agreed
to accompany him only upon a pair of his assurances: she'd get the

easier job; she wouldn't take an involuntary swim. When they reached the lake, Brendan cut the motor and raised the main, which vaulted the boat forward as soon as he trimmed it. The tack he designated for his helmsman was straight across the lake, hard at the Toronto skyline thirty-five miles away. The spinnaker aloft and suddenly taut, the boat leapt forward again and heeled considerably.

She understood that her job was to keep the sails "tight," but Brendan was up near the bow. "If you go over..?" she called. "Is there a man-overboard drill?"

Brendan laughed. "Drop the sails and have a beer." He gathered the lines he'd need, then retreated to a position near her.

As the yacht heeled hard to leeward, a cool spray shot off the caps of the waves that the bow sliced through. Brendan hooked on a simple shoulder harness and stepped over the railing, hiking out to windward, nothing but the toes of his worn boat shoes on the edge of the deck.

An inadvertent turn of the wheel or luffing of the sails might drop him into a lake grown chilly with autumn, yet he arched out into space, like a circus acrobat waiting for someone else's vault to restore the laws of gravity. His hair whipped about wildly; his hands took or gave what lead the sails needed. Linnie found it appealing, his capacity for adventure; James had lacked it entirely.

Brendan's exhilaration was contagious. If the sun hadn't started to set, Linnie would've had no idea of how long they'd been out sailing. By the time they returned to the mouth of the river, with the motor engaged, she steered while he put away the spinnaker and furled the main. After he'd hooked and tied to his mooring, she got a couple of beers out of the cooler in the cabin, where Brendan soon joined her. The temperature outside dropping, he turned on the range's burners for heat, but left the hatch open. Stars were boring holes through the darkening sky.

Linnie looked into the small forward cabin, where the V-berth mattress was piled to the ceiling with bags of old sails. "Bring a lot of women here?"

"I have to work on that." He took a sip of the beer she handed him. "Murphy, my co-owner, keeps buying old sails we don't need."

"Can't you cure him of that?"

"Maybe at the end of season."

"Isn't this it?"

"Start of next?"

"I do like your boat," she said.

He turned to her, put his hand on her shoulder, and the next moment they were kissing. Linnie hadn't expected it, and imagined that Brendan hadn't either, the immediacy, the passion. Her arms were around him, her legs spreading at the slow tug of a hand up her thigh. Her clothes came off in batches, the bra with the sweater, the underwear with the pants. He kissed her nipples, her neck, the gap between her breasts, then slid his lips down her abdomen, while his hands massaged her calves, the hollows behind her knees, the flesh inside her thighs. She wanted him inside her, wanted his weight on her, and she pulled him down onto the bench seat, but his fingers roamed and lingered, triggering her release before he finally thrust into her. She wondered at the noise they made, the whoosh-clap of flesh, the slap of buttocks on the vinyl mattress, the groans of delight. Partly comic, partly wonderful, and a little pathetic, she thought, the way their hunger trumpeted itself so insistently.

When she finally let go of him, let his cock slip out of her, she pulled him close and laughed. "Do you think anyone heard?" A number of boats were moored nearby.

"The wind's blowing hard," he smiled. "Or they'd have heard us in Canada."

They lay facing each other on the narrow berth. She was stirred by how much she wanted the simple press of flesh against flesh, the warmth of him, but the sudden bleat of an air-horn startled him onto his feet. He threw his shirt on and poked his head up the hatch; a motor was idling nearby. "Let me lock up," he called.

He ducked back into the cabin, naked from the waist down. "The girl who runs the launch," he explained. "She likes to quit early this time of year."

They threw their clothes on and locked the hatch behind them. She called Nick from the car and said they'd pick up an extra order of spaghetti for dinner.

The house was dark when they arrived, the night so clear and the sky so wind-scrubbed that Linnie could imagine her eyesight had suddenly improved, the heavens made closer. Constellations were crowded and well-etched, galaxies brushed with radiant dust. Yet once inside, she felt the absence of Ted in the front hall, a stillness she didn't have to disturb in order to locate him, and turned on enough lights to make the house seem welcoming when Nick returned.

Brendan poured himself a glass of wine in the pantry and toasted her. "I think you're amazing."

"I'm half-employed and half-divorced, and I'm halfway out of here." She grimaced. "Why don't you move? Try Seattle."

It surprised her, the amount of time it took him to reply. "I don't know if their state bar has reciprocity with ours."

"They've got sailing, it's all water. You could teach sailing."

"You'll have a real job, space on your couch?"

She shrugged. In her last conversation with Beth Jauron, who'd been lobbying to employ her, her friend had mentioned a starting salary that was not much more than half of what had first been suggested. Linnie was still attracted to the city, to its vitality and opportunities, but she'd been instantly dissuaded from working for her friends, who didn't behave like them once money was at issue.

Brendan put his glass down and ran his hands along her neck and through her hair, then traced her lips with his. "Spend the night," she said.

Nick was happy to find Brendan in the kitchen and a spaghetti dinner waiting, his favorite. He spoke reluctantly about the LoveHope home, the way it hung onto an odor like an empty garbage pail or smelled like a cloud of cheap air freshener. He didn't have the energy to watch television and went to bed early.

Later, after more lovemaking, Linnie lay under the covers and ran her fingers across the silky blond hair on the bronzed forearm nestled alongside her ribs. She felt sated and happy, and a little sore in those parts of her that had been too long ignored, yet she wondered, as she imagined Brendan did, at their prospects. Evelyn and Paddy hadn't been able to sustain more than a devout friendship, any chance of a tighter knot unraveled by the random tugs of family and the taut lines of guilt. Their families – and it extended to the two of them – had a history of choosing partners unwisely.

And Linnie thought of Ted and what he must be feeling, locked away in the unfamiliar. She felt guilty at the way her day's pleasure had blotted out her concern for him. "It's funny," she said, rising up on an elbow. "Every so often I find myself listening for Ted. It becomes a habit, making sure he's here. He goes out at night, prowls around."

"It's dangerous for him. And God knows Margot will argue that in court."

44

NICK'S JOURNAL

Oct. 22

*Janet said she wanted to keep him at LoveHope, he was so gentle
the whole time. It wasn't gentle Ted was, it was scared.*

*Janet said they might hire me a day a week I was so good with
everyone, but I put Ted in the car and said we had a birthday
party to go to. Just to say something to get going. What is the
hurry? Somebody else will want that space, and Ted doesn't want
it anything at all. He was all balled up in the car, his hands
squeezed till they were red, and his eyes looked like water.*

*We could put a heater upstairs in the bunkhouse, and I
could keep him there. We did it before, program people came
and stayed for months. That would work for Ted, why don't we
do it for him.*

*The first thing he did when he got home was hurry up to
Evelyn's bedroom, only it's pretty much empty. Maybe Linnie
should stay in that room, it's bigger, and Brendan could too
if he sleeps over. He was here Saturday night, which was nice.
He laughed more easier, and he kept looking at her. He did
homemade cinnamon rolls for Sunday breakfast. They are Very
Good, I saved two for Teddy-bear.*

45

I s Brendan with you?"

Margot's voice could be piercing, even after one had braced oneself with a cup of coffee, except it was six a.m., and Linnie hadn't gotten out of bed. "What's up?" she asked drowsily. "I wasn't."

"Sorry. I have an early breakfast meeting and thought I'd see if you'd confirmed a court date with Brendan."

"No."

"I gather you're seeing him."

"Tomorrow morning." Linnie sat up, deciding to tackle Margot head on. "Do you want to meet us? In Buffalo? At the historical society."

"I'll mail my contribution in." Brendan had reached an agreement with the historical society to mount and maintain an exhibit of Evelyn's collection, provided certain initial costs were covered. "Long live Saint Evelyn," Margot added.

"And then we're going to see where the institute used to be," Linnie said, "the one Ted was in."

"It sounds ghastly. No thanks. What I want is to set a date with Judge Hood."

"Go ahead."

"I hear the weekend at the home went well."

"Did you ask Ted?"

"I asked Judy Urbanski. She sends me copies of everything that goes to the court."

"You read them? Christ, Margot. Do you need me to recommend some good books? Reality TV?"

Margot laughed, a real burst from the belly. "Sometimes I forget how funny you are. So tell me, Linnie. How is our loving lawyer?"

"Bridge*wart*? You tell me. That pervert's not a wall I'd climb, I don't care how long it'd been since I'd had sex. You remember what that's like?"

"I was hoping you'd tell me. Brendan — I really do like him."

"Margot?" Clearly, Nick had mentioned the overnight stay.

"I'm curious, I want details, and feel free to make them candid ... unless it's truly sordid. Brendan's so good-looking. Plus, he's so smart and cautious he must be scared to death of any possible conflict of interest."

"Is that what you want to tell me?"

"No. I mean it. I can't see him betraying his duties with the trust, it's not in him. I don't know about the business in court about Ted's guardian. It's probably no conflict for Brendan."

"I'm sure Squire Bridge*wart* could find one."

"I don't think I need to tell him. It's hard enough in this world to find someone. That's what I wanted you to know."

Margot, brandishing a sword, was pretending otherwise. "Why don't you help with Ted?" Linnie asked. "If he's got to be sent to a home, maybe you could find one."

"Evelyn is dead."

"You didn't see LoveHope. Don't you hate that name? 'Love-hope,' like some goddamn herbal-tea optimist smoked a little crack and flipped out with glee."

"You'll never replace Mrs. G.," Margot said. "Half the people in Niagara County are retired, and anybody young and unemployed is on food stamps and assistance, and they'd no more be a domestic than a prostitute. We have immigrants in Toronto. There'd be a good chance of hiring someone who gave a damn and would stay more than a few months."

"Is that an offer? Move everybody up to Toronto?"

"It's going to get much worse with Ted. Seizures, possible dementia, the horror of whatever's going on in Lewiston. You can pretend otherwise, you can throw yourself in front of the speeding truck, but there it is."

Off the phone, Linnie wished Brendan were with her; she couldn't imagine anyone else who, there and then, could make her laugh. She wished she could drape half her body over his, and if the embrace encouraged them to early morning sex, she wouldn't turn him loose until she'd escaped the reach of Margot or anyone else's unwelcome claim to her attachment.

April, when told of the pre-dawn phonecall, laughed. "You two sound like sisters, I swear."

"You sound like Judge Hood."

"I have two half-sisters, full-blood to each other, and every year each one insists the whole family's gotta gather for Thanksgiving in her house, no matter the weather or drive. One lives here in Tonawanda, one all the way to Jamestown. They keep no track of turns, always argue the other's kitchen is too screwy for cooking. Every year, right about now, I stop taking calls. I just say I'll bring whatever, wherever, tell me in an e-mail."

"This is different."

"Not so much. Margot's got family. And with no children of her own and no one else in charge, who else is she gonna scrap with if not you?"

"I don't see it."

"Honey, it's the mess of *family*. You can pack your bags and sing adios, you have that freedom."

"Is this a lecture?"

"Make it an invitation. I'll call a bit later. We'll grab lunch, and you can catch me up."

The call was from Dan Pataki, not his girlfriend. "Linnie," he said, "there's someone I'd like you to look at, if you're up to it. He's about fifty, with a brush haircut: like your description of the guy from the gorge."

"You found the fisherman?"

"I don't know. All I know is we have a new victim."

Pataki made certain someone could look after Ted before dispatching a squad car to pick Linnie up. She sat in the front seat beside the deputy, who cut down Pletcher Road and turned south on the parkway. She could see the activity as they got close. Their flashers on, police cars had followed a narrow jogging trail through the woods and parked in low brush about a half-mile outside Lewiston. The asphalt path looped through town, ran north along the river, east on Pletcher, and back to Lewiston through the forest lining the Robert Moses Parkway.

The deputy escorted Linnie through the police roadblock and into the woods, then left her by a bend in the path where two men in "CORONER" windbreakers huddled by their van. The deputy disappeared into a grove of trees, then reappeared with Dan Pataki, who signaled Linnie aside.

"This time the wound's ugly, not neat," Pataki told her. "The other victims were likely deceased before their skulls were fully penetrated. Now we've got ancillary injuries and bruising, and the body was dragged into the woods. This time," his voice took on an edge, "it seems more of an attack. The killer may have known the victim, I think he must've known the victim, but this time the victim apparently didn't submit or lose consciousness."

"When did it happen?" She'd turned on the alarms the previous night to prevent Ted from wandering.

"Late last night or early this morning. A guy walking his dog found it. And then the brother reported the victim missing."

Pataki guided her, circling into the woods in order not to disturb evidence. Linnie saw a camera flash before she saw the site and the forensics scouring it. Draped with a coroner's tarp, a body was sprawled on the ground beside a fallen trunk. Pataki asked a coroner's assistant, "Can we see the face?"

The man bent to the body and pulled away the black sheet, exposing the left side of the face, which looked relatively unscathed. The thickened pool of blood beneath his head had tinged the bristles of his hair; the familiar red sweatshirt was visible at the neckline.

"That's him." Linnie turned away. She was scared if she kept looking at the "fisherman" she'd picture Ted's dead face in place of his.

"His name is Richard Kieffer," Pataki said, leading Linnie out the way they'd come in. "He's lived with his younger brother since his parents passed. I gather he liked being on his own, not in a structured program."

They reached the clearing where squad cars had flattened the brush beside the asphalt. Linnie recognized the man seated in the back seat of one of them: he was the person she'd seen in the supermarket parking lot with the fisherman.

"That's the victim's brother," Pataki said. "Maybe we've been a bit tough on him. But I don't get it. He let his brother do what he wanted, go anywhere anytime."

"I saw the victim again. At Stella Niagara."

"He's a custodian there." Pataki nodded at the brother. "Most of the people who work there know the victim."

"There was this other guy — tall, thin, a cap pulled way down. It's hard to imagine him working at Stella."

"I'll ask."

"How old is the victim?"

"Fifty-two."

"I wonder if he was at the institute with Ted. His brother would know. Brendan located someone who used to work at the institute. We're meeting him tomorrow."

"If you could get a list of former patients, maybe we'd find a name that isn't on our lists, someone to look into. Otherwise," Pataki shrugged, "what we have is a small area. Everything's happened within a three-mile radius of Stella Niagara. Or your aunt's house. You keep a close eye on Ted and your doors locked."

46

L innie was surprised at how imposing a landmark the Buffalo
Psychiatry Center was. The complex had been through numerous
name changes since it had been commissioned in 1870 – the State
Lunatic Asylum, Buffalo State Hospital — until its virtual abandon-
ment a century later. Twin towers, topped with sharply peaked copper
caps, rose above the administration building, a Romanesque classic
designed by H. H. Richardson. It and other once handsome buildings
were heavily caged by afterthoughts of screens and bars, and later
gouged by massive piles of collapsed bricks and boarded with sheets
of rotting plywood while they awaited a wrecker's ball or a rich angel's
restoration. Olmsted, the great landscape architect, had designed the
hospital's grounds, including the attached farm behind it that buffered
the patients from the city and provided them jobs and food.

What remained of the asylum was surrounded by rusting wire-link
fence, the bottom of which disappeared into mounds of rotting leaves.
The retired psychologist who'd responded to the e-mails led Brendan
and Linnie down Forrest Avenue while dodging puddles that rain
had left in the buckled sidewalk, then turned to a padlocked gate and
produced a key. "A friend's on a city panel," he said, "hoping to make
something of these ruins."

The gate unlocked, he led them into the grounds, where they were
careful to keep to the paths. Huge roof tiles and other debris had
fallen close to most of the walls. At the west end of the complex, the

psychologist pointed out a building's ground level windows. "They used to leave the blinds open," he explained, "for the light."

The blinds were long gone, but enough daylight spilled into the basement room to reveal the old-fashioned square refrigerator doors lining a wall. Had a six-foot long metal tray not extruded from an open door, Linnie might have thought the room a kitchen, rather than a morgue.

"There used to be a smaller gate just up Forrest." Their guide pointed across the street. "Storey-Davis was right over there. Patients from the Institute could use the field and clinics. One day I brought eight kids over to the dental clinic, and some staffer watched the other kids while I stayed with the one in the dentist's chair. When everybody was done, I found the group gathered right here, the damn staffer was taking a nap. The kids were maybe six to ten-years-old and watching an autopsy, full-blown, right through these windows."

The psychologist looked through the fence at a parking lot. "Odd. I guess I was wrong." He pointed at the empty lot. "I thought a small building was left. The big ones came down decades ago."

"Who were the patients?" Brendan asked. "When you were at the institute?"

"Mostly young, some only months old. That was Storey's theory. Get a kid early, mold him closer to normal with heavy intervention."

"Is there any way to get a list of who was there?" Linnie asked.

"No chance, I'd think. It was private. And psychologists and psychiatrists don't keep many records. Too many lawsuits."

"What did you mean," Linnie asked, "'heavy intervention?'"

"Rigorous training. And corporal punishment was allowed if it made the child more compliant. But it rarely did. Storey had someone else run the place so he'd be free for his research."

"On what?"

"He called his theory 'Managed Stimulation.' He had the idea you could slow down and manage unwanted stimuli, that a retarded child would learn best if his brain waves had flattened out. The shame is, you could test that theory easily now, except no one's inclined. The theory pretty much went the way of his career ... which went the way of the institute."

"My cousin was a resident there. He left, I think in 1963."

"I'd left by then, but it was close to the end."

"Why did it close? What happened?"

"I don't know. But I called a colleague after I'd agreed to meet you. He said there was a rumor at the time that a kid died and an investigation was underway."

"Who investigated? Doctors from the hospital?"

"If anyone did, it would have been the police."

By the end of the afternoon an investigator who worked for Brendan's law firm had the answer. In December, 1963, criminal charges had been prepared but not filed, and an off-the-record settlement had been reached with both Storey and the institute's assistant director. A boy Ted's age, eight years old, had died after being administered an insulin coma, and another child had broken bones in his excessively restrained limbs during a grand mal seizure suffered in a similar coma. At the time Insulin Coma Therapy was a recognized, if dangerous, treatment for schizophrenia and other maladies, and its aftereffects included a prolonged sense of calm and increased cooperation, but the procedure's one-per-cent mortality rate required a level of medical supervision not in place at the institute. Storey had begun by injecting moderate levels of insulin to create stupor in his young subjects, then glucose to reverse the effect. Encouraged but dissatisfied, he and his staff physician increased the dose of insulin and induced outright comas in the less cooperative patients. Parents had only been told that the children's sugar levels were being moderated. Inspite of the letter written by Brendan's father, or because of it, Storey had procured consents from most parents for "sugar level modulation."

"And Ted?" Linnie asked. "Did they do that to him?"

"He was named in the initial complaint," Brendan said. "Apparently, Ted was heavily bruised from the treatments."

Eight years after she had dropped him off, Evelyn picked her boy up. Eight years in which Margot had no idea that her brother existed. Eight years in which Evelyn, a charming hostess at her houses in

Buffalo and north on the river, had twice been The Buffalo Philharmonic's Woman of the Year. Eight years, and on three afternoons
among them, Ted's little body sweated out quarts of fluid, shook as
violently as any fish landing in a boat, and collapsed into the peace of
a nearly lethal coma.

47

I feel dirty knowing it," Linnie said. "The whole business is so awful."
She and Brendan were in a coffee shop on Elmwood late that
afternoon. The rain, which had let up that morning, had returned
in force, sheets of it drumming the canopy over the front window,
rivulets cascading from a tear in its canvas. The weather had turned,
the prospect of winter arriving in a four-day rainstorm.

"I feel bad for Ted," Brendan said. "Terrible. But at least he had
Evelyn to take him home. Think of the other kids."

"I can't." Linnie crumpled up her napkin and tossed it into her
empty coffee cup. "So what do you tell Judge Hood?"

"I'll write a letter about how traumatic the institution must have
been for Ted, how that experience argues against a group home."

"Will he buy it?"

"I don't know." He looked doubtful. "What I've come to realize
is we're looking through the wrong end of the telescope. Most of
the Surrogate Court's tough decisions involve the opposite: removing
someone from his home, often against his will, because it's the humane
thing to do. And the judge wants resolution by the holidays."

"Is there any chance of reinstating Nick into the middle of the
guardian business? I still think he'd be okay, looking after Ted."

"Nick may be competent enough, I honest-to-God don't know. But
the judge has another problem. Corpses of disabled adults keep turning

up. The judge is going to be reluctant to make any decision that might let Ted be the next victim."

Linnie declined his invitation to stay in town a while longer. Mrs. G. was paying a visit to the house that evening, and the rain hit with torrential bursts that slowed traffic to half-speed. Linnie was thankful she had a new car, new tires, all-wheel drive; the new windshield wipers could barely keep pace with the giant wakes of water hurled up by tractor-trailers.

Mrs. G. was upstairs, looking through Nick's closet, when Linnie found her and swept her up in a hug. "Aren't you a sight," Mrs. G. said, brushing rain-slick hair from Linnie's face. "I don't like no girl a' mine drivin' in this weather."

"You did."

Mrs. G. resumed her household inspection, looking in a bureau drawer in the bedroom and hoisting a pajama-top. "She don't know how to fold a shirt." A local service had supplied a housekeeper, who was coming two days a week. "The bathrooms, an' the floors, now they look okay."

"You come any time and tell her what to do."

Mrs. G. refolded the pajama-top, with two creases parallel to the buttons, and returned it to the drawer. "I'm half-scared to ask – how's our Ted?"

"You heard about LoveHope, the group home they made him stay at?"

"I suppose I figured it'd come to this." Worry-lines overlapped the furrow in her brow. "Prayed it wouldn't fall upon Miss Evelyn to see to it. But she had her way with him like no one, not even Nick. It's him I trouble about."

"Nick?"

"He won't leave, you know. You joke about packin' him up with you, but he won't leave his brother here. An' if Nick's in the house alone, see, a woman in need may scheme herself in. Maybe a hard woman, 'cause she's broke, an' he won't know to be hard on her."

"Margot. She'll chase them out."

"She'd chase a good one out. But a bad one'd be a match for Margot."

"I don't know."

"Nick'll listen to you."

"I'd tear the hair out of anyone who'd hurt him."

"That's what I want to hear. It's your eye on it that matters."

Ted was buzzing audibly with the excitement of Mrs. G. staying to dinner. He shuffled around the kitchen, made little cackles in the back of his throat, and finished a large meal with two slices of the cake she'd baked. Her leaving fell hard upon him, notwithstanding the rub she gave his neck, the kiss she forced on his forehead. Nick turned on a TV cartoon, Linnie made chocolate milk, and yet the house had gone empty.

Rain clattered on the roof, sloshed out of gutters, and slapped off what leaves remained on the trees. Nick fetched a pair of ponchos, an umbrella, a flashlight, and made an excursion of it, hustling Ted out into the car, driving up to the bunkhouse, dashing for one of its doors.

Linnie cleaned the dinner dishes and turned on the television. A newscast featured footage of a mid-day news conference: Niagara County Sheriff Anthony Pellini, dressed like a cavalry general, was speaking to a crowd of reporters and cameramen. When it was clear he had no new information to offer about the attacks, Linnie muted the sound, but took another look at his outfit. Sheriff Pellini had four gold stars on the shoulders of his heavily starched shirt, and his pants were tapered like riding pants and disappeared into his boots. His chest was puffed out, and he'd rotated the hip with the firearm on it towards the camera. Fidgeting on one side of him were two men in suits, likely FBI agents, and on the other side were Dan Pataki and two deputies.

Linnie's eyes gravitated to Pataki, who stood perfectly still. His pale green uniform was wrinkled, his top buttons were undone, yet he exuded respect. Linnie was struck by the improbability of her having the ear and the friendship of the county's chief criminal investigator. She wanted him to marry April. Both of them possessed an unshake-able decency that would survive economic or personal catastrophe; they, and others like them, were the best argument for living in Western New York. But the TV camera zoomed in on Sheriff Pellini, and Linnie turned the TV off.

Outside, the wind shifted, gusted. Rain, slung against the windows like fine gravel, rattled panes already opaque with water, and branches scratched back and forth over the shingles. The ground-dwelling animals had surely taken their shelter: leaving what, leaving whom?

48

NICK'S JOURNAL

Oct. 30

We made a game, get to the car and up to the bunkhouse, try not to be soaked. Ted got sulky when Mrs. G left. I took the key and got the upstairs door open and Ted worked the bunkhouse TV. There aren't many channels, no cable, and the picture can slide up the screen or be real fuzzy in a storm, and it won't sound like fun, but Ted will watch real close, and he laughs at screwy things. Like I got blankets because it was cold and wrapped myself into a caterpillar on the floor and he would try to find my face and hoot when he did.

The radiators haven't been on since we had program clients stay there, but Evelyn used to have a small plug-in heater for her office, so I went downstairs. Her office still has furniture, but it looks empty. There's things nobody wants, but Evelyn's books and stuff is gone. Linnie packed them all up and a truck took it. Now the downstairs rooms look neat except for mouse droppings. I didn't find the plug-in heater.

Ted was tired after a couple shows, so I took him out and put him in the car. The lights were out, but the motion light went on up front of the bunkhouse, and I thought I saw someone by the lilacs on the way to the road. It was raining, and the bushes are thick with branches, but the leaves are fallen, and it looked like a shape right behind the lilacs, the size of the man I saw at night in the park. I waited to see if it was a man and what he would do, or would he come up and tell me what he wants. He backed away towards the road quick, and Ted left his car door open and was getting wet, so we went to the big house.

49

innie was reconciling accounts at April's Niagara Falls office when the lunchtime call came. "Evelyn?" Judy Urbankski, probably with a file in front of her, quickly corrected herself. "I mean 'Linnie.'"

"Yes?"

"Nick's last entry in his journal: As soon as I read it, I called the police, but the house isn't in the village, so they put me into the sheriff's office."

"Why?"

"Nick said he thought he saw someone on your property. He didn't tell you?"

"No. He would have if he were concerned."

"He should have, with what's going on. Where is he? I assume he's with his brother."

"No. Nick's on a neighbor's tractor. People are rushing to get leaves up before the snow comes."

"He's not with Ted?"

"No."

"That..," she took a long time settling on a word, "is unfortunate. I couldn't get you on your cell. The sheriff's department sent a deputy. In case someone is lurking. I'm sure they'll have it under control."

Less certain, Linnie drove back to the river, where one squad car was parked by the bunkhouse. She continued to the house, where a deputy was waiting near his squad car.

"You live here?" he asked, as she got out of her car.

"Yes. Where's Marcie? The cleaning lady?" Linnie had left Ted with her for a few hours when she went to work.

"She's the one who got the key?" The deputy nodded towards the bunkhouse. "She went up with the other car to let us in. She's been there a while."

"Where's Ted?"

"Is that his name? The retarded fellow? Lord, he's a handful." He cast his eyes at the squad car. "He was all calm, and then he got wacky. I was helping him sit in the backseat — he wanted to sit there -– and then he bit me."

Linnie saw Ted as he reached the squad car. He was lying on the back seat, rocking frantically. "Open it."

"Lady, he sat in there on his own." The deputy opened a front door and hit a latch; the back door opened. "I just closed the door to keep him put. After he bit me."

Before Linnie could join him, Ted lurched forward and smacked his head against the screening that separated the back from the front. He'd wet his pants. Wild-eyed, he wailed, pure terror keening high and holy. She dove into the car, wrapped him in a hug, and whispered, "Honey, it's okay, okay, it's okay."

Ted tried to push Linnie away, then moaned while she held him in her arms and whispered endearments. A minute passed — it might have been five — before they climbed out of the car. "Into the house, Honey. We'll go to the house." Linnie started him off towards the front door, then turned to the deputy. "What were you thinking?"

"The damn guy bit me." The deputy waved his wrist to show a shallow scratch. "I could run him in or file charges. Goddamn, I may go to a doctor. Who knows what germs he's carrying?"

"You didn't need to lock him up like a dog." Linnie was trying to hold onto her tears.

"Lady, he bit like one."

"How dare you?" She was screaming; she'd never been half as mad in her life. "This is his home! How dare you treat him like that? Don't you ever, ever, treat my family like that."

"Hey, I'm glad he's not mine." With that, the deputy headed towards the bunkhouse.

Dan Pataki arrived an hour later and joined Linnie at the house. "How's Ted?" was the first thing out of his mouth.

"Sleeping. He went right in, dropped on a couch, put himself right to sleep."

"Can't blame him. I'm sorry. I spoke to the officer. I think we want to make this go away quietly. There's the matter of biting."

"Ted didn't know what was happening."

"I know it, I'm on your side. But if we make the deputy feel threatened, he may put the biting episode in a report, and even though we're not going to press forward with anything, it'll find its way to your court."

"That's not fair."

"Maybe not." He spoke more sternly. "Look, you might not like that group home Ted went to, but that's as homey as any of them get. I've been touring all the halfway houses and institutions because of this case, and there are a couple you don't want to see. They're for the unruly, the one-on-one clients with disposition to violence: they have the charm and razor-wire of a criminal facility."

Linnie looked toward the bunkhouse, where a pair of cars were parked. "Do you think someone is lurking around here?"

"I don't know." Pataki drew a slow breath through his teeth. "Every night I run two cars through all the parks and public spaces. I'll make sure they start giving this place some slow drive-bys."

50

NICK'S JOURNAL

Nov. 8

The clock changed hours, but it was still cold first thing this morning, a day when little clouds are upside down and rise off the river. I wonder who will look at it to see what Evelyn did and where will I be. If Ted's not here.

I put bolts high on the doors where Ted won't reach them and an extra smoke detector on the ceiling so he won't be able to go out at night unless a fire alarm wakes up everybody. Linnie helped buy them.

You asked if I ever saw Meadowland which is a home for disables and run by the same people as do LoveHope. They had a Christmas party one time I picked Ted up there, and they don't have a rug in the whole place. It's all floors like a hospital. Thick rugs are on the walls of one room, which is to send somebody for a timeout. It isn't like any house I know and clients are not nice.

I think you are a liar or Janet is. She said Ted would be good at LoveHope, and you say maybe at the other house run by those people, and it's something Janet thinks too. You want me to help move Ted, how many times. Yes it's easier if I do it, but will he think I'm the one who did it to him?

I don't like the questions and writing this any more. You don't listen to me, I know Ted better than you. I could keep him okay, and you say well maybe and maybe not.

This is my end to this writing, your one last question, and I won't talk to you again unless Linnie says I have to.

Would Ted know anybody in the park, like maybe the man I saw? The park gets wide across River Road and runs all the way across to Pletcher, and it also runs the other way, with a tunnel under River Road to the part on the river. I remember Evelyn used to walk Ted to the park so he could ride his bike on the paths. I'd be working those summers on Mr. Grayson's farm, it's out of business now, but I know Ted met a few people like himself. They might all ride bikes in the park, or play. Evelyn would leave them alone in the park, or let Ted walk himself to the park, that's what she told me. She thought they'd be more grown-up if only a grown-up wasn't always yelling this and that at them. She'd go off an hour on errands, she was proud they could do it without her.

Except they couldn't. One day two ladies came by the house and said a group of four retarded men had no business in a public park, not even when an adult was with them, and without an adult it was like running baboons wild. They said their children were scared, and one man did his peeing where they could see, and they called the police, and they would call the police again if they saw it again. They said if their husbands found out about the peeing, they'd bring a baseball bat and beat hell out of the retards. So that was it for days in the park, Evelyn didn't let Ted go by himself. I don't know what happened to the friends he had there.

51

E die Patterson brought a stack of microwaveable TV dinners to the house on the river, as well as some laundry, since her washing machine had "fried" a day earlier. Linnie was in Buffalo by late afternoon, letting herself into Brendan's home on Middlesex Road with a hidden key. The downstairs rooms were elegantly, if simply furnished, though the house somehow looked uninhabited to her, like a model home undisturbed by stray books and unfinished newspapers. The refrigerator was a joke stale as its contents: a pint of thickening half-and-half, four apples in an early stage of fermentation.

Brendan arrived shortly, with a bottle of cold wine and a package of gourmet cheese crisps. The plan was to linger over a glass of wine and head out to dinner, but they wound up in bed so quickly that it undermined Linnie's determination to keep control of things, as did an orgasm that left her gasping. What she didn't want was an unappeasable hunger: a yearning for someone too rooted to a spot from which her own roots had been pulled up. Yet she found herself wanting exactly what would be hardest to forego: the intimacy, his proximity.

Two hours later they were still in his bed. Her elbow on the mattress, she rested her chin in her palm as she turned towards him. "I've been trying to think how this doesn't end badly."

"And?"

"I don't know. In a week or two Judge Hood is going to turn things over to Margot, and she should have control. She feels so cheated. Margot and her hundred-page petition to the court. What I'm not going to do is hang around like a sponge of a relative. No home, no job."

"April?"

"I do her books. Things are shaky. I'm not going to mooch off anyone, and I'm too old to keep drifting sideways. You know the law firm I worked for? They offered me a job managing its D.C. office."

"Will you take it?"

"Maybe. I would if the job were in Seattle."

"And Nick? What of him?"

"It's him I worry most about. Even more than Ted. Or you and whatever you want."

He rolled flat onto his back and put both hands under his head. "What I don't want is to get run over on your way out of town."

"I could try to take you with me. But you wouldn't go."

The next evening after dinner, Ted started rattling the kitchen door, which was held firm by the new latch. Linnie heard the commotion and grabbed her cellphone, a Swiss Army pocket-knife, and a heavy flashlight. Thus armed, she made her way to the kitchen and opened the door.

Ted ambled out into the chill and paused on the steps, as if something had been forgotten. Linnie supplied it, a blue wool pea-coat hung in a nearby closet, and helped him get his arms into the sleeves. He stumbled down the steps and started up the drive.

She let him get halfway up the driveway before following in her car. Not long after Ted headed south on River Road, she pulled up alongside him and had him get in the car. They continued to Pletcher Road and turned away from the river, passing the small senior center, empty at this hour. One of Stella Niagara's buildings was a checkerboard of lights; the others were dark.

Linnie drove into the convent's back parking lot on the chance of getting a reaction from Ted, but he sat quietly in his seat until she restarted the engine and pulled back onto the road. Only then did he take notice of his whereabouts. She continued towards the overpass over the parkway, but stopped short, parking on the road that provided a back entrance into the state park. Once the door had been opened for him, Ted settled one foot on the ground, then the other, and started to walk further down Pletcher Road, the same route on which she'd followed him before.

Past the parkway overpass the road was an odd mix, the suburban's piecemeal encroachment upon the rural. Homes were close enough to the road to provide a fine view of the television playing in the front room or tucked a distance away. Linnie followed fifty yards behind Ted, but he never looked over his shoulder. She worried that she wouldn't recognize the last place he had paused on this road: it had been under an oak, but the remaining leaves would have fallen and the acorns would have been claimed by squirrels. She didn't trust herself to know an oak, bare, from any other hardwood.

She was wrong. He stopped under the same tree as he had before, past a macadam drive with a rusting newspaper delivery box, and he waddled in little half-moons in front of the trunk. Past the tree, a dirt drive shot straight back towards a few small buildings, the dim light from one spilling faint pockets of illumination towards the others. A door to the lit building opened briefly and closed, although nothing passed through the doorway, not even a dog.

Ted had begun to watch that house, his sideways shuffle inching him towards the head of the dirt drive, and paid no attention to two cars, one closely trailing the other, that turned off Creek Road. Linnie hurried towards him. She didn't know what the approaching drivers would make of Ted, loitering on the side of the road, and figured her purposeful stride his way might lay claim to him, if a curious driver needed that comfort.

The cars shot past, each driver crossing the yellow line to give both pedestrians the extra margin of safety. The arc of the trailing vehicle's headlights traced the arc of the one in front, until the two cars had rounded the corner and a single glowing cloud shrunk towards the river. Ted had reached the driveway and started down it when she caught up to him.

"Ted?"

He turned at the sound of her voice and mumbled in protest. "Ted, is it time to go home?"

52

On the way to her car she considered whether Ted knew the residents of the house on Pletcher. Years ago, Linnie knew, Evelyn had sent him to help pick fruit and vegetables at homes where a few crops produced a side-source of income, but Mrs. G. had said that not a lot of people struggled anymore for those extra dollars, not when the supermarkets were full of cheap produce from California and Mexico.

Linnie planned to head back to the place and introduce herself, once Ted was settled at home, but realized it wasn't a conversation to spring on a stranger at ten o'clock in the evening. The following morning, she put on a suit and heels, in hopes of making a better impression, and drove to Pletcher Road. She found the dirt drive easily enough and saw a powerline strung all the way back to the simple, single-story house that had been lit up the previous night.

Her front right wheel quickly bottomed-out in a rut of the drive, and there were worse ruts ahead. Rain and run-off had followed the slope of the property and cut knee-deep channels across the drive. Linnie parked in place and set off for the house, her heels burying themselves in mud.

She hadn't brought the arsenal she'd had the night before, but she had her cellphone and daylight. As she got closer to the dingy gray house, she noticed cheerful arrays of plastic flowers sprouting from coffee cans nailed to the posts of the front porch. Beyond the house the drive curled around a shed, then surrendered itself to waist-high weeds near a wooden shack, most likely a former chicken coop, and a barn fifty yards beyond. The eastern half of the barn had toppled, and the underlying sections of walls had been cut away to let that half of the roof hang all the way to the ground, thereby fashioning a rough eastern wall for what remained of it.

Linnie stepped up onto the house porch and called out a few hellos, hoping not to startle any elderly resident, then knocked on the door. She'd rehearsed her greeting in order not to garble it: *Sorry to bother you, I live over on the river, and I have a cousin...* No one answered, but she heard a gentle clanging at the back of the house.

Linnie stepped off the side of the porch and continued along the wall to a kitchen window. An elderly woman, two layers of sweaters over her flannel pajamas, was working at a low, free-standing sink. Her thin white hair had gone severely bald; her hollow cheeks needed more teeth to fill them out. She was using a brush to clean a pot, which kept clattering into an adjacent one. Finally, she hoisted the pot to her face, which she all but put inside it. Satisfied, she returned the pot to the sink.

"Hello?"

It wasn't clear the woman heard Linnie, but she took a step towards the window. She looked directly at the visitor but didn't see her: the colored parts of the old woman's eyes were totally clouded over by cataracts. She twisted her head, trying for a bit of peripheral vision, then gave up. "Ed-dee?" she called. "T'at you, boy? Git in." She waited a moment and tried again. "Ed, boy?" She turned back to the sink and dropped her hands to locate the edge of it.

Linnie backed away. Beyond the house, the chicken coop's roof had a hole at the bottom of a section that had buckled, and the door was cockeyed in its frame, but the half-barn appeared half-substantial. A stable door was swung open to a stall, where a bulb hung on a long cord.

On the way to the barn she further regretted her outfit, heels and a skirt. The weeds sprouted low shoots and runners that tangled with one another, creating a cross-hatch of thistles, and she had to follow a narrow path trampled through the stinging, sticky plants.

The barn's stable door swayed as a gust blew past. Linnie kicked her shoe into it twice to announce herself; she didn't want startled birds or angry dogs rushing her. Inside, two adjacent stalls had been converted into a single workshop. A workbench ran the length of one wall, with tools hung above it. A few power tools were set up, but most seemed to be a carpenter's hand tools, delicate saws and intricate chisels.

She passed through the stable into an empty tack room, where a large door hung on overhead rollers and closed off access to the barn's central room. Linnie pushed that door far enough along its bent track to slip into the main room. The morning sun was blocked by the roof that now fashioned the eastern wall, but a high window let light sift to the dirt floor, which was centered by a flat wooden wagon covered with books.

As her eyes adjusted, she turned to the wall that she'd passed through. Diagrams and pictures hung everywhere. The first poster she noticed had photos of an "Adult Cretin," so labeled, his naked body superimposed with arrows pointing at anatomical abnormalities. A second picture had to be a reproduction of a print from an earlier century. A man was strapped in an armchair; a profusion of miniature demons escaped into the air around him through a small hole in his head. Linnie recognized the adjacent illustration, done in the style of Heironymus Bosch; she'd seen it in Evelyn's collection, from which all this horrific material had to have been stolen. A tortured soul stood inside the gates of an inferno; malicious spirits flew out of his mouth, fled from his ears and nose, and tore his eyes out as they exited. He couldn't scream; a small serpent was twisted around his tongue.

Nauseated, Linnie surveyed the rest of the display. A page torn from a textbook featured a skull with a huge rectangular hole in it; the caption explained that the hole had been made while the Inca was very much alive, in order to let the madness out. Trepanning. Trephination. A textbook on the dirt floor lay open to a well-thumbed page; it noted several spellings and various cultures that had practiced the cure. It even supplied a diagram, a drill pointing at the side of a figure's skull.

The treatment was remarkably simple: drill a little hole and let the pain of confusion and the tongue-tying serpents out. Evelyn would have assembled this collection and grouped it in a portfolio.

A large assortment of slender drill bits and two hand-powered drills were scattered over ratty blankets spread on the floor. Each drill had the hand-crank and gears on the side; the larger one had extended casing and a platform an inch square to steady the bit as the drilling progressed.

Linnie wished there were a portable tank of gasoline, or a lawn mower with fuel in it, and someone to start a fire; the wretched building should burn past any possible chance of recognition. She couldn't stand the idea of Evelyn's inadvertent participation.

She heard the footsteps a moment or two before she could focus on them. The man stood, quite erect, inside the sliding door that she'd opened.

53

He would have been more handsome with a haircut that tamed the ringlets of wiry, dark blond hair that hung to the tattered collar of his baseball jacket. His features were well proportioned, nothing large enough to stand out and take note of, nothing lacking, pale eyes and pale ringlets of hair that hung, like sideburns, forward of his ears. It was the face she'd seen in the kitchen window. It was the man she'd seen with the fisherman, except his hair had been hidden by a cap.

He turned his shoulders to glance at Linnie, and then surveyed his domain — his posters, books, blankets, tools — and grunted. *Mmm-hmmmph.* A guttural affirmation. He didn't seem surprised that a visitor had found his barn; rather, he appeared proprietary, even proud.

Linnie circled behind the wooden wagon, putting it between them. Her heart raced, and the muscles in her calves contracted, while the fright itself receded. Linnie felt its aftereffects, what the rush of adrenaline had unleashed. She was increasingly sure, and smart enough to watch for disproof, that she was in no danger, and she suspected that the other person had reached a similar conclusion. He avoided eye contact, his attention claimed by a fingernail that he bit: she presumed autism was on the list of his disabilities.

"Eddie?" she asked. "Is that your name?"

"I don't know you."

"Are you Eddie?"

"I don't know you. I know your cousin." His shoulders hunched, and he dropped his chin into the gap between them. "Are you sick?"

"No."

"You're not sick, I see that. You're not in pain."

"No."

"I see that, too."

"Do you follow the ones who are sick?"

"I can't follow them all the time. But I know them, where they gather, where they hide. I know when the end is near."

"Don't they belong in a home? A hospital?"

"They hate group homes - locked in and scared. They don't trust hospitals."

"Are you a doctor?"

His eyes swung her way, stopped just short of eye contact. His chest puffed out. His tone was earnest. "I want the pain to stop, I want them at peace, especially those who've never known it. *'Pax aeterna.'*"

"Latin? I studied Spanish .. and forget a lot of it. *'Peace?'*"

Eddie considered her choice of words, then put his hands to each side of his head. "*Everlasting.* These people, their minds aren't empty, a void. Imagine the ones who have ten thousand emotions and thoughts raging inside of them and no way to express or realize them. Torture, your head exploding. A lifetime of it."

"It has to hurt."

"I've seen what it does."

"What about Richard Kieffer? Didn't he express himself at times?"

"He had a seizure. Sudden. He swallowed his tongue. He was choking."

"An emergency. I see," Linnie said as she pulled her phone out. "You know what a cellphone is?"

The man looked directly at Linnie; there was, for the first time, full eye-contact. "I don't have a phone," he said.

Linnie understood the accusation: where was she, or anyone else with a cellphone for that matter, when the fisherman had his seizure in the middle of nowhere? She dialed a number for the Sheriff's Department and was grateful she got Dan Pataki quickly.

An hour and a half later, with deputies and Crime Scene Unit officers standing by and a task force from the FBI's Buffalo office en route, Pataki stood with Linnie in the barn, making his own quick assessment. The man named Eddie had been escorted back to the house.

"It's not fair," Linnie said, "that these posters were Evelyn's."

"Look," he replied, "a few months from now no one will remember this part of it. I don't see the investigation remaining public. I can't imagine this case being settled in trial." He looked at the tools on the ground. "Do you think Ted knows this guy?"

"Yes."

"Let's hope Ted's involvement stops there."

"Nick has him at home."

"Keep him there. He probably doesn't know what's happened, and he can't incriminate himself if he can't talk sense. Which may be the saving grace of this mess." He considered the idea briefly. "Meantime, you've got to promise you won't let Ted leave the area."

"I won't." The assurance, and his request for it, drained her; she would have dropped onto a chair, if there had been one.

On her way out the driveway Linnie shielded her face from curious onlookers; her car had been moved down the street. A crowd of photographers and newsmen was clustered at the head of the driveway around Sheriff Pellini, who was dressed for the occasion in his battle-gear, while a TV cameraman positioned a shield for the sun. Linnie slipped away.

Linnie didn't have the chance to talk to Brendan till that evening, when he stopped by her house with cartons of take-out food for everyone. "Are you okay?" he asked.

"I guess. It was a strange day."

"I don't know about your hiring out as a deputy." Brendan smiled sweetly. "Is this a career move?"

"Did I screw up?"

"I doubt it."

"What do we do?" She found great relief in the use of the pronoun, first person plural.

"We'll push the court date back. And you'll keep Ted at home until we see what today brings."

54

I t no longer surprised Linnie that Margot was the first to pick up on bad news and the first to call with it. "Do you believe it?" she complained. "How goddamn unfair. Have you seen it? I can't stand to see my mother belittled. My God, is this her bloody epitaph?"

The *Niagara Gazette* had headlined a front-page article about the case: *Eccentric Collector's Curiosities A Factor.* "I called the goddamn idiot editor. It is the *'collection'* that's eccentric, goddamnit, not the *'collector.'* How dare they?"

Brendan didn't imagine many people were influenced by the article. "I don't think the piece maligns Evelyn," he told Linnie, "and people will forget it. One day, the whole awful business may increase interest in Evelyn's collection and the reason for it."

Linnie spent the rest of the morning being interviewed by a pair of investigators, whose primary interest was to establish Ted's whereabouts at such times as the drilling incidents took place, a task made all but impossible by the absence of a clear timeline for much of what had happened. Nick had driven to the Sheriff's Department, too, for his turn. Fortunately, a consensus was building among law enforcement agencies that Edward Krysinski, the "surgeon," had acted alone. The suspect had gone off the radar years earlier, having been released from a home for autistic adults. A long unopened file recovered from the facility would reveal that a therapist thought, "Edward's perspective capabilities may one day trump his disabilities." And somehow Eddie had been allowed to wander endlessly, aimless and unschooled, ultimately to settle with a severely aging aunt. Linnie tracked the developments: she understood that a collapsing economy, and perchance a well-intentioned infusion of a number of severely disabled adults, had over-taxed the region's resources. This was Ted's region and his scanty "resources," which Evelyn had hoped to spare him.

Before leaving, Linnie tracked down Dan Pataki for his assessment. "Where do we stand?" she asked.

"It can change — you know that's my refrain, right? But I have a hard time seeing anyone else charged in this. We've got no witnesses or concrete timeframe. And as for Ted, Judge Hood's already ruled him incompetent. So I'm not concerned about a criminal court. It's Surrogate Court, the guardian business, they're the ones who'll send Ted up the river."

Once she and Nick got back to the river, she called Brendan. "Hey," he said when he picked up, "you need bail?"

"Not funny."

"So what happened?"

She reviewed the morning's interrogation and attempted a verbatim recitation of Pataki's assessment. She concluded with a list of her possible miscues.

"You did great!" Brendan said. "The county's chief investigator is telling you as much. Don't be hard on yourself."

She was startled by the strength of her reaction, how his simple reinforcement fed into something she felt starved for. "Will I see you? If it's tonight, it has to be here. Ted's unsettled by all this. I should be with the boys."

"It may snow."

"We have heat."

"Has Nick put the plow on the tractor?"

"Of course. He's way ahead of us. He's going to make beef stew."

"I'll get there about seven, if the weather holds."

The weather held until a week before Thanksgiving, when Buffalo got eighteen inches of lake-effect snow. A few inches fell, and this time didn't melt, at the house on the river, which lay north of the path of Lake Erie's mischief. As anxious as Linnie had been to resolve everything by early November, so as not to be in flux during the holidays, Judge Hood had rescheduled guardianship hearings for the Friday before Thanksgiving.

The prospect terrified her; she didn't want to feel the way that Nick did, steamrolled. The court had a mountain of material, from the lawyers, Judy Urbanski, and others, all of it outside her control, and the bulk of it probably argued for everything Evelyn had hoped to prevent.

She'd assumed that she'd have to stand in front of a whole courtroom and answer pointed questions about her character and the basis of her opinions, and was relieved to discover the morning proceedings would all take place in Judge Hood's chambers. Nick had visited the judge the day before so that he'd be free to look after Ted.

The morning of the hearings, the temperature dropped into the mid-teens. Nearly cloudless, the sky was pale blue on top, pale gray on the horizon, and the little jet-trails that cars emitted rose quickly off the pavement and dissipated. Linnie drove by herself.

In Lockport she parked next to Brendan's car in the courthouse lot. Margot and Bridgewater were sitting outside the judge's office, while Brendan was already inside. Margot handled the awkward moment by getting to her feet and hugging Linnie. "What a morning. Freezing."

"Why didn't you spend the night at the house? To drive from Toronto so early..?"

"I'd have to have driven at night. I don't mind, but my eyes do."

Linnie looked at Bridgewater. "Hi."

"Morning," he said cheerfully.

Linnie didn't want to make nice and noticed sections of a newspaper discarded by his feet. "You through with these?" she asked as she picked them up and immersed herself in them. It was a painfully long quarter-hour before Brendan emerged and tipped his head at Margot. "Your turn." She and Bridgewater got to their feet and entered the office. Brendan laughed when the door closed behind them.

"What's so funny?"

"I can't see Judge Hood keeping Bridgewater in there for long."

"Why?"

"Because I'm there as Evelyn's lawyer and spokesperson. I drafted her will. I'm also a close family friend and the trustee. But at this point I can't imagine Bridgewater saying anything that interests the judge."

"Are you sticking around?"

"I can't. I've got a conference later this morning. And Hood won't make his decision today." He kissed her on the cheek, and turned to leave, but stopped. "Oh. The judge is going to ask if you're sleeping with me."

"What do I say?"

"Tell him I rock. Tell him lawyers from Buffalo are ... fill-in-the-blank."

"Jesus, that's lame."

"Tell him what you think about your family, what you want. That's all he cares about."

Linnie would have badgered him for more advice, but the door to Judge Hood's chambers opened, and Bridgewater stepped out, looking sheepish. Brendan marched off down the hall before Bridgewater could make an excuse.

"I wanted to make sure she was comfortable, get it started," the lawyer told Linnie.

"Don't stick around on my account."

Twenty minutes later, Margot exited the chambers and left for Toronto. Linnie stepped inside tentatively. "You have to help," she said, surprised at the sudden toll her nerves took: her legs weak, her stomach stabbed, her voice shaky.

"How?" Judge Hood asked.

"Explain things." She sat down, so she didn't have to concentrate on standing. "The questions or whatever. So I don't say something that might hurt Nick or Ted."

Judge Hood squinted with such profound sympathy that his eyebrows stretched across the bridge of his nose and nearly touched. "How? I can't imagine you saying a thing that would hurt your family."

"I don't want to screw up anything for the brothers."

"Let's assume I have a pretty good grasp of what they want. I even read Nick's journal. The question today is what you want."

"Me?" The subject threw her: she'd imagined she'd discuss the boys and their best interests.

"You." He smiled gently. "We can kick it off with gossip, so it's out of the way. I know you and Mr. O'Connor had a date or two, and I presume it's none of my business. I don't expect him to confound duty and dating."

"Does Margot?"

"I don't care one whit about her opinion on this. And I told her so. I've got two possible candidates for guardian, and Nick's not one of them."

"But Nick could–"

"He's not one of them. You are. And if you state you want to be the guardian, I want it to be for Nick and Ted's sake. Evelyn Phillips made it clear there were two people she most trusted, Mr. O'Connor and you. Your aunt wanted you as the guardian, and in my mind that says a world about you."

Her tears started and wouldn't stop. It was the judge's kindness, and the clear appearance of Evelyn in it, that stunned her. "I'm sorry," she managed.

"You've got nothing to be sorry for. Whether you want the business of guardian or not."

"Brendan?" she said. "I can't even begin to know what's going to happen with him. He seems too good to be true, which is what my ex-husband seemed at first, and that was desperate and fucked – excuse me, there's-no-other-word-for-it. And I don't know what Brendan wants. What I want is kids, marriage, and if I don't have a husband I'll adopt, because my family has all but disappeared. But right now Nick and Ted, what they need trumps anything."

"It's what you want that's going to trump anything else at some point, so don't stuff that down to the bottom of your wish list."

She brushed away tears. "I need a job."

The judge was clearly at a loss. "On that..?"

"No, you have to listen, because maybe you don't think it's a good job for a guardian or would pay enough, but the various entities and their local homes and programs for DDs lack much in the way of accounting software, efficient record-keeping, computer-filing, and they have to hire out payroll, etcetera. I think a bunch of these programs would welcome management geared to their needs, and at the property there's a bunkhouse that would make a good office. It'd need a new furnace, AC, an ADA bathroom, other upgrades. And as soon as I could, I'd hire Nick, who often winds up volunteered for free shifts at day programs."

"A director of a program here in Lockport once described chasing funds from government agencies and private foundations as 'playing hopscotch backwards.' But I have no concern about or interest in your job. You understand Ted can't go out wandering anymore? We're on one skinny sheet of ice there."

"I know."

"And another thing. Dementia, it's probably his future if he lives long enough. You talk about having children, and you've got a responsibility to them. If Ted gets demented, you have to be willing, if you're the guardian, to make the hard choice and put him someplace where he's safe and so are others."

Linnie found herself imagining the presence of Evelyn in the room, her aunt keeping vigil under the guise of the avuncular, sweet judge. She chose her words carefully. "I'd want to be sure he no longer understood where he was, and I'd build a little addition or redo the upstairs at the bunkhouse. I don't care what it costs or what money remains after Ted and Nick, but when it's necessary I'll hire round-the-clock staff for Ted. He isn't leaving the property, if I have my say, unless he needs a hospital."

The judge shrugged his assent. "Of course, we're talking about everything except what's in my purview. We need to pick a guardian. Margot wants to take that on, she long ago petitioned for it, and she makes a strong case for herself and her opinions. The state favors siblings in the role. You? You haven't said you want to do it, not permanently. So that's the question. Can you tell me, in all certainty, you'd want to jump in with both feet?"

55

Brendan hosted Thanksgiving dinner and roasted the turkey. The rest of the meal was brought by his sister and her family, and by Linnie and the boys. The best cook of the latter group, Nick had blanched and sautéed French beans and baked two pumpkin pies.

Linnie thought it odd that she'd rarely met Brendan's sister over the years. Lisa and her husband had three boys between the ages of four and seven, who every quarter-hour went tearing through the house with an abandon interrupted by tears and a fight. Assigned to babysit her cousins, Kiley had turned on TV cartoons and started feeding them ice cream the moment they walked in the house.

Once dinner was served, Lisa seated herself at the oval table between Nick and Ted, thereby instantly winning Linnie's affection. Kiley parked herself on the chair between her father and Linnie, with whom she quietly shared her opinion of her young cousins. "Gawd! Has my aunt never heard of birth control?"

Linnie laughed. "You know you're way too young to be such a mean, old bitch."

"Not."

"They're really cute," Linnie insisted. "When I was your age, I wanted brothers and sisters so badly. Wouldn't you love to have a sister?"

Kiley looked at her father, then at Linnie, as if the question might be related to the two of them. "Why?"

"You could have fun with her, be the boss, take her shopping."

"A sister might be okay." She made a face. "But suppose it was a boy? Like he'd want me to buy him a lacrosse stick or shit like that."

The meal ended just in time. Ted had been wonderfully calm thus far, but decided he didn't like his dessert and sprayed a mouthful of apple tart across his plate. Brendan's nephews laughed and mimicked him. If Ted had gotten away with it, why couldn't they? They put whatever remained on their plates in their mouths and spat it out, as their laughter propelled food across the table. Kiley, after a "Gawd Almighty!" attempt at disapproval failed, was made young again by the laughter she couldn't contain. Confused at first, Ted started to whoop, convulsing with his staccato chuckle.

Nick supervised the clean-up, and still had the energy to drive home. Linnie slept the whole way.

The next morning, she rose early and stepped outside. The moon, a few days past full, was hung low in the western sky, the shadows of its valleys clearly stenciled by the sun rising behind her. Across the river cannons boomed, a volley of noise to chase birds from the vineyards that were holding their grapes for the frozen ice-wine harvest. As she got into her car, Linnie looked up at Ted's window, its shade drawn askew, and tried not to imagine the room straightened-up. Empty.

She drove to the supermarket for a pair of newspapers and added warm donuts for the boys' breakfast. Margot favored sugarless cereals and low-fat muffins, the sort of wholesome food also served at group homes and institutions. After stopping for a latte, Linnie got back to the house in time to answer the phone that started ringing.

"Is this Linnie Carson?" It was Judge Hood's voice.

When the call was over, she phoned Brendan with the news and then took herself to the river, which was inextricably connected with everything she thought or knew about her family. The day hadn't yet stirred the water, slick as speckled granite and moving with a speed that tricked the eye, the glass surface suggesting a glacial creep, unless floating debris swept past with it, cues to the real pace. The Canadian banks were sheer, banks of red mud timbered by trees without their cover.

Evelyn had once told her a story about her grandmother — Linnie's great-grandmother. The first person to go over Niagara Falls in a barrel and survive, a woman, had done so on the presumption of fame and a resulting fortune, both of which proved fleeting. Her grandmother was an absolute beauty, Evelyn had said: "She's where you and your mother got your looks." And she was convinced that the stunt's first survivor, an overweight and mustached female, lacked the makings of a celebrity that could cash in on the stunt.

"Grandmother told me her scheme," Evelyn had said. An accomplice would make himself noticed and launch a flimsy barrel right above the Falls, with only a big anvil in it, at a spot where it was certain to cascade over the edge and drop into the closest boil of the Horseshoe. The barrel would be torn to smithereens in the many minutes it spent submerged; scraps of it would be unrecognizable. Down below, in the basin past the Falls, a rescue boat would set off from the shore, its well-submerged line dragging an otherwise identical, but sturdy barrel into the river from its disguised perch on the shore. Once released, with tourists watching from the heights, the barrel would pop to the surface, where accomplices in the boat would rescue the battered, brave, beautiful heroine. New York audiences would thrill to her story.

Something happened – the rescue boat's paddle-wheel caught on the line it was dragging and tore it – and by the time the barrel surfaced, downriver from the boat, it was streaming towards the lower rapids, almost as deadly as the Falls themselves. With the rescue boat having to abandon the chase, the barrel coursed through some of the world's more violent rapids but was intact when it reached Lewiston and calm water. A few miles further downriver, a fisherman put a rope on the barrel, towed it to shore, unlatched it, only to find the barrel full of an angry woman, rather than whiskey, salt, flour, or anything remotely useful.

"Our ancestor," Evelyn had said, "claimed she'd been put rudely ashore by the fisherman, who claimed the barrel. Now, I don't know if any of the story she told me about the stunt gone sour was true. Grandmother was old when she told me; it's the age where everything is gospel truth, a deathbed confession, or a perfect and shameless lie. But I choose to believe it was true, a wonderful rascal in our family.

My grandmother said she'd made her way to the road and walked upriver a bit, when she noticed what might have been a forty-room hospital being built. The workers told her, no, it was a summer house they were building, and then they had to explain what a summer house was, because she had no idea of such a thing, a huge house open merely for the summer. She told me what followed was deliberate. She made her way into Buffalo, her background always a mystery, and met and married into the family building the summer retreat. Your great-grandfather, the well-behaved son." Evelyn had paused telling the story and pointed down a steep incline to an outward curl of the pebbly shore. "I like to think the barrel landed here, what with the back eddy – that this is what she stumbled into."

In the living room there was a portrait of the woman, done up in a society gown and family jewels. Linnie had begun to see her own mother in the picture: the gray-green eyes, the upper lip straight and the lower one bowed, angel and victim, slick imposter and diffident matriarch, and impossibly, recklessly lovely.

"There're still forms, I hope you know," Judge Hood had said in the phonecall. "And regular reporting to me. Oh, yeah. Your lawyer friend, Mr. O'Connor, knows this, but there's an oath you'll take as guardian, all formal. I just hope you're as pleased with it as me. And Ted and Nick."

Linnie decided that next summer, when the river was warm again, she'd have Brendan sail upriver and drop her not far offshore, for the view her great-grandmother might first have had, and then she too would fight the current to get home. After a look back at the house, she figured she'd better get back to it before Ted got to the kitchen. He'd sample all the donuts if he found them, and it would be fun to watch him enjoy his share.

THE END

AFTERWORD

In the early 1950s it was not uncommon for a wealthy family to send an obviously disabled baby off to an institution, where she or he would spend her or his entire life.

The State of New York has now removed the initials M.R. from the acronym, the words from the title, of the organization that monitors the treatment, etc., of the Developmentally Disabled. Also, the *Robert Moses Parkway* has been renamed the *Niagara Scenic Parkway*. Lastly, the two copper-topped towers and magnificent central building of the H.H. Richardson-designed complex at the Buffalo State Hospital has been restored and turned into a hotel on what is now named the "Richardson Olmsted Campus."

The institutions named in this book all existed with the exception of the Storey-Davis Institute, a name that's fictional.

ABOUT THE AUTHOR

Duncan grew up in Buffalo, N.Y., and spent his early summers 30 miles north on the lower Niagara River. He moved to Los Angeles, where he wrote film and tv scripts for years, then ran a small business while writing some novels and plays on the side. He and his wife Kathy Hallberg - an entertainment lawyer - raised two wonderful daughters there and now split their time between Florida and an old family summer house on the Niagara River. He often writes about characters or events from Buffalo and environs. One can learn more about him and his work at his website, www.duncanrsmith.com.

The author greatly appreciates his readers and hopes that, should you like a book, you will give it a positive review on Amazon and social media and recommend it to friends. Word of mouth - yours - is important for my work.

Thanks,
Duncan

OTHER NOVELS
BY THE AUTHOR

Jumpers

When The Nights Were Long

Made in United States
Orlando, FL
20 January 2022

13815883R00161